TRIAL BY FIRE

By Danielle Steel

Trial by Fire • Triangle • Joy • Resurrection • Only the Brave • Never Too Late
Upside Down • The Ball at Versailles • Second Act • Happiness • Palazzo
The Wedding Planner • Worthy Opponents • Without a Trace • The Whittiers
The High Notes • The Challenge • Suspects • Beautiful • High Stakes • Invisible
Flying Angels • The Butler • Complications • Nine Lives • Finding Ashley • The Affair
Neighbours • All That Glitters • Royal • Daddy's Girls • The Wedding Dress
The Numbers Game • Moral Compass • Spy • Child's Play • The Dark Side • Lost and Found
Blessing in Disguise • Silent Night • Turning Point • Beauchamp Hall
In His Father's Footsteps • The Good Fight • The Cast • Accidental Heroes • Fall from Grace
Past Perfect • Fairytale • The Right Time • The Duchess • Against All Odds
Dangerous Games • The Mistress • The Award • Rushing Waters • Magic • The Apartment
Property of a Noblewoman • Blue • Precious Gifts • Undercover • Country • Prodigal Son
Pegasus • A Perfect Life • Power Play • Winners • First Sight • Until the End of Time
The Sins of the Mother • Friends Forever • Betrayal • Hotel Vendôme • Happy Birthday
44 Charles Street • Legacy • Family Ties • Big Girl • Southern Lights • Matters of the Heart
One Day at a Time • A Good Woman • Rogue • Honor Thyself • Amazing Grace • Bungalow 2
Sisters • H.R.H. • Coming Out • The House • Toxic Bachelors • Miracle • Impossible
Echoes • Second Chance • Ransom • Safe Harbour • Johnny Angel • Dating Game
Answered Prayers • Sunset in St. Tropez • The Cottage • The Kiss • Leap of Faith • Lone Eagle
Journey • The House on Hope Street • The Wedding • Irresistible Forces • Granny Dan
Bittersweet • Mirror Image • The Klone and I • The Long Road Home • The Ghost
Special Delivery • The Ranch • Silent Honor • Malice • Five Days in Paris • Lightning
Wings • The Gift • Accident • Vanished • Mixed Blessings • Jewels • No Greater Love
Heartbeat • Message from Nam • Daddy • Star • Zoya • Kaleidoscope • Fine Things
Wanderlust • Secrets • Family Album • Full Circle • Changes • Thurston House • Crossings
Once in a Lifetime • A Perfect Stranger • Remembrance • Palomino • Love: *Poems*
The Ring • Loving • To Love Again • Summer's End • Season of Passion • The Promise
Now and Forever • Passion's Promise • Going Home

Nonfiction

Expect a Miracle
Pure Joy: *The Dogs We Love*
A Gift of Hope: *Helping the Homeless*
His Bright Light: *The Story of Nick Traina*

For Children

Pretty Minnie in Hollywood
Pretty Minnie in Paris

Danielle Steel

TRIAL BY FIRE

MACMILLAN

First published 2024 by Delacorte Press
an imprint of Random House
a division of Penguin Random House LLC, New York

First published in the UK 2024 by Macmillan
an imprint of Pan Macmillan
The Smithson, 6 Briset Street, London EC1M 5NR
EU representative: Macmillan Publishers Ireland Limited, 1st Floor,
The Liffey Trust Centre, 117–126 Sheriff Street Upper,
Dublin 1, D01 YC43
Associated companies throughout the world
www.panmacmillan.com

ISBN 978-1-5290-8566-2 HB
ISBN 978-1-5290-8567-9 TPB

1 3 5 7 9 8 6 4 2

A CIP catalogue record for this book is available from the British Library.

Typeset in Charter ITC by Palimpsest Book Production Ltd, Falkirk, Stirlingshire
Printed and bound by CPI Group (UK) Ltd, Croydon, CR0 4YY

To my beloved children,
Beatrix, Trevor, Todd, Samantha,
Victoria, Vanessa, Maxx, and Zara,

Be happy, be brave, be safe,
and take the right risks.

Make wise choices about who you love,
and when you find the right person,
put all your chips on the table,
winner take all!

With all my heart and love forever,

Mom / d.s.

Maybe love isn't possible unless
you're willing to take a risk.
Maybe that's what makes it
worthwhile.

You can't love someone unless
you put all the cards on the table,
and all the chips,
and you're all in.

—D.S.

TRIAL BY FIRE

Chapter 1

Dahlia Johnson de Beaumont sat in her elegantly designed office in the building she owned on the Rue du Faubourg Saint-Honoré in Paris, on a warm day in late June, and consulted her list of appointments and the calls she had to make that morning. She was the CEO of the venerable, highly successful perfume firm she had inherited as an only child. It had been founded by her maternal grandfather, Louis Lambert. Dahlia's mother, Constance Lambert Johnson, also an only child, had inherited it from her father, the founder. Constance had passed away when Dahlia was in college in New York. She had bequeathed the company in its entirety to Dahlia. Dahlia had always known she would inherit the business one day. It was expected. She just didn't know it would happen so soon. She had a normal, happy childhood, except that her career path had been chosen for her, almost like royalty in a way.

They were one of the most important perfume manufacturers in the world. Louis Lambert Perfumes were as well-known as Guerlain, and followed as many of the original traditions of perfume-making as was possible at a time when some natural ingredients were no longer available or legal and had been replaced by synthetics. It was a technical challenge, but as much as was possible, and with great care, their perfumes appeared to be unchanged.

Dahlia's mother, Constance, was a gentle, genteel woman. She had never worked in the firm, once she'd inherited it, but she had a deep love for the company her father had founded. It was run by the competent directors, executives, and managers her father had put in place before his death at eighty-seven. Their perfumes were in some way old-fashioned, or traditional, and yet they had been subtly adapted to the modern world and to what women wanted today. Many new scents had been added to the originals, which were popular around the globe. The managing board of directors had run Lambert during Constance's entire ownership. Her husband, Hunter Johnson, had been on the board, was one of the overseers of the company, and had protected Constance's interests and invested the company's assets wisely. He had suggested several times to Constance that they go public, but she had preferred to maintain private ownership. She knew her father would have wanted that, just as the Dumas family kept Hermès private, and the Wertheimer family owned Chanel. Lambert was easily as profitable as Hermès, and had stores where their perfumes were sold around the world.

Hunter, Constance's husband, was American. They had met at a party at the American embassy in Paris, and he had been dazzled by her. He was twenty-five years older than Constance when they met. She was twenty-one, one of the most beautiful young women in Paris, and he was a childless widower of forty-six. He was one of the early founders of venture capital. They married within the year they met, and Dahlia was born in New York a year later. Hunter advised Constance brilliantly on the company's investments during her ownership of Lambert. Her death while Dahlia was in college in the States was a heart-breaking blow to Dahlia and her father. He adored his wife, and Dahlia and her mother were very close.

Constance and Hunter had lived in New York in the early days of their marriage, and Dahlia attended private school there. They remained in New York until Dahlia went to college, Hunter retired, and he and Constance moved to Paris. They had gone back and forth to Paris frequently before that, and Dahlia was equally comfortable in Paris or

New York, in English or in French while she was growing up. She had strong family ties to France, and had spent her early years in New York, with summers spent in their summer home in Saint-Paul-de-Vence in the south of France, and once she was in college, she worked at the Lambert offices in Paris for a month every summer and loved it.

Two years after they moved to Paris, Constance had died of breast cancer at forty-two. It had gone undetected until too late. Her mother had died of it at an early age too. Dahlia had inherited the Lambert empire at twenty, finished college at Columbia, attended the Wharton business school, moved to her parents' house in Paris, and entered the company she owned at twenty-four. The people who had run it until then taught her what she needed to know. They had been grooming her to run the company for years. Her grandfather had begun talking to her about the business since she was a child. She was fascinated by it. She benefited from his managers' experience and her father's wise financial advice for a year, as she was assigned to lower-level jobs where she could learn the business from the bottom up, just as she had expected to.

Hunter Johnson died suddenly at seventy-two, less than a year after Dahlia came home to France, five years after his wife had died. He had never recovered from the loss of

Constance. Even his deep love for his daughter didn't raise his spirits once his beloved Constance died. He had developed a heart condition which killed him in the end.

Dahlia was an orphan, and the sole owner of one of the most profitable businesses in the world, just before her twenty-fifth birthday. Slim, graceful, blonde, green-eyed, she had been taught everything she needed to know about the business by experts, and she had strong support from the managers and the Board, but nothing had prepared her for losing her parents' world. They had been the source of joy and emotional support, wisdom and love, for her entire life, and without them she felt lost. Her father had died of a heart attack with no warning. She stood alone at his funeral with the church of Sainte-Clothilde full to the rafters. She continued to live in her parents' house in Paris, and felt like a lost soul.

Her father had died a year after she had graduated from business school at Wharton and gone to live in Paris. At the same time, she ran into Jean-Luc de Beaumont a month after her return from graduate school. He was a childhood friend. His family had spent their summers in Saint-Paul-de-Vence too. They saw each other every summer in the south of France and had known each other all their lives. He was comfortable and familiar.

Dahlia was a perfect hybrid, a combination of two

cultures, two countries, and two worlds. Her look and style and attitudes were more French than American because of her mother's influence, but she had grown up in New York, been educated in the U.S., and had an American perspective about business, based on what her American father had taught her. It was an ideal combination. She had the romance and femininity of a Frenchwoman, and the education of an American businesswoman, which she brought back to France with her. She was a dual national, and felt at home in both countries, although she privately admitted that her heart was more French, and she felt stronger ties to France once she lived and worked in her business there. France was home to her now, and with her father's death, her ties to the United States evaporated. Since he'd been much older than her mother, he had no living relatives during her lifetime. And once he was gone, she had no adult family members to protect and guide her, but she was a sensible young woman with a fine mind, and her parents had taught her values that served her well. She was a woman of integrity, substance, and power at a young age.

When they reconnected, Jean-Luc de Beaumont added an element of joy and levity to her life. He had a lighthearted attitude about most things. He had studied in France, but never seriously. He preferred the outdoors and extreme athletic challenges to intellectual or academic pursuits. His passions were ski racing, driving fast cars, mountain climbing, and anything dangerous and exciting that gave him an adrenaline rush. He was as handsome and dashing as Dahlia was beautiful, and an only child like her. They were the same age, and his family's fortune allowed him the luxury of not having to work, and Dahlia was financially independent. Being with him counterbalanced her awesome responsibilities and the strong sense of duty that had been part of what she'd inherited along with Louis Lambert Perfumes. She was serious about her obligations to the family name, which was a heavy burden at times.

Being with Jean-Luc made everything seem brighter and more exciting, and his parents always welcomed her warmly. He became her first serious love. They married six months after her father's death. He moved into her large family house in Paris with her, which she had inherited too and wanted to keep. They were children playing at marriage with youthful innocence. They had fun together and were in constant evidence on the Parisian social scene, with doors open to them everywhere. They were the golden couple of the hour. By day, Dahlia went to work to learn more about the business her mother had left her, and her father had felt confident she would run with great competence one day. She had a good head for business and a flawless instinct for perfume, like her grandfather. She hired some of the great perfume makers in the business.

She learned her job well while adoring Jean-Luc and encouraging and celebrating his adventures. She loved how fearless he was. They opened their hearts to each other without reserve, and their first child, Charles, was born on their first anniversary. They were both twenty-six when he was born. Their life was full, with the vast empire Dahlia was learning to run by day, and the fun they had at night, going to parties, seeing friends, and holding balls in their splendid home on the rue de Grenelle. It was one of the most distinguished, beautiful homes in Paris. Dahlia had spent a great deal of time there as a child, so she knew it well. It was familiar and home to her. And she traveled often for business to their stores around the world, to better understand their customers.

When they brought Charles home from the hospital in Paris, they put him in the nursery that had once been hers as a visitor, and her mother's as an infant. Dahlia and Jean-Luc filled the house rapidly, despite the demands of her job. Dahlia gave birth to a baby every year for the first four years of their marriage. Alexandra arrived less than a year after Charles, Delphine thirteen months later, and Emma fourteen months after that. And all the while, Jean-Luc continued his mountain climbing, ski races, and car racing. Even marriage, fatherhood, and four babies couldn't slow him down. He was the consummate aristocrat going to shoots in Spain, hunts in England, and balls in Venice. He learned to fly his own plane. They were the golden years of the 1990s when everything was about having fun, and there was plenty of money to do it. Dahlia's business was booming, although Jean-Luc took no interest in it. Dahlia loved working, and Jean-Luc admired her for it. It didn't bother him that she did. It gave him more free time to pursue his passions. She made her work seem effortless at night when she came home, and what she was learning energized her. Emma was born on her mother's twenty-ninth birthday, and by then Dahlia was CEO of the company, the youngest CEO in France, while Jean-Luc roamed around Europe, visiting his equally aristocratic friends and having fun. Dahlia never objected to his carefree life. She loved him as he was, beautiful and brave and wild, while she had all the responsibility for them both, which suited her. No one in his family had ever worked, so they thought him normal and Dahlia unusual.

He was staying with friends in Courchevel in the French Alps when they decided to ski the Three Valleys, enjoying the trails that were familiar to him and that he knew well, when disaster struck. He and his two friends went out early one morning before the mountains had been cleared with dynamite, to shake loose the excess snow and provoke avalanches so no one would get hurt later. They went out ahead of the dynamite squads and were buried by an avalanche. Dahlia was in Paris, working, but had promised to come that weekend, bringing the children and a nanny with her. The ski patrol found Jean-Luc and his friends three hours later. His friends survived, but Jean-Luc was dead from suffocation under the deep snow and his neck was broken. Dahlia became a widow at thirty after five years of marriage and with four young children under five.

She was devastated when the police called her in the office to tell her. She was in shock when the company's driver took her to Courchevel to identify her husband's body and they followed the hearse home to Paris a day later. Jean-Luc was the love of her life, and the only family she had, other than their children. It brought back all the painful memories of her mother's death ten years before, and her father's five years later. Dahlia had thought that she and Jean-Luc would grow old together. She had imagined them with their grown children around them, and their children's children. And now that wasn't going to happen. They had talked of having two more children, or even four. Jean-Luc never balked at the size of their family because Dahlia made it so easy for him, with nannies taking care of the children while she worked, and she loved taking care of them herself on the weekends. Like everything else she did, she made it look effortless.

Jean-Luc was the joy in their lives, the magic. She was the responsibility and made things run smoothly. She had never expected him to leave them at thirty.

She managed to organize his funeral, and barely remembered it later. She was traumatized to the depths of her soul. She couldn't eat, she couldn't sleep, she couldn't think. She felt like a ghost in her own home, while trying to be present for the children. Charlie and Alexandra were barely old enough to understand that their exciting, happy, fun father wasn't coming home again, and Delphine and Emma were too young to tell. Dahlia had to bear her soul-wrenching grief alone, and be strong for them.

Jean-Luc had been an only child, and his parents were devastated. Having had him late in life, after many stillbirths and miscarriages, he was their miracle. His mother was in her seventies, his father in his eighties now, and they turned into very old people overnight, as though someone had turned out the light in them. They had always been kind and welcoming to Dahlia, but she and the children were a painful reminder of their lost son. They took to traveling to escape the memories for what remained of their lives. Neither of them lived long after the tragic loss of their only child.

It was up to Dahlia to keep the family going, to keep them together, comfort them, give them strength even while she felt empty and broken herself.

Three weeks after Jean-Luc died, she went back to work, still in terrible pain and trying to create a new normal for the children without him. It was a very long time before she felt even remotely normal herself, and even laughed at something Charlie said.

She knew that she would never be the same again. The loss was too enormous, and she felt as though he had taken a part of her with him, the fun part. What was left was duty. She was the single mother of four children who needed her, and the CEO of her own business, which needed her too. It seemed like a long time before she could concentrate on anything again. She just worked doubly hard to compensate for it.

Jean-Luc had died without a will, since he was so young. Death hadn't crossed his mind at thirty, despite the dangerous sports he pursued. According to French law, what money he had was divided in five equal parts for her and the children, and she had her part reapportioned to the children. She wanted them to have it, and she didn't need it. Although he had played well on it, his fortune was much smaller than Dahlia's, which was enormous due to the lucrative business she owned.

She brought the children up alone, enjoying their company, cherishing the time she spent with them and shepherding them gently toward the business she hoped the four of them would run one day. As they grew up, she taught them about Lambert's history, and all about how fine, high-quality perfumes were made and marketed.

Dahlia couldn't imagine ever loving a man again as she had Jean-Luc, so she embraced her children instead. She turned down all social invitations for a year after he died. She had no desire to go to parties, or any kind of social gathering, once he was gone. For years, her days were occupied by Lambert Perfumes, her evenings, weekends, and holidays by her children. Taking care of her children when she had time allowed her to hide from the fact that the years were passing. The children met all her emotional needs, as she met theirs, and she never felt alone as long as she was with them. Motherhood was an easy place to hide by night, and business by day. The children became a substitute for the husband she had lost. She never had to go home to an empty house, as they were always waiting for her with open arms. There was no sweeter moment in her life than being with them. The memories of her passion for Jean-Luc faded with time, and he became a hero to all of them, more than he had been in life. His parents had died by then, so her children had no grandparents. They only had her, as she had only them as family.

She occasionally had dinners with men, but none of them ever measured up to her glamorous idolized memories of Jean-Luc. He was the biggest and bravest of men, and had suited her when they were young, though he might not have later, as she grew into her business and the demanding role of CEO of an enormous international enterprise.

She was nearly forty, ten years after his death, when romance entered her life again, with a man she took seriously for a short time. The romance faded quickly, when she realized that he was more interested in what she could do for him than who she was as a person. She saw it within a few months and ended the relationship. He also had no desire to share her with another man's children and made it clear. Her family was her priority, and then her work.

After that, Dahlia never introduced her children to the men she went out with. She didn't care enough about the men, or she would have. She always kept herself aloof and guarded her heart. There was no room for passion or a misstep in her life. She had her massive business to run, her children to love and to love her. She needed nothing else.

She was more excited by her business every year. In a major decision to expand, she had added cosmetics to the perfumes, which proved to be an immensely profitable decision. Dahlia made few mistakes in business, and when she did, she corrected them quickly. She did the same with men. She never got too attached, and when she sensed she was starting to care too much, she retreated. She let nothing interfere with her family or her dedication to the empire she had inherited and that had grown exponentially due to her hard work.

There were men on the fringes of her life, but no one she cared about intensely, and her brief affairs were discreet, remained below the radar, and attracted no attention. She went to most events alone and preferred it. She could leave whenever she wanted if she had a heavy workload in the office the next day.

On Dahlia's fiftieth birthday, friends gave a dinner for her at a discreet, elite club. Like the Dumas family of Hermès, and the Wertheimers of Chanel, she kept a low profile and preferred to stay out of sight, although she was still beautiful, professionally powerful, and didn't look her age. She didn't enjoy public attention and stayed out of the press whenever possible. She had no desire to be famous or even personally known to the public. Her privacy meant more to her.

There was a man at the dinner whom she'd never met before. Philippe Vernier was the CEO of a major French corporation that did a great deal of business in Asia, a major market for her as well, and they talked about it at dinner, and found that they had a lot in common, and even some mutual friends in Paris and Hong Kong. He was the head of a major luxury brand of clothing, which wasn't entirely unrelated to her world, and his company dabbled in cosmetics too, though not on the scale that Dahlia did. He was obviously impressed by her talents. He knew who she was and had read about her. She was a legend in the business world. They had a pleasant evening talking to each other, mostly about their work, and he invited her to dinner the following week. He wore no wedding band, and never mentioned a family on that evening or the several others that followed. She had to discreetly call a friend who knew him to find out if he was married. She got no clues from him.

Dahlia was disappointed to discover that in fact he was married, which in her mind made him ineligible for a romance. Until then, she had found him very attractive, but considerably less so once she knew his marital status. He was not unique in Paris society, or the French business milieu. He was one of many men who didn't want to go through a costly divorce but had long since abandoned the pretense of a marriage that still worked. These men no longer shared their lives with the women they were married to. Philippe Vernier was a prime example of the breed. Distinguished, well educated at the best French academic institutions, successful, charming, cultured, vital and powerful, and still handsome at fifty-eight, he gave off the vibes of a single man during his evenings with her, but he wasn't. On the fourth or fifth evening they spent together, he explained simply and directly that he and his wife Jacqueline had married at an early age. It had been a union that had pleased their families, but a romance that had evaporated quickly, and a mistake that had left them each with a partner they had no lasting attraction to, and nothing in common with.

He had an only son, Julien, whom he said he wasn't close to, and who was a spoiled boy with no real ambition and a weakness for Russian gold diggers. Philippe admitted that he spent little time with his son and hadn't been an attentive father. His wife spent most of her time traveling, preferred London to Paris, and was more interested in the horse shows, hunts, and house parties she attended in England than she was in life at home. They had long since agreed to lead separate, independent lives, while officially living at the same address, and being in the same city and sleeping under the same roof as seldom as possible. Philippe said the arrangement worked well. The only time they spent together was on their summer holiday in the south of France with their son at Saint-Jean-Cap-Ferrat. The rest of the time Philippe was free to do as he wanted.

Dahlia was leery of what he said at first, but in the next few months of dining with him more and more frequently, she found it to be true. She had never dated a married man before, and didn't like the idea, but the reality was simpler than she had feared. He was always good company. In the past six years, he and Dahlia had been seen together often at important social events. They were not an official couple but were an accepted unofficial one. It wasn't a passionate love affair, but their relationship had grown into a comfortable, compatible alliance for both of them. They lived in their own homes, spent weekends together regularly, when they wanted to, spent the evening together twice a week, on Mondays and Thursdays, and took vacations together once or twice a year, if they had the time and both liked the destination. Philippe and Jacqueline had never discussed his relationship with Dahlia. He was sure she knew, and she had an English friend, a lord, with whom he suspected she had a similar arrangement.

Neither Philippe nor Dahlia ever considered marriage, and he had told her early on that divorce was not an option and would have been a financial nightmare. The arrangement they had was warm, even if not passionate, and it met their needs well enough. They frequently talked business, which was of interest to both of them, and it was pleasant for her to be with someone who understood the challenges she faced every day.

Jacqueline had absolutely no interest in how Philippe spent his time at the office, and he liked being able to talk to Dahlia about his work, and Dahlia had no one else to discuss work with at her level. Philippe was a respectable escort at any event, and she was the person he preferred to have on his arm at any important social gathering, not his wife. Dahlia had only met Philippe's son a few times, and never his wife, much to her relief. His marriage was never a topic of conversation between them, and she suspected that Jacqueline had made her peace with their separate lifestyles long ago. Dahlia and Philippe were two enormously successful people with much in common, and a warm affection for each other, which had grown into a kind of companionable love, or that of best friends, and they were familiar to each other now. She couldn't imagine her life without him, and she even forgot he was married sometimes. They knew when either one of them needed to be left alone and respected it. Not living together gave them the space and independence they both required.

Her children were grown now, and had their own lives, careers, apartments, and relationships, except for her youngest daughter Emma, who lived with her and studied at the Beaux-Arts. And two of her children, Delphine and Charles, worked for her. She was grooming them to run the firm one day, when she retired, although at fifty-six, she couldn't even imagine retiring.

Her son Charles, at thirty, was the age that she had been when she became CEO of the company. He wasn't as sure of himself as she had been when she had to run the company herself. He had a strong financial mind like his maternal grandfather, and was Assistant CFO, and when the current head CFO retired in two or three years, Dahlia expected her son to take over as the head financial officer.

He was still unmarried, and had lived with a woman for three years whom Dahlia wasn't crazy about and hoped would fall by the wayside before too long. Catherine was nine years older than Charles, at thirty-nine, had a mediocre job in PR and, by her previous lover, a twelve-year-old daughter whom Dahlia hadn't met and didn't wish to. She had met Catherine, was unimpressed, and didn't like the age difference. She thought there was an element of greed there. Charles was kindhearted, trusting, and naïve, a little too much so, but he was still young, and easy prey for greedy women.

Alexandra, Dahlia's second child, was twenty-nine, fiercely ambitious, a producer of a successful TV show. Alex was competitive and often jealous of her siblings and her mother. She looked a lot like Dahlia, except for her dark hair, but she had none of her mother's gentle ways and finesse in dealing with people. Alex preferred to confront people head-on, which had won her success in her job, but not the admiration of her coworkers, who found her cold and hard and ruthless. She was much tougher than her brother. Alex had had a revolving door of partners and had recently married the producer of a rival TV show in a civil ceremony. The civil ceremony was in anticipation of their upcoming big social religious wedding. The civil ceremony was a necessary legal formality in France. He was even tougher than Alex, rough around the edges, sexy and good-looking, but Dahlia questioned how happy they would make each other in the long run. Alex had no interest in the family business and never mentioned her connection to it, although her future husband, Paul Ferrand, appeared to be impressed by it, which worried Dahlia as to his motives.

Delphine, her third-born, was Dahlia's soulmate, at twenty-eight now. She was the easiest of her children. She and Dahlia were always in harmony with each other, and their relationship had been easy for all of Delphine's life, unlike Alex, who had battled with her mother forever. Delphine had married young, at twenty-three, after going to college in the States as her mother had. She went to Brown, and was more interested in the American side of her bloodline than Dahlia was, or her siblings were. She returned to Paris right after she graduated from college, joined the family business, and had worked for her mother for six years, rising steadily to the top, due to her natural instincts for finance and the perfume industry. She had recently added antiaging products and skin care to their existing line, which had done extremely well.

When Delphine was twenty-three, she had married Francois Mattheiu, from a respected family. He had a genius instinct for start-ups and had made a fortune of his own. He was the consummate nice guy, a big teddy bear of a man, a great husband, and a loving father to their two little girls, Annabelle and Penelope, or Penny, who were two and four. Dahlia had little time to spend with them. Delphine was very close to her mother and valued her advice. Dahlia joined the family for dinner occasionally after the girls had gone to bed, and invariably they talked business, which was what interested both women most. Francois was very tolerant of it, and had no sense of competition with his wife due to his own success. He genuinely liked his mother-in-law and was impressed by her strengths. He thought she was a remarkable woman. She could have led an indolent life, and instead she worked hard and was dedicated to her family and her business.

In contrast, Charles and Alex spent very little time with

their mother. Alex was too involved with the show she produced to have much spare time, and was often at odds with her mother. Charles was always with Catherine and her daughter in his spare time, and had a family life with them, although they weren't married. But marriage was clearly Catherine's goal, despite the nine-year age gap between them, and she wanted a child by him before it was too late. She was very vocal about it, which worried Dahlia too. She wanted Charles to meet a nice girl his own age.

Emma, Dahlia's youngest child at twenty-seven, had always been different from the others. There was nothing obviously wrong with her, but she had her own ideas, which were nothing like those of her siblings. She was artistic and expressed herself through her drawings and art and scribbles rather than eloquently with words, which always seemed to fail her. She couldn't compete with her siblings and didn't try. She ignored them. She was a dreamer. She had talked later than the others, had read late, and didn't have their high grades in school. She had no interest at all in the business and seemed unrelated to the others. She had a funny, punky style and a dry sense of humor. She seemed to see the humor in the situations her family took seriously, and she called life as she saw it. She loved Delphine, but had nothing in common with her, and liked playing with her two little nieces. Dahlia worried a lot about what would become of her later. Emma always seemed freshly arrived from another planet, and looked at her family as though they came from Mars and spoke a different language than she did. She was happy on her own, as long as she had a pencil and a notepad tucked into a pocket so she could draw. Her art style was primitive, and it had a sophisticated naivete to it, which was very much like her. She was child-like and womanly at the same time, sexy and innocent. She was an observer of life more than a participant.

Dahlia's family were her pride and joy, much as the business was. She loved it when the firm came up with a new perfume, or reintroduced an old one that she was proud of, and knew her grandfather would have been happy about. But her children's accomplishments and happiness meant even more to her. She was sad that her parents hadn't lived to see her children grow up, or Jean-Luc, who would have added another dimension to his children's lives, which would have been so different from what Dahlia had to offer them. She taught them intelligent, academic, worldly things, but Jean-Luc had a big heart and would have loved his children unconditionally, and given them the experience of physical adventures. He had loved them as babies, but never had the chance to know them as they grew up. They were still so young when he died, and Dahlia had done her very best with them as a single parent. It was harder with Charles because he was a boy. Delphine gave her credit for being a good mother, having children of her own, and being generous and forgiving by nature. Alex always complained about some element of their past that hadn't been to her liking, and she thought her mother could have done better and didn't hesitate to say it. She was harsh in her judgments, which always had a sharp edge to them. Dahlia was a much gentler person, and so was Delphine. Dahlia was a kind person despite her immense success. Alex was all sharp edges, with a long list of grudges dragged along from the past. Alex never forgot one's failings or the time someone had screwed up. She was jealous of her siblings, and even of her mother.

The siblings got on fairly well, except for Delphine and Charles, who sometimes had opposite goals for the business, and battled it out. They all found Alex harsh and uncharitable at times. And Emma was a mystery to them, except to Delphine, who understood her gentleness and differences instinctively, even when Emma's words and explanations, and vague philosophical meanderings didn't make sense. Emma's theories made sense to herself, occasionally to Dahlia, and almost always to Delphine. Alex didn't even try to understand her, nor did Charles. Emma could see it in their faces, so she never paid attention to them either.

Emma lived in her head and her own artistic world, and at twenty-seven, she still lived at home. She needed protection from the world. She was oblivious to anyone who'd want to hurt her. There was a sweet innocence about her that Delphine loved and that touched Dahlia profoundly.

Dahlia left her office early that night. She was flying to New York in two days, on the first leg of a tour of the United States, to check out the Lambert stores there, to make sure they looked right and the staff presented well and were gracious to their customers. She was going to the stores in New York, Chicago, San Francisco, L.A., and Dallas. It was the twenty-first of June and she was going to start the trip with a week in New York.

She had no emotional ties to the city anymore. She had grown up in New York and had lived there with her parents, with frequent trips to France, until she left for college and they moved to France for her father's retirement. She had lost touch with most of the old friends that she grew up with in New York, having moved to France thirty-two years ago. But she still had contact with a few. She had more in common with them but no time to see them. Her quick trips to New York were always too busy and brief. Her mother had been happy to move back to France, and her father had looked forward to it for years. It took the sting out of retiring for him. He had always loved Paris, its beauty and all the culture it offered. And their moving there thrilled him. Ever since her father's death, Dahlia had felt divorced from her early life and education in the United States. Her mother's influence and ties to France had been stronger; Europe suited Dahlia better, and she had lived there for more than half her life now herself. But she enjoyed visiting New York, the energy of it, the creativity, walking around, seeing familiar landmarks, and looking at the people she passed on the street and saw in Central Park. But it wasn't her city anymore. It was just fun to visit and exciting to do business there.

Alex and Charles felt no pull to the States. Only Delphine had always been intrigued by it, loved her college years there, and wanted to work in the U.S.—until she met Francois. Everything changed when she came back to France to work for her mother, and she had been satisfied and fulfilled ever since, both personally and professionally. She was happy with her life, unlike her sister Alex, who always wanted more or something different.

Dahlia looked into the glamorous shop windows on the Faubourg Saint-Honoré until she reached the car parking attendant, who went to get her car as soon as he saw her. She liked winding down at the end of the day, and often took work home with her. She had no plans with Philippe

Vernier that night and hadn't seen him in a week. She was spending that evening with her children before her trip, which was what she usually did before she left to travel.

Dahlia had remained unusually close to her children, in part because she had never remarried and there was no serious full-time man in her life and never had been since Jean-Luc. He was the love of her life. She and Philippe had kept their relationship just unengaged enough that she had plenty of time for her children and her work. And in part, she was closer to them because two of them worked in the family firm with her and they had constant daily contact. She was the kind of mother hen who kept a close eye on all of them. She was always available to them to solve a problem, to help with a crisis, or to cover a financial need they couldn't afford themselves. Her primary goal was always to make life easier for them and spare them pain. She was aware that she would have to let go at some point, and let them deal with their own problems, but she had never found an opportune moment to sever the cord entirely. She knew she should, and Philippe reminded her of it regularly, but it was very hard to do, and she never had. His parenting style was very different from hers and he had very little contact with his son.

She was leaving for three weeks, so she had invited them

all to dinner. She always made sure to spend an evening with them before she left.

Dahlia was well aware that her relationship with her children was unusually strong, and she loved it that way. They were the hub of her world, the center of her universe, more important than any man in her life since their father. She was closer to them than most women were to children their age. She appreciated each of them for who they were, with their weaknesses and their strengths. Charles, with his talent for finance, his loyalty to the family business and to her, and his attraction to women who were stronger than he was, she wanted to protect him and knew she couldn't. She understood his inability to express his love for her at times. She knew he loved her whether he showed it or not. She didn't expect more from him than she got.

She accepted Alex with all her sharp edges and occasionally razor-sharp tongue, more often than not used on her mother. Alex would have to soften that one day, or she would hurt all those she loved. She hadn't learned that lesson yet, but she was a talented woman with strengths of her own that she hadn't even discovered, though Dahlia thought she would one day.

Dahlia was grateful for the bond that she and Delphine had. It was an unexpected gift that she treasured, the confidences and common ground they shared. Delphine was all love, for her husband, her children, her mother, the business she helped to expand. She had made the right choices in her life, and shared the blessings of that with all who knew her. She was a bright ray of sun in Dahlia's life, and Dahlia was grateful for her every day.

And Emma was the gentle elfin soul who seemed to come from another place, with a universe all her own. Her touch was so light it felt like butterfly wings. Beyond her unusual, different style, she radiated goodness that flowed through her art into the world.

Dahlia was grateful for all of them, and for Philippe Vernier, who kept her earthbound with the limited time and affection he was able to give her, whatever the reason for his limitations.

Jean-Luc was the past, with all the love of youth, and he had given her the children who were her greatest gift. That had been his reason for being in her life even so briefly.

As Dahlia got in her car to drive home to have dinner with her children before she left on her trip to the States, she was a woman comfortable in her own skin, satisfied with the life she had built on what others had left her. It seemed like more than one could expect of life. She felt like a lucky woman, and she drove home happy and looking forward to seeing her children, even Alex with her prickly exterior. She was excited about her upcoming trip. If anyone had asked what more she wanted or would wish for, she couldn't have thought of a thing that was lacking. As far as Dahlia was concerned, she had it all, and realized just how fortunate she was. She smiled, thinking of them. Her children were the spice and the sunlight in her life. One couldn't ask for more.

Chapter 2

Dahlia's children arrived for dinner at her elegant hôtel particulier on the rue de Grenelle. There was a guardian's lodge inside the big dark green painted outer doors, tall enough for carriages to have driven through in the eighteenth century when the house was built. Louis Lambert had inherited the house from his father and left it to his daughter Constance, who had kept it. Constance and Hunter stayed there when they visited Paris, and then moved in when they left New York after Hunter retired. Dahlia had visited often when she was a child, and felt at home in her big beautiful room. She and Jean-Luc had lived there when they were married. Their children had grown up in that home and Dahlia still lived there now. Emma resided on the top floor, in the rooms with the round oeil-de-boeuf windows.

Dahlia had renovated the house several times since she had inherited it. The kitchen was high-tech now. She had added air-conditioning years before, which was a rarity in Paris, and had done the exquisite decorating herself. The house had been lived in by five generations now, and had aged well. Dahlia kept it in perfect condition. Inside the big carriage doors, which were kept closed, with a code to enter, or swung open by the guardian for deliveries and guests, there was a cobblestoned courtyard. The original bronze loops to tie up the horses were still there, regularly shined to a burnished glow, a historical detail that Dahlia loved. The stalls for the carriages were used for storage or cars now, and there were immaculate white marble steps leading to the front door. Henri, Dahlia's ancient butler, let each of them in when they rang the bell, and greeted them warmly. He loved it when they came to dinner. He had been there since they were children. He used to give them piggy-back rides and had taught them to ride their bikes.

Behind the house there was a beautiful garden, planted in all white flowers, and the lawn the children used to play on; the trees they hid behind when they played hide-and-seek while their mother watched them, or the nanny who took care of them when she went to work. The house was rich in their own family history, not just that of the people who had built it three hundred years before. Dahlia had kept the bedrooms modern and up-to-date, with bright, cheerful colors, and pastel silks in her own rooms, with heavy satin drapes held back with thick silk cords and long tassels in the formal rooms. The family living spaces were warm and comfortable with inviting couches, state-of-the-art video and stereo equipment, and fabulous contemporary art. Her children still loved being there and visiting Dahlia. She made everything so pleasant for them, and they were happy to see her before her trip.

Charles arrived first, from the office, after a long day's work. He was always happy to catch a few minutes alone with his mother, in a setting other than work, before the others arrived. He always said that once his sisters were in the room, it was hard to get a word in, especially with Alex there, who always had something to complain about and needed center stage. His girlfriend Catherine was meeting him at the house, and she always came late, terrified that the others would be even later, and she'd get trapped alone with his mother, since she knew Dahlia didn't approve of her. Dahlia was always perfectly polite, whatever her private feelings about her, but Catherine felt awkward being with her without Charles to hide behind. Catherine was from a simple working-class background in Clermont-Ferrand, a particularly unattractive city, and hadn't grown up with Charles's advantages or education.

She'd never had an important job and hadn't gone to university, and she'd had her daughter Rose in her teens without the benefit of marriage, all of which she knew worried Charles's mother. She and her daughter had been living in a rented room in a bad suburb of Paris when she met Charles, and two months later, she moved, with her daughter, into his very nice Left Bank apartment in the 7th arrondissement. Dahlia thought she was a gold digger, and Catherine could sense it, although Charlie never confirmed it in so many words, and his sister Alex was suspicious of her too, and outspoken on the subject to the point of being rude.

Before the others arrived, Charles chatted with his mother for a few minutes. Neither of them mentioned Catherine, which was a bigger topic than either of them wanted to address right before a trip. His mother liked to keep those evenings stress-free and enjoyable for everyone. They talked about work, and a trip to Rome Charles was taking soon. And then Henri let Delphine in, and she joined them in the library they used as an informal living room. There were family photographs on every surface, and on the shelves of a floor-to-ceiling bookcase. Delphine kissed both of them and sat down on her mother's other side, on the couch.

"How do you like those new shades of lipstick I sent you

this afternoon?" She gave her mother a broad smile and sank into the couch after a long day. She hated to miss giving her two little girls a bath and putting them to bed, but she was willing to sacrifice it for a family dinner before her mother's trip, a tradition they all loved. "I like your haircut, by the way," Delphine complimented her. They were both naturally blonde with long hair and looked like sisters. Dahlia was wearing hers down, and Delphine had hers pulled back in a bun for work. She tried to look businesslike to compensate for her youth.

"I gave Catherine a bunch of the last ones," Charles added, "and she loved them."

"We still need a great pink to flesh out the summer looks," Dahlia responded, and Delphine nodded agreement, as she took a sip of the white wine Henri handed her in one of her mother's elegant glasses. He knew exactly what they all drank, and their preferences. Dahlia was drinking champagne, and Charles was having a short scotch on the rocks. He needed something to calm his nerves for dinner with his mother and sisters. The scotch would give him patience and courage, and a boost after a long day at work.

Alex arrived next, looking windblown and frazzled. She collapsed into one of the oversized brown leather chairs and waved at her mother and siblings. "I had the worst day," she said breathlessly.

"Problems with the show?" her mother asked her, not too concerned. Alex frequently had "the worst day."

"No, they lost the order for my wedding shoes. Thank God I checked." Delphine suppressed a smile, and took a sip of her wine, as Henri handed Alex a dirty martini with extra olives, chilled ice-cold the way she liked it. "Thank you, Henri." She smiled at him. He used to help her sneak back in at night through the kitchen, when she stayed out past her curfew when she was younger. He had done it for the others too, which their mother knew, and grounded them anyway. Dahlia was loving and generous, but had run a tight ship when the children were in their teens. "I have a list of things I need my assistants to check on while you're away," Alex said to her mother, ignoring the others. She was obsessed with her wedding plans. She still had two fittings to do for the dress, being made by Dior. "Paul can't come to dinner tonight. He has a production meeting. I told Henri when I arrived." Delphine's husband Francois wasn't coming either. He had a business dinner. She had told her mother the day before. Their dinners were relaxed evenings. Dahlia didn't treat them as command performances, and her own children rarely declined. They all got along very well.

Catherine arrived next, shook Dahlia's hand, kissed Alex and Delphine, squeezed in next to Charles on the couch, and let the small talk fly around her without contributing. Alex had hair as dark as her mother's and Delphine's was fair, though her features were similar. There was a definite family resemblance between all of them, whatever their coloring. And Catherine's hair was dark brown with highlights in it. It fell in waves to her shoulders. She was a nice-looking woman and didn't look her age, but she wasn't as beautiful, as well-dressed, or as confident as his sisters, and she was acutely aware of it whenever she was with them. They were all very striking and she looked ordinary next to them, and felt it. Charles didn't seem to notice or care. He loved her.

As they sat drinking and talking, Emma arrived, as silent and ethereal as ever. She was delicate, with bright red hair, a pale ivory face, and huge cornflower blue eyes. She didn't say a word as usual, until Dahlia noticed her and put an arm around her. Emma had a way of entering a room that was almost ghostlike. She hated drawing attention to herself. She smiled when the others saw her, and then went to kiss all of them. She had paint splattered on her hands. She had a studio in the attic, where she spent hours, working on her abstract paintings. Her dream was to have an art show, which hadn't happened yet. She was taking classes at the Beaux-Arts. She had graduated from there five years before and was still studying. The Beaux-Arts was the best art school in Paris. Emma was as serious and dedicated to her art as the others were to their jobs. They treated her art as less important than their work, except Dahlia, who believed in her talent and encouraged her.

"I'm sorry I'm late, I was working on a painting and I couldn't leave it." Emma did acrylic paintings that looked like oil, in a riot of colors. She was wearing jeans splattered with paint too, with a clean T-shirt, and work boots, and her red hair was a wild mane of curls. Her looks were vivid, but her personality was pale. She seemed almost translucent.

The conversation at the table was lively as the prelude over cocktails. Alex talked incessantly about her wedding, ad nauseum—they were all sick of hearing about it. Delphine said to Charles in a whisper that it would be a relief when it was finally over in six weeks. They'd been hearing about it for a year, since she had gotten engaged to Paul. Charles and Delphine talked about the Lambert cosmetic line during dinner. Dahlia assured Alex that Agnes, her main assistant, had everything in total control for the wedding and would be following up while she was away. Catherine and Emma were engaged in quiet conversation, while the others bantered back and forth. Conversation was fast and lively at the table.

"It's just a quick trip," Dahlia told them, "to check out

our stores in five locations, New York, Chicago, San Francisco, L.A., and Dallas. I want to get a look at some of the American stores in person, and make sure they're up to our standards. If you don't visit them from time to time, they get sloppy and do whatever they want."

"Can't you send someone else?" Charles asked her, as he finished the excellent meal of soft-shell crab that Dahlia's cook had prepared.

"I could, but I'd rather see for myself. Nothing wakes them up like a visit from the boss," she said simply. "I'll be back in three weeks, or a little less."

"That's only three weeks before the wedding, Mother. You'd better be back here on time," Alex said ominously, and Delphine and Charles exchanged a smirk. They had both known she'd say that, and she had said it at least twice at dinner.

"I'll be back in plenty of time," Dahlia reassured her. She had expected the reminder too, and she always tried to be patient with Alex. "Concentrate on your show and leave everything to me and Agnes. We have it all in hand," she said confidently.

They stayed to chat for a few more minutes after dinner, kissed their mother, and hugged her tightly. She had one more day in the office the next day, so she would see Delphine and Charles again to say goodbye, and Emma at home, but she wouldn't see Alex or Catherine, and she hugged them both when they left. Even before the last of them left, Emma scampered back upstairs like a mouse, to work on her painting again. Dahlia smiled. She loved her evenings with her children. They were helter-skelter and informal, and reminded her of their dinnertimes as kids. She was looking forward to their coming to stay with her in Saint-Paul-de-Vence in August after Alex's wedding. She couldn't wait for that to be over. She was tired of hearing about it too, after a year, but it would soon be behind them, and then they could get back to normal life again and think of something else.

She sat down at her desk in the little office next to her bedroom and took some folders out of her briefcase. It was only ten o'clock, and she could get in a few hours of work before she went to bed. She knew that Emma would be up until all hours, but Dahlia never saw her once she went upstairs to her own floor. It was her private world that Dahlia didn't invade. Sometimes Emma worked all night on her paintings. Dahlia never intruded or interfered, and she had enough work to keep her busy until she went to bed. It had been a lovely relaxing evening with her kids. She knew she would miss them while she was away. And if they had a problem, or something went wrong, they always knew where she was, if they needed her. She had never been out of touch, unavailable, or too far away since the day they were born. She was their only parent, after all, and she took that very seriously. She had played a double role as mother and father almost all their lives. She was determined never to let them down, and never had so far.

She wouldn't be away for long, and then she'd be back to make Alex's wedding as perfect as she could. Dahlia always delivered what she promised, to them and everyone else.

Chapter 3

Dahlia's last day in the office before her trip was always hectic, as was her first day back, playing catch-up. Before she left, she tried to think of everything that could go wrong or might need her attention, and tried to tie up every loose end. She was a perfectionist, which was why her business was so successful. She wanted every customer who bought a Louis Lambert product to be satisfied, even thrilled.

She had meetings back-to-back all day. Some of them included Delphine, others didn't. She met with Agnes at the end of the day to go over wedding details that were still pending. Agnes was sixty-two years old and had worked for Dahlia for thirty years. She knew the business as well as Dahlia did, and she could second-guess what Dahlia's choices would be almost every time. Not always, but very close. Agnes was devoted to Dahlia and her children, and had loved working for Lambert Perfumes for almost her entire career. She had been married, was widowed now, and had no children. The business was her family and her job, and she had enormous respect for Dahlia. Agnes was an extraordinarily efficient assistant.

"She's nervous about all the details," Dahlia said to her about Alex. "She thinks we're going to forget something."

"She should know us better by now," Agnes said with a smile. They went over a checklist together again, and everything seemed to be accounted for, and most of the details had already been taken care of.

"I'll be back in time to put the finishing touches on it with you. I'll go to the final fittings with her. It's cutting it close, but Dior will have the dress ready for sure," Dahlia said confidently. Agnes didn't doubt it for a second. Alex and Paul were going to Greece on a sailboat for their honeymoon, and Alex's future husband was taking care of that. A friend was lending them the boat, with a crew of twelve.

Charles had already said goodbye to her when he left the office, and Dahlia stopped in to see Delphine to give her a last hug. And then Dahlia left. She had plans that night with Philippe. She had texted him the day before, and he was coming to spend the evening with her. Her children knew about the affair that had begun six years ago and had met Philippe at various times. They knew he was married, and it was clear he intended to stay that way. Nothing had changed during the last six years. Dahlia did not discuss him with her children, and they wouldn't have dared to comment. He was a well-known, highly respected person, the CEO of a very successful luxury brand. Dahlia went out with him publicly from time to time and saw him privately at her home twice a week. Whatever arrangement they had seemed to suit her, and she kept it to herself. The children knew he visited her in Saint-Paul-de-Vence in the summer after they left. She didn't make a secret of it, nor did she explain it to them. They were always with her for the first half of August, and he came for the second half. He spent four to six weeks with his wife and son in Saint-Jean-Cap-Ferrat before that, which Dahlia didn't tell them. If he made her happy, that was good enough for her children. He didn't interfere with them or their relationship with their mother, which was most important to them. It wasn't an unusual relationship in France, where most men who weren't happily married chose to maintain their marital status, lead separate lives from their spouses even if they lived in the same house, and not get divorced. Divorce was often viewed as an expensive American practice that was far less common or popular in France.

Dahlia had always steered clear of married men who pursued her, but Philippe was so attractive and appealing, and they slid into their attachment to each other so effortlessly that it seemed normal to her now, and their six years together had flown past. He never tried to hide her—they went to public events together, and she enjoyed the two nights he spent with her every week. It gave her companionship, they shared many similar tastes and opinions, and their part-time arrangement left her the time she needed for her business and her family. He didn't detract from her life, he added to it, which was key to her. Since she didn't want to marry again, it no longer bothered her that he was married. She wouldn't have had time for a full-time man, an overly demanding relationship, a marriage, or a difficult man. Philippe wasn't. The arrangement worked perfectly for both of them. And with her children out of the house with their own lives, except for Emma, she had the freedom to do what she wanted. She had just enough room in her life for Philippe now, and their time together was wonderful. She was fifty-six and he was sixty-four. They both felt old enough to structure their life the way they wanted. What she shared with him was warm, intelligent, and familiar. She could talk to him about business or anything else. He wasn't particularly good for advice about children, because he had been so uninvolved with his own son, and barely saw him even now as an adult. Dahlia loved her relationship with her children. Philippe was disappointed that his son, Julien, was more of a player than a worker or serious person.

Dahlia's relationship with Philippe was a purely private pleasure. They were almost like good friends or an old married couple. It wasn't the kind of relationship she had expected to have, but it was the one they had fashioned in the circumstances, with the time they both had available and were willing to share. There were nights when she actually preferred being alone to do whatever she wanted. And it wasn't easy for Philippe to be close. He had spent years before he met her guarding his emotions, having affairs with women he didn't really care about, and having a fraudulent relationship with his wife. He kept a distance between himself and Dahlia that was comfortable for him. Dahlia realized that he was afraid of closeness, even though he was at ease with her now, and she kept a safe distance from him too by not being with him all the time. Whatever it was, or the reasons for it, it worked for them.

She was happy to see him when he arrived in time for dinner. He brought a bottle of her favorite champagne, and Henri had gotten caviar at her request. They liked spoiling each other to make their time together special. There was always something festive about it. She was wearing white satin lounging pajamas, with high-heeled silver sandals, her long blonde hair swept up. He loved the way she looked and how elegantly she dressed. He loved being out with her, and being seen with her, and she was proud to be with him. And what happened between them was no one's business. There was a touch of mystery to it because no one knew what it was for sure. What they lacked in deep emotion they made up for with intellectual attraction, comfortable companionship, and good sex. She didn't think she had a right to expect more at her age, and was convinced that true love only came around once, and she'd already had hers, so what she shared with Philippe was enough, and more than many people had at their age. It was romantic in a superficial way, and warm at the same time. After six years, they knew each other well. She couldn't imagine having more than that now, and Philippe had made it clear right from the beginning that divorce would never be an option, nor remarriage. He intended to end his days legally married to Jacqueline, even if they spent little time together, had never had an honest exchange, and according to Philippe had never been in love. It had been an appropriate joining of two important families and nothing more.

At least what he shared with Dahlia was sincere. It was a bond between two people with bright minds who enjoyed each other's company, were attracted to each other, and were surprisingly at ease with each other in parallel lives. There was no pretense that it was more than it was. She felt she could say anything to him. Philippe had been an unexpected gift in her life, and she was always surprised that it had lasted this long, given his circumstances.

He wasn't what she had expected or wanted, but she was happy to have him in her life. There were definite limitations to their relationship, but she accepted it for what it was. He had warned her early on that he had a fear of women who wanted too much from him, and deep emotions weren't his strong suit. She had accepted that about him, which he appreciated. She never tried to make more of their affair than what it was. She was an unusual woman in that respect, and never tried to change him. In her own way, she loved him as he was. She wasn't disappointed by him, because he didn't pretend to be more. She missed what she'd had with Jean-Luc sometimes, but she had no illusions about finding that again. She was content with Philippe.

Jean-Luc was ancient history, a youthful dream that hadn't lasted long. What she shared with Philippe, however limited, was her reality now. She never tried to alter it or asked him to leave his wife. She knew he wouldn't have, and she accepted the timetable he set, and his limited emotions as the price she paid for being involved with a married man. It wasn't perfect, but it worked well enough for them, and particularly for him. The American in her would have preferred a cleanly divorced man, even if they never married and didn't live together. But Philippe was who life had put on her path, and she made the best of it with good humor and grace, and never made him feel he was falling short, even when he was. At sixty-four, he was never going to change. He had made the ground rules clear right from the beginning, and had never deviated from them, or deepened their relationship, which was precisely what he didn't want.

"How long will you be gone?" he asked her over lobster salad. She knew all his favorite meals and had them for him whenever he dined with her. He took her to the finest restaurants and liked to eat well. He was a bon vivant, a man of sophisticated tastes.

"About three weeks. I enjoy trips like it occasionally, checking on our image in other countries and cities, and seeing how well our representatives are upholding the standards we set here. I enjoy going to the States now and then."

"I always forget you're half American," he said, smiling at her. "You don't seem like it."

"I don't feel like it. I've been here for a long time. It felt more real when my father was alive. Delphine has always been attracted to life in the States. The others have no interest in it whatsoever. It's funny how different they are."

"You've done a good job with them." Philippe was always surprised by how close she was to her children, a little too much so he thought. He often advised her that she should let them fly on their own, without providing such a strong safety net under them. He thought they needed a chance to fail too, but she never wanted them to get hurt, and was determined to protect them. He found it touching and startling at times. His parents had never done that for him. He'd been raised in boarding schools from a young age. His parents had manifested very little interest in him, and expressed no emotion, which was why he found deep feelings unfamiliar and alarming and had no idea how to navigate them.

He had married a cold woman because it was all he knew of relationships. He had thought that good breeding and good manners were enough, and yet had always found something lacking, until Dahlia came along, and he was attracted to her like a moth to a flame. But when he got too close to her, her warmth seared him, and he backed away immediately.

She was a loving person, and he admired that about her, but he had no role model to follow, and no idea how to reciprocate. Philippe took no risks with his heart—the only risks he took were in business. He only got as close to her as he could tolerate, like sitting near a warm fire in winter, but never getting close enough for the sparks or flames to touch him. The fire within her burned much more brightly than the fire in him, but he appreciated the fact that she accepted him as he was, without forcing him to come closer, or expecting more of him. The deep love she had described to him that she had shared with her husband in her youth would have terrified him.

As expected, after dinner, which had been excellent, they disappeared to her bedroom. Henri had left by then, and their lovemaking was testimony to how well they knew each other and enjoyed each other, rather than being inspired by deep emotion. He left her at midnight, and would have preferred to spend the night as he always did on their nights together. But she was leaving early in the morning for her flight to New York and had to get up at dawn. Her suitcases were packed, and after he dressed, still basking in the haze of their very satisfying lovemaking, she walked him to the door in a pink satin dressing gown that outlined the lithe figure that never failed to arouse him—even more so than some of his younger partners had before he met her. He had never cheated on her in their six years together, which was new for him, and always surprised him. He knew she was faithful to him and was touched by it. Fidelity had never been part of his marriage.

"Don't go falling in love with an American," he said in a raw whisper, as he kissed her when they reached the front door. She looked beautiful and tender in her pink dressing gown and bare feet. He would have liked to make love to her again, but she only had a few hours left to sleep. "A handsome New Yorker, a movie star in L.A., or a cowboy in Texas."

"I'll try not to," she said, as she kissed him. They both knew that would never happen.

"I'll call you," he said. It was the unspoken agreement they had. She very rarely called him, not wanting to get him at a bad time, if Jacqueline was around. And she knew that soon, before she got back from the States, he would be leaving for his annual summer vacation with his family in the south of France. It was the only time all year that he, his wife, and son Julien went anywhere together. He would be leaving sometime in early July and staying in Saint-Jean-Cap-Ferrat until mid-August, when he joined Dahlia in Saint-Paul-de-Vence. He would already be gone when she got back, and he wasn't coming to Alex's wedding. They had discussed it and agreed that he didn't belong there, as he wasn't close to Alex. Dahlia would be busy overseeing the wedding, so she wasn't going to be seeing him for a long time, about seven weeks, until he came to Saint-Paul-de-Vence in mid-August—longer than usual this year, because of her trip.

He left a few minutes later and walked to his car in the courtyard. It was a balmy June night and she stood in the doorway and waved as he got to his car. He stopped the car at the big outer doors, and the guardian came out to help him. After he drove out onto the rue de Grenelle, she closed the door and went back into the house.

She had her own life to live, and Philippe had his, in their separate worlds, with the distance between them that he needed and that she told herself was best for her too. But now and then she wondered what it would be like if he wasn't married, and he wasn't afraid that love was too great a risk to take, even after six years. He always retreated to the distance where he felt safe. Seven weeks apart now would be easy for him. It gave her the time she wanted with her children, and for her work. She told herself that this way no one would get too attached, and no one would get hurt. The distance between her and Philippe kept her life orderly and predictable, even though she knew it wasn't what love could be, with all the ups and downs that made it exciting and so much sweeter. Philippe had never experienced what that kind of love was, and didn't want to. And Dahlia was happy enough being his lover twice a week. It was what destiny had given her, and she accepted with grace.

Chapter 4

Dahlia's flight landed in New York on schedule. She went through customs and immigration with no problem, using her American passport. She never used it, except on trips to the States. The rest of the time, in Europe and Asia, she used her French one.

"Welcome back to the United States," the customs officer said by rote without looking at her, handing her dark blue passport back to her. It always reminded her of her father when she used it. She collected her luggage, found a porter, and left the terminal to find the car and driver Agnes had booked for her. Dahlia preferred a discreet SUV when she traveled for business. It was hot outside the terminal. The summer had already gotten started. It was late June, and considerably warmer than Paris. She had traveled in black slacks, a white T-shirt, and a light tan jacket. The driver was holding a small discreet card with her name on it. She identified herself to him, and he got her bags from the porter, whom she tipped. Minutes later they sped away from the airport toward the city.

There was always a feeling of excitement arriving in New York. There was an undeniable electric energy everywhere, even driving through the suburbs. With the time difference in her favor, it was only ten A.M. in New York, but traffic was already heavy on the highway. She had slept briefly on the plane, and wasn't tired, despite the obscenely early hour she had to get up in order to be at the airport at six to check in for the eight A.M. flight. She had left her house in Paris at five-thirty, when it was still dark. She'd be at the hotel at eleven A.M. New York time, which gave her all the time she needed to change and be at their uptown store at noon. She was going to confirm her arrival to their rep when she got to the hotel. Everything had gone like clockwork so far. She was going to visit the downtown store on Monday, and she had appointments after that with their American PR firm, and the head of their local business office to analyze some numbers with him.

She called Delphine from the car. It was only four P.M. in Paris, so Dahlia knew she'd still be at the office. She called her on her cellphone in case she was away from her desk, as she often was, checking on things all over the building, from production to marketing, to the design office about the packaging they were working on for their new cosmetic line. Dahlia had just approved the testing for a costly antiaging line Delphine had convinced her to launch, in order to stay current against their competitors. It would cost them a fortune to develop, and Dahlia was always skeptical about those products. She didn't believe in them herself, or use them, but people loved them, men and women, and they swore by the best ones out there. Lambert had cautiously entered the market with one or two products, but now they were going to go after that market segment full bore, and were making rapid strides in becoming competitive with the others.

Delphine answered on the second ring as soon as she saw her mother's number come up. She was out of breath. "Hi, Mom, sorry. I was running up the stairs from the basement."

"What were you doing there?" Delphine always surprised her, and impressed her.

"There was some crazy computer bug in shipping today. I went down to make sure they were dealing with it. It turns out that it's at the warehouse."

"Don't you have assistants to do that?" Delphine amazed her.

"Yes, but I wanted to make sure they were dealing with

it properly, and the tech guys were down there for a meeting. You'd have done the same thing," Delphine reminded her, and Dahlia laughed.

"You're right. I probably would have." Dahlia liked laying eyes and hands on situations herself. Delphine had learned it from her. Charles was more of a delegator, which Dahlia thought was a more male point of view. Delphine felt there was nothing too low or too inconsequential to deal with, which was Dahlia's philosophy too. "What did I miss today?" Dahlia asked her.

"Nothing." Delphine sounded more relaxed. She had gotten back to her office and slid into her desk chair. "It was pretty quiet today. I had marketing meetings this morning, nothing you don't already know. Are you at the hotel yet?"

"I'm on the highway. We'll be there soon. I'm seeing Madison Avenue today. I'll spend Monday in Soho."

"What are you doing this weekend?" Dahlia was thinking of contacting an old school friend she hadn't spoken to in two years. Her college friends had been from all over the country and dispersed after she graduated, and she hadn't seen any of them in a long time. She got Christmas letters with photographs of people she didn't recognize and whose names she barely remembered. It was hard to live in another country, have a busy life, and stay in touch.

"I'll walk around, shop a little. I brought a mountain of reading with me. I have a lot to read to get up to speed on the stores in the five cities I'm visiting. I keep a close eye on New York and L.A., but I have to read up on the others." Chicago, San Francisco, and Dallas. "I thought I'd drop by the Soho store and see how they treat me as an unknown customer. That's always good to know. What are you doing this weekend?"

"I'm taking the girls to visit Francois' parents. They haven't been to see them in ages, and I promised them a ride on the carousel. We're having dinner with clients of Francois tonight." She had a fully rounded life between her job, her husband and kids, and their family life. It was no different from what Dahlia had done at Delphine's age, except her world had only had one parent a few years later. Delphine's children had two.

They ended the call a few minutes later, as Dahlia's driver crossed the bridge into the city, sped down the FDR Drive, and then cut across the East Side to get to the Four Seasons Hotel at Fifty-seventh Street, between Park and Madison. The doorman and a porter rushed forward to take the bags, and Dahlia told the driver she wouldn't need him for the rest of the day. She was going to walk to the store five blocks up Madison, and she was planning to have dinner in her room that night. It would be late on Paris time by then.

Agnes had pre-checked her in, and all Dahlia had to do was sign at the desk. They took her to her usual suite on the fiftieth floor. It had a bedroom and a living room, a dining room she could use as a conference room if she needed it, and a small kitchen that was well stocked with snacks and amenities. The minibar was equally so, and the view was spectacular. The décor was spare and somewhat cold, but it was her favorite hotel in New York, impeccably run, and less than five blocks from the store, in the same block as Hermès. She could cast an eye inside Hermès on her way back to the hotel. She liked checking to see what they had in New York that they didn't have in Paris, and Madison Avenue was a perfect location for the Lambert store, since they had a similar client base to Hermès's, and both were prominently located on Madison Avenue. Lambert had a two-level luxury store that looked like a work of art. They had spent a fortune on it, which their sales figures justified. Dahlia thought it was one of their most beautiful stores after the one on the Faubourg, which she had kept as close to the original as she could, while bringing it up-to-date subtly over the years. Their customers expected their stores to have a certain opulent, elegant look.

She opened her bags once the manager and porter left the suite and helped herself to a bottle of sparkling water at the minibar, while she admired the view. There was an enormous bouquet of white roses in the room from the manager. Her phone rang as she was about to undress to take a shower and put on a chic black linen suit she had taken out of her bag and dropped on the bed. She was surprised when she saw the number. It was Philippe.

"You have been gone a day and I already miss you," he said when she answered, and she laughed. "You've ruined me. How was the trip?"

"Uneventful. Two movies, a salad and some very good Brie, and a nap."

"How's New York?" He loved just hearing the sound of her voice. Memories of the night before flooded into his mind, and he wished that she was still in Paris so he could spend the night with her, before going to his country home for the weekend. She had been there with him before, when the servants were off, and Jacqueline was out of town for a horse show or a hunt. But Dahlia was ill at ease about going to one of his homes, even if he was alone, and preferred to see him at hers. She thought it disrespectful to his wife to go to his.

"It seems as lively as ever. I just got here. I haven't been to the store yet," she said of New York.

"I miss you." That was a big admission for him, and it touched her. He always seemed fine whenever she was away.

"I miss you too," she said, although she really hadn't had time to yet. She would miss him when she got back to Paris and he had left, but she'd be busy then too, with Alex's wedding two weeks after she got home, and afterward, moving to the house in the south of France. And two weeks after that, Philippe would come to visit her there. She had a busy two months ahead of her. His vacation was starting a month before hers, so he'd have time on his hands.

"We should go to New York together again one of these days, maybe in the fall," Philippe commented. They always had fun when they did, seeing people they knew, going out to dinner in fabulous restaurants. She liked traveling with him, which they did once or twice a year, and always for a short time. It was hard to get away from their jobs. "I like L.A. too," he continued, "but it's so damn far. You can go to New York for a weekend, but not the West Coast. Between the nine-hour time difference and an eleven- or twelve-hour flight, it's too much."

"That's why I'm here for three weeks. Everything after New York is a big trip."

"Well, don't have too much fun," he said, and almost sounded jealous. He never was, and it made her happy that he'd called her. Sometimes she didn't hear from him for a week or two while she was away, or he was. But once he was in the south of France, she knew he'd get busy seeing friends and probably wouldn't call her again. After six years she knew him well, and his habits and his quirks.

They talked for a few more minutes and then got off. She took a shower, ordered coffee from room service, and had a cup while she put on the black linen suit. She didn't want to fall asleep during her meetings. At some point the long day and the time difference would catch up with her. She was used to it. The rep had told her they would order food for lunch at the store. She wanted to get some work done first.

Her first impression of the store would be important, about how the sales staff looked, how respectfully they wore the uniform—a neat black jacket and black slacks or a skirt, stockings, and high heels, hair impeccably cut or pulled back. No facial jewelry or piercings, no visible tattoos. The uniforms had been designed by Dior. Dahlia was a stickler for how her employees looked. She wanted nothing about their person to distract from the beauty of the store, and the exquisite bottles they had lined up on display. Dahlia wanted everything to be perfect, and she had asked the rep not to tell the sales staff she was coming. She wanted to see how they looked for real, not how they dressed up to impress her.

Twenty minutes after she spoke to Philippe, Dahlia was wearing her black linen suit with high heels, diamond studs in her ears, and carrying a black leather Hermès Kelly bag as she walked up Madison Avenue, glancing in the shop windows she passed, admiring their wares. Hermès had an enormous black leather horse in the window, with a saddle made of red and black silk scarves, just for display purposes. As always, their windows were incredible. And there was an enormous red alligator Kelly bag next to the horse, and a crop and feed bag next to it. She stopped for a minute to admire the display. It was hard to resist.

Half a block later, she was standing in front of her own store, under the handsome sign that said LOUIS LAMBERT, with exquisitely done decorative creations in the windows. They couldn't compete with the life-size black leather horse in the window at Hermès, but their bottles were beautifully designed, and there were two giant ones they had had made for display purposes. The entire store was done in gray silk faille, with a navy blue ceiling sparkling with tiny stars embedded in it, upholstered gray walls in the faille, and gray and white marble cabinetry and a gray marble floor. It was the epitome of chic, with samples of all their bottles on display. The bottles alone were works of art. There were two long counters of testers, which the sales staff was supposed to know everything about, both the history and the contents. Every perfume came in eau de toilette, eau de parfum, and perfume, with derivative creams, soaps, and other products. And there was a small room in the back, in black marble, for all the men's products and scents as well, with a young man in a white shirt and black suit to demonstrate them. Their men's products had become increasingly successful since her grandfather's day and represented forty percent of their sales now.

Marie-Helene Roberts, the head rep, was waiting outside, per instructions. Dahlia greeted her warmly and shook hands with her. She was a woman in her fifties who had worked in the perfume industry for her entire career, previously at Chanel, and Dahlia had met her before. They walked into the store.

There were five women and a man working when they walked in. Dahlia looked them all over quickly. She noticed immediately that one of the women was wearing a black sweater instead of her uniform jacket, and the youngest-looking one had on pink running shoes and not plain black high heels. They glanced at Dahlia without recognizing her. At a nod from Dahlia, Marie-Helene introduced her, and for an instant all six of the sales staff froze, then greeted her politely and shook hands with her. Marie-Helene was French but had lived in New York since Chanel transferred her there twenty years before. Dahlia could hear that two of the saleswomen were French as well. It was a decidedly French brand, and she liked having French people on their staff. It somehow gave them more credibility as a venerable French company.

The sales staff clustered around, and Dahlia opened cupboards to look at the stock, and asked them questions about their customers and their bestselling products. They were well versed, and Marie-Helene could see Dahlia's look of approval as she nodded, but she knew there would also be hell to pay for the sweater and the running shoes. She didn't want a hair out of place or the slightest deviation from the uniform, and they had to look immaculate. At least none of them had tattoos, or not where anyone could see them. Dahlia was intransigent about that, and it was nonnegotiable. Their customers could have as many tattoos as they wanted, but not the sales staff. That was not the image Dahlia wanted for Louis Lambert around the world. And there had to be a certain uniformity of the kind of people who sold their products. She didn't care about race, but they had to be impeccable, well-spoken, polite, and perfectly groomed. The image they cultivated was that a Lambert perfume would make you feel like royalty when you wore it, and as far as Dahlia was concerned, royalty didn't have nose piercings and tattoos. The company paid for manicures twice a week for the in-store sales staff, for the men as well, and she expected them to take full advantage of the benefit. She didn't want them demonstrating the perfumes with broken dirty nails or chipped nail polish. She noticed that they all had immaculate hands as she chatted with them. No detail escaped her notice, and after an hour in the store, as customers came and went, Marie-Helene and Dahlia went upstairs to a private room with the store manager. Dahlia took a pad out of her bag the moment they sat down and made rapid notes as Marie-Helene and Aimee, the store manager, chatted.

"I'm sorry about the running shoes and the sweater," Aimee said sheepishly to Dahlia before she could hand her the list. "They know better. I said something to both of them this morning when they came to work. Margaret said that her jacket got lost at the dry cleaner, and Josette said she had warts removed yesterday. I promise you, we maintain a high standard most of the time, but things happen."

"I'm sure you'll find her a new jacket quickly. Marie-Helene can help you with it, and maybe Josette can find some suitable black ballerina flats until her foot heals."

"I'll see to it," Aimee promised.

"I was very impressed by their knowledge of the products," Dahlia praised them with a smile, "and Steve gave me some very useful feedback about the men's products that's good for us to know," she said, handing the store manager the list. There were nine items about their setup of the displays that she wanted corrected, and when Aimee read the list she didn't disagree with her. Dahlia had an incredible eye for detail.

"I'm sorry, you're absolutely right. I didn't notice any of these things myself. They're easy to correct once you see them."

"Don't feel bad." Dahlia smiled at her. "I straighten the paintings in people's houses when they're not looking when they invite me to dinner. It may sound silly, but the details matter, and have an impact on how people react to the store and the products we're selling. And personal appearance is a big factor too."

"I'll take care of it immediately," Aimee promised. They had set up one of the major displays backward, and she hadn't even noticed. It was a new perfume they were introducing, and someone had followed the diagram backward for the installation.

Marie-Helene suggested a restaurant two blocks up the street then, instead of ordering in. "You must be exhausted." It was almost three o'clock, nine P.M. in Paris.

"No, I'm fine, it's normal dinner time for me."

They left the store a few minutes later and went to the restaurant the rep had suggested, where they had authentic French bistro food. By the time they came back an hour and a half later, Aimee had implemented all of Dahlia's corrections, which she saw immediately when they walked back into the store.

"Perfect," Dahlia said, smiling broadly. And Josette had been sent to Bloomingdale's to buy a pair of black ballet flats with rubber soles. Everything was in order, and Dahlia shook hands with all of them and thanked them. There were three customers in the store then, and Dahlia was pleased to see that they were doing a brisk business with the clever, discreet guidance of the sales staff. It was one of their most important stores, she wanted it to be perfect, and now it was.

Dahlia and Marie-Helene parted company on the sidewalk at five o'clock, and Dahlia was pleased by everything she'd seen, and the minor corrections they'd implemented.

"You have a good staff there," she praised her.

"They're very responsive, and Aimee does a good job with them. I'm sorry for the slipups, and your comments about the displays were very helpful."

They were meeting again on Monday at the store in Soho, which was liable to be less precise than the Madison Avenue store. It was going to be another visit without warning, which was one of Dahlia's hallmarks, so she could get a real impression of what the customers saw. "See you on Monday then," Marie-Helene said to her in French, and Dahlia left her to walk back to the hotel. She was tired by then, but she wanted to get on local time, so she didn't want to go to bed early. She wandered into a couple of shops on the way back and enjoyed seeing the merchandise. Madison Avenue was one of her favorite shopping streets in the world, though not as much so as the Faubourg Saint-Honoré in Paris. That was still Mecca for shoppers of the finest luxury brands, but Madison Avenue was a close second, and always reminded her of shopping with her mother when she was in college. Constance had exquisite taste and had taught Dahlia a great deal about fashion. She was one of the most elegant women Dahlia had ever known, and she used to love to watch her dress. Her own daughters had their own style too, but people didn't dress the way they used to in Constance's day, with the same quality, elegance, and attention to detail. The world had changed. Dahlia loved dressing well too, but she had her own moments of wearing jeans and running shoes on the weekends, especially when she went on long walks with Philippe on a Sunday when he was in town. She had brought two pairs of jeans with her, to wear on the weekends she would be in California.

She went shopping the next day at her favorite New York stores. It was Saturday, and after she shopped in midtown, she had the driver take her down to the Soho store, to get an advance impression. The store was crowded and the staff were selling well, but they looked noticeably less polished than the Madison Avenue staff. It was all minor details, and she was pleased at how she heard them converse with the customers and the information they shared with them. There was nothing glaringly wrong, and she made a list in the cab on the way uptown, of things to mention to them on Monday.

Dahlia had dinner in her room again that night. Philippe didn't call her, nor did any of her children. They were busy. She watched a movie and fell asleep. She would have liked to go to a restaurant if she had someone to have dinner with, but she didn't. She woke up early the next day, on Sunday, and wanted some exercise. She had slept well, and she put on a pair of the jeans she had brought, and her running shoes, and walked to Central Park. There were couples out with their children. It was a hot, sunny day, and she sat on a bench and watched them for a while, soaking up the sun. She had worn a starched white shirt and rolled up the sleeves. Even in simple clothes, she had a crisp, chic look, with a heavy gold bracelet on one arm and a denim Kelly bag that had been her mother's that was no longer made. It was a collectors' treasure now and she loved it.

She walked around the reservoir, and just being there reminded her of her youth and growing up in New York. It was so blissfully familiar to her, and a memory of a happy time in her life with her parents, when she went to the Lycée in New York, and then Columbia. New York was an echo of the distant past for her, it wasn't home anymore, but she enjoyed being there and savoring it. At lunchtime she bought a hot dog and a Coke from a food truck and felt like a New Yorker for a minute. But she wasn't a New Yorker. She was a Parisian, and she looked it, even in jeans and running shoes. It was something about her, the way she did her hair, just an attitude that French women had. She didn't look like an American, she was too carefully put together, with her sneakers and her mother's Hermès bag.

After she ate her hot dog, she sat on a bench in the park for a while, watching couples strolling, holding hands, families sitting on blankets or playing ball. A steel band was playing and added to the festive atmosphere. It was like a carnival in front of her, and she thoroughly enjoyed it. She stayed in the park all afternoon, then walked back to the hotel. It was too late to call her children by then and Philippe hadn't called her all weekend, which didn't surprise her. She was comfortable being there. She hadn't walked by her parents' old home in the East Seventies, because it would make her sad. New York was always nostalgic for her when she wasn't busy working. But she had a feeling of warmth and well-being after the day in the park. She had a glass of wine when she got back to the hotel and ordered a salad for a light dinner. She watched another movie and it felt like a brief vacation. From the next morning on, she knew she would be working. She had the store visit lined up in Soho the next day, a meeting uptown that afternoon, and a day of meetings with the advertising and PR agency. On Wednesday she was leaving for Chicago, and had two days of meetings there, and a press event to attend to launch their new perfume. On Friday, she was flying to San Francisco. She'd have a day off on Saturday, another on Sunday, and then hit the ground running, with store visits and meetings in San Francisco before heading to L.A. It was a full schedule from now on, which was why she was there.

The visit to the Soho store went smoothly the next day. She noted the corrections she wanted, made a few changes, and reminded them of the uniform requirements and how important they were for their image, whether downtown or uptown. They had many high-end customers from Tribeca, Soho, and lower Fifth Avenue who expected to see the same high standards as they did at all of Lambert's stores worldwide. The manager of the store, a young man originally from Hong Kong, took it well, and was quick to react to the improvements Dahlia wanted. She liked him a lot, and was pleased with the visit, much to Marie-Helene's relief, and her meeting afterward went well.

Her day with their ad agency was a big success, and by the time she left for Chicago on Wednesday, Dahlia was very happy with her stay in New York. It had been productive, and all of her New York–based employees had been responsive, and she thought Marie-Helene was doing a great job. The night before she left for Chicago, she reported to Delphine, who was delighted to hear her mother sounding so pleased. All was well in Paris, and Dahlia realized when they hung up that she hadn't heard from Philippe in a week. It was typical of him. He was sad when she left, but busy with his own life now. She knew he was going to his house in Saint-Jean-Cap-Ferrat that week with his son and wife.

In Chicago she checked into the Peninsula hotel. She had stayed there before, but not in a long time. Her suite felt like a yacht, and had every high-tech luxury feature currently available to add to the comforts of the elegant rooms. She was always fascinated by the architecture in Chicago. It was designed for the brutal weather they had in winter, with snow and blizzards and ice-cold winds, when people would do anything to avoid going out. Numerous buildings were used for multiple purposes—twenty floors for a hotel, another twenty for apartments, or offices, a movie theater, a supermarket, a department store—fifty and sixty stories, which made it possible not to leave the building for weeks. Dahlia found it fascinating, and had been intrigued by it when she'd gone there before.

In the warm weather, the lake was beautiful, and there were sailboats on it, and people enjoying water sports. It was entirely different from New York. Chicago was a small, sophisticated city, with an elegant feel to it. It didn't have the frantic electric energy of New York, but it wasn't a sleepy city either. It felt just right, and was a completely different experience from New York City. She enjoyed being there.

Her meetings went well. The Lambert store in Chicago was beautiful, and the staff was extremely pleasant and looked impeccable when she met them.

She had meetings there for three days and was sorry to leave as she boarded the plane on the last night of June, heading for San Francisco. She had a day off the next day, Saturday, and she wanted to enjoy the city before her meetings started on Monday. So far, her American tour had gone well, and she was happy when she boarded the plane at O'Hare Airport for the four-and-a-half-hour flight to San Francisco on Friday night. The two-hour time difference was in her favor again. She fell asleep before they took off and didn't wake up until they landed. She woke up feeling refreshed, and ready to enjoy another city on her trip.

Tuesday was the Fourth of July. She hadn't spent a Fourth of July in the States since she was a child. It was going to be fun! She was smiling as she disembarked from the plane and headed for baggage claim to collect her bags.

Chapter 5

The driver Agnes had hired for Dahlia in San Francisco found her at baggage claim and gave her a hand. He was young and energetic, got her bags off the carousel, and left them with her on the sidewalk when he went to get the car. He had a big friendly smile, and on the way into the city, he told her he was a graduate student at UC Berkeley, and driving was his summer job. He said he had met a writer and two movie stars so far, and asked her where she was from. When she told him Paris, amused by how chatty he was, and how open and agreeable, he said he had a French girlfriend freshman year, but she'd gone back to Paris two years later, and they still wrote to each other. She was from Lyon, he told Dahlia. He was from North Carolina. He was going into his second year of school.

He told Dahlia she should visit the Napa Valley while she was there, saying it was beautiful and looked just like Europe. She enjoyed talking to him and thanked him with a big tip when she got to the hotel. She was staying at The Ritz-Carlton halfway down Nob Hill, at the edge of Chinatown. She had stayed there before and liked it. It was a short walk, although down a steep hill, to Union Square, where all the high-end shops were. She had a beautiful view of the Bay Bridge from the windows of her suite. It was her favorite hotel in San Francisco, and the service was excellent, better than the other hotels she'd tried before.

At the top of Nob Hill was small, elegant Huntington Park; the old Flood Mansion that was the Pacific-Union Club now, the most elite men's club in the city; the Fairmont and Mark Hopkins hotels; and Grace Cathedral, with its spectacular carved bronze doors. San Francisco was a small city, with a thriving financial district, composed of a cluster of skyscrapers, that were out of step with the rest of the architecture in town. The city boasted a still-busy port, full of cruise ships—it was mostly a tourist town now—and the residential area was full of old Victorian homes, some of which had been turned into apartment buildings, but many of which were still grand homes, where the wealthy population lived. None of the buildings, or very few, were more than six stories high, and there was still a genteel feeling to Pacific Heights, full of family homes, and a few very impressive ones. It was a city that had known great wealth and had had a resurgence with all the young investors in technology who had made big money. Many of them lived south of the city in Palo Alto, where Stanford University was, while others lived in Marin County, some on the island of Belvedere, or in the city proper. And curled around the city was the Bay, with the Golden Gate Bridge at the mouth of it, leading to the Pacific Ocean. Dahlia had heard that there were some lovely beaches nearby but had never been to them, nor had she been to the wine country in Napa Valley, so highly recommended by her young driver. On a spur-of-the-moment whim, she asked the concierge at the front desk how far the Napa Valley was from the city, and if it was worth the trip just for the day.

"Definitely," he said, agreeing with what the driver had told her. "It's lovely country, with many excellent wineries you can visit. The vineyards are beautiful to see. You shouldn't miss it. It's an hour and a half away, and an easy drive. We can get you a car and driver, if you'd like, or arrange to rent a car for you. It's directly north of the city, with gorgeous warm weather, and some of our best restaurants. Would you like me to arrange a car for you, Ms. de Beaumont?"

In the spirit of the moment, Dahlia decided to try it. She

could always change her mind and drive around the city instead, or go across the Golden Gate Bridge and visit the charming town of Sausalito on the other side. It was all very picturesque, which was why it was so popular with the tourists. The Lambert store in San Francisco was on Post Street, half a block from Union Square, where the department stores were, and it shared the block on Post Street with the most exclusive jewelers in the city: Harry Winston, Graff, and Cartier. And once again, Hermès was their neighbor a few doors away, around the corner, with Christian Dior across the street. The Lambert customers in San Francisco were mostly Asian and European tourists. Their second store was in the Stanford Shopping Center in Palo Alto, where all their high-tech customers lived. The city had been home to people of great wealth since the Gold Rush days. For a small city, the Lambert revenues from the two San Francisco stores were very impressive, and warranted her attention now, more than several other American cities where they had stores.

The concierge promised to rent a car for her and have it ready in the morning, since she told him she'd rather drive herself. She thought it would be relaxing after a week of meetings in New York and Chicago for the last week and a half, and more to come in San Francisco, Los Angeles, and Dallas. The Fourth of July was going to be the only break in her schedule for the rest of the trip, and a day in the Napa Valley appealed to her. She had enjoyed trips to the wine country in France, near Bordeaux, and two people had now told her that Napa was very similar. It sounded like the perfect respite from her busy schedule.

The suite was large and pleasant when the manager took her upstairs, and she liked the view of the colorfully lit Bay Bridge, leading to Oakland, Berkeley, and the East Bay. It was an easy city to find one's way in. It was all laid out in a very straightforward way.

The management had sent her a bottle of champagne, which she didn't open, chocolate-dipped strawberries, and a box of chocolates. She was tempted to try one of the Chinese restaurants nearby for dinner, which the concierge had told her were excellent, but she was too lazy to leave her room, after the flight from Chicago, and ordered room service. If she was driving to Napa the next day, she wanted to go to bed early. It had been another long day of meetings and travel. She was about halfway through the trip now, and everything had gone well so far.

She showered and got into bed, and thought about Philippe. She would have liked to tell him about the trip, but he hadn't called in over a week, and she felt awkward calling him on his family vacation, or even texting him, in case someone saw it, like his son or his wife. She had met his son Julien a few times, but he had introduced her as he would any casual friend, and Julien hadn't seemed suspicious, but calling him on their family vacation seemed like too much. It was one of the inconveniences of being involved with a married man, which she was well aware of.

She fell asleep as soon as she turned off the light, before she had even watched the movie she had paid for, an old favorite she'd seen before, but the only one she liked on their menu.

When she woke up, the sun was streaming into the room, and she felt energetic and refreshed and eager to get on the road and head for Napa, to discover something she hadn't seen before. She had toast and coffee, dressed in her jeans and sneakers again, took a sweater in case it got chilly, and was at the concierge desk promptly at ten. They had the car ready for her. She hastily signed the rental car forms. They had rented it from a large, well-known international company, so she was sure the insurance was adequate, and didn't check the box for the additional insurance. She wanted to get going and there were three people behind her, eager for the concierge's attention. It was a weekend and everyone seemed to have a plan they needed his help with.

"Will you be returning it when you come back at the end of the day, or would you like to keep it for your stay?" the concierge asked her. She thought about it for a minute and couldn't decide.

"Can I let you know when I get back?" she asked him.

"Of course." She thought it might be convenient instead of taking cabs. She vaguely remembered that taxis were hard to come by in San Francisco, and a rented car might be a good idea. It was an easy city to drive in, and she had an international driving license for her travels.

The car was waiting for her in the hotel driveway, and as promised, the doorman handed her the keys when she told him her name. It was a small dark blue SUV that suited her purposes perfectly. She didn't want a big fancy car, and she was looking forward to the drive. She turned the radio on, as she left the hotel. There was a map in the car, but the concierge had already given her a printout of the directions and she used the GPS. She drove west toward Pacific Heights, and then right all the way down to the bay, where she easily got onto the feeder street to the Golden Gate Bridge and headed toward it through the old military preserve, the Presidio. She was on the bridge a few minutes later, and followed the signs and the flow of traffic heading north, driving through Marin County. Eventually, clearly marked signs on the freeway directed her toward Napa. She took the appropriate turnoff, headed right, and drove through farmland, small ranches, and vineyards toward the

Napa Valley. And after several miles of green fields, she reached a smaller highway, which ran through the Napa Valley. She had driven past Sonoma on the way, which sounded less interesting to her. She drove straight north, until she began seeing signs to the wineries she was passing, which offered tours and tastings.

She visited two of them, only taking a sip of the wine she was offered, since she was driving, and drove as far north as Rutherford to the Auberge du Soleil, a French hotel the concierge had told her had an excellent restaurant. She parked the car and walked up to the deck off the restaurant, where she had a clear view of the valley. It was every bit as beautiful as the young graduate student had said when he drove her from the airport to the hotel. She sat down to admire the view, and wished that her children were with her, or Philippe, someone she could share it with. It seemed too bad to be alone with such a magnificent view. She asked for a table, and the hostess led her to one with the same view. She had a delicious lunch, sat relaxing with a cup of café filtre, and left the hotel two hours later.

She drove through the Napa Valley for another hour, and then headed back down the valley to return to San Francisco. It had been a perfect day, and they had told her that she would have a front row view from her room of the fireworks on the Fourth, if the fog didn't roll in. San Francisco was famous for its summer fog and chilly temperatures, particularly in August. But so far, it had been a hot, very relaxing day, without a whisper of fog. The drive back was as easy as the drive to Napa had been.

She was driving through Marin County on the way back, as the fields and ranches gave way to a more suburban landscape, when she noticed dark black streaks in the sky. It looked like someone had painted black brushstrokes on the blue sky and it seemed ominous. It looked like smoke, and had appeared very suddenly. She saw it more clearly from the Golden Gate Bridge. There was obviously a fire somewhere, and the sky was filling with smoke as she drove across the bridge into the city and headed toward the hotel.

She could even smell smoke when she got out of the car at the hotel, and she told the doorman she was keeping it. He said he'd let the concierge know.

"Where is all the smoke coming from?" she asked him.

"A fire started in Napa a couple of hours ago," he said seriously. "It sounds like a big one. It's already devastated one of the wineries." He mentioned the name of a winery she had driven past before lunch. "It's dry as a bone up there, we haven't had a decent rain in months."

"It must have happened so fast. I was there this morning."

"That's how these fires happen." They could smell it

distinctly now, as she thanked him and went upstairs to her room.

She turned on the TV in the living room of the suite, and there was live coverage of a raging blaze. It was hard to believe that the fire had gotten so big in only a few hours. The reporter covering it said it had been started by a campfire that was left unattended. A brisk wind had come up and started a brushfire, and it was raging out of control by six o'clock. It was frightening to watch it, and awesome to see the force of nature. Driven by the wind, the fire had jumped from the winery, which was already gutted, to a row of houses that were in immediate danger, and the area had been evacuated. The television cameras showed groups of shocked and crying people a safe distance from the blaze, hugging each other as they watched their homes start to burn, and no one had been able to stop it so far. The commentator added that it was everyone's hope that the fire wouldn't grow to proportions of previous fires in the area, which had taken weeks to control, and had devoured millions of acres and thousands of homes.

It was incredible to Dahlia that only a few hours before she had been where the fire now was, and it had looked so perfect and peaceful and now this tragedy had happened. They went on then to show animals fleeing the area—flocks of deer, cows escaped from a dairy, some sheep, two horses that had gotten loose and were rearing on camera, and some cats and dogs yelping and running away from the flames. The whole scene was terrifying.

Dahlia sat mesmerized by the TV until late that night, as the fire leaped over roads and rivers, driven by a strong wind and setting fire to everything in its path. A huge area had been evacuated by then, and firefighters were doing everything they could to stop it, with no success so far. She couldn't tear herself away and kept watching the TV as the devastation continued.

She stayed awake until three A.M., and it continued getting worse, advancing relentlessly. A dairy had been burned by then, and two more wineries, houses, churches, schools. The firefighters said they were going to do an airdrop of water and fire-retardant chemicals, but they would have to wait until morning to do it.

Dahlia finally fell asleep in front of the television, and woke at seven in the morning, to the acrid smell of smoke coming in the windows she had left open to get some air in the room.

The news was still live then, and they reported that the fire was not contained, and more firefighters were being called in from other counties. The situation was very serious and still out of control.

She kept one eye on the news, while getting her papers

ready for her meetings the next day. It was hard to concentrate, watching what was happening, as the cameras jumped from one reporter to the next covering the fire, reporting one disaster after another. One firefighter had died so far, and a first responder trying to save a ninety-two-year-old woman from a burning building. She had recently suffered a stroke and couldn't get out of bed on her own, and her family was out when the fire started and engulfed their home. The ninety-two-year-old woman had died too, as well as several others while trying to save their homes or flee them. One man had died trying to save his dog. They had died together with his arms around the husky.

Dahlia turned the TV off while she dressed. She couldn't stand it anymore. What she had seen so far was so horrible she couldn't bear it. Her site visit to the store and her meetings the next day seemed so insignificant compared to what was happening in Napa. It was even more real to her and more poignant because she had just been there the day before. The fire continued to rage all day, with heartbreaking coverage on TV. She went for a walk, but the smoke made it hard to breathe and her eyes burned, so she went back to the hotel.

In spite of feeling distracted, Dahlia appeared at the store on time to meet their regional rep on Monday morning, who was talking frantically on her cellphone when Dahlia got there. She explained apologetically that her parents had just been evacuated from an assisted living facility in Sonoma that had burned to the ground. They were uninjured, but understandably distraught.

"Do you want to go up there now?" Dahlia asked her, feeling guilty for meeting her at all. The entire city seemed in distress and a state of emergency had been declared.

"No, it's okay. My brother and sister are on their way up there. My sister lives in Marin and she'll get there before I could. The poor things have lived through this twice in the last three years. We can't go through it again. My other sister lives in New Jersey. We're going to send them to her. This is the third time for them." Dahlia felt as though she had landed in the eye of a hurricane, and she felt terrible for all of them.

She tried to pay attention during their store visit, but the regional rep, Mary Thomas, kept getting calls, and Dahlia felt sick as she listened. First she talked to her mother, then her father. She went outside to talk and came back with tears rolling down her cheeks.

"I'm so sorry," she apologized. Dahlia had made a sketchy list of things the store needed to improve on, which seemed irrelevant now. They didn't stay long, and spent the entire meeting with the manager talking about the fire.

She let Mary go after that, and she thanked Dahlia, who went back to the hotel, and watched the news for the rest of the day. It was like an addiction she couldn't stop. There was a whole segment of the news focused on animal rescue—cats, dogs, horses, goats, cows, ferrets, coyotes. Two mountain lions had been at the top of a flaming tree and the rescuers got them to leap to safety into a net, then sedated them in the net so they could take them to a wildcat rescue facility to be treated for burns. Dahlia was crying as she watched. Her site visit to the store had been meaningless and she didn't care.

They showed a pet rescue center, mostly for cats and dogs, birds, rabbits, hamsters, guinea pigs, and small animals that people were lovingly saving from the fire, some of whom had been badly injured, and whose rescuers had risked injury to themselves to save them. In some cases their owners had died. In other instances, the animals were found in the debris or running down the street, yelping and burned.

Philippe called her at midnight, when it was morning in Paris.

"What in hell is going on?" Philippe asked her. "Are you still in San Francisco? You should get out. Go on to your next stop, or come home."

"I still have meetings tomorrow. The city is safe, except

you can smell the smoke. We're not in danger here. It's just so tragic to hear what's happening. People, animals, homes, it looks like hell on earth." She had tears in her eyes as she said it. She had been watching tragedies unfold all day, and she couldn't stop watching into the night.

"Fire is a terrible thing," Philippe agreed. "I'm worried about you, Dahlia. The smoke is dangerous too." The air quality had gone from green to orange alert that afternoon.

"I'm fine. I just feel so awful for the victims. I went to Napa on Saturday, before the fires started. It all happened just hours afterward, and it's happening so fast."

"I think you should leave," he said again.

"I'll fly out tomorrow night. My meetings are all south of San Francisco tomorrow. Far from the fires. My meetings today were a disaster. Nobody could think straight and people were crying."

"Come home," he said firmly.

"I really should do L.A. and Dallas, as long as I'm here. How are you?" she asked him. "Everything okay?"

"Perfect. Everything is fine. Julien and I went out on a boat yesterday and were fishing together all day. He was actually pleasant and interesting to talk to. Maybe he's finally growing up." His relaxed family vacation on the Riviera was hard to relate to compared to the immediacy of the fires, and how close they were.

"I'm glad," she said, sounding distracted again. He could tell she really didn't care about his vacation.

"Let me know where you are and if you're coming home early. I might be able to fly to Paris for the day." It was the first time he had ever offered to do that, and she was touched. He sounded worried about her. The French media had made a big deal of the Napa fires. They were a big deal, and she was only an hour or two away from them.

"I will. Thank you for calling." She got off when Delphine interrupted the call. Charles was in the room with her, and they were on speaker.

"Are you all right? Shouldn't you leave?"

"I just want to see the store in Stanford tomorrow, while I'm here. I'm not in any danger in the city," except from the smoke. There was a new store manager in Palo Alto and Dahlia wanted to see how she was doing, and if it was the right fit. They talked for a few minutes and Dahlia assured them she would leave after the meetings and fly to L.A.

After they hung up, she watched another segment about the pet rescues. A San Francisco vet had set up a whole field hospital in Napa, with vets and volunteers, to save the animals who were injured. There was a separate one for animals in nature coming out of the hills, looking for food and water and to escape the fires. But it was the pet rescue hospital which seized Dahlia's heart. The animals all looked so pathetic, and some were badly burned.

She slept fitfully that night and was up early the next day. The sky was black with smoke, and the smell was much stronger than the day before. The hotel distributed N95 masks to all the guests, and told them not to go out without them, and to stay in the hotel if they could.

Dahlia was less worried because she was driving an hour south to Palo Alto, away from the fires. She was sure the air would be better there.

Mary Thomas joined her at the hotel so they could drive down together. They didn't speak in the car, and listened to the radio the entire time. The fires were still out of control. The water planes were dumping thousands of gallons of water on the fires, with no effect so far. Mary Thomas told her that her sister had brought their parents to Marin. They were shaken but they were all right. Her brother was flying them to New Jersey that weekend. They had lost all their personal possessions in the assisted living facility fire, but were handling it well. They were just grateful to be alive. Two of the other residents had died.

The visit to the Stanford store went more smoothly than the one the day before. They were doing a good job, and the new manager was excellent. One of their best customers wanted to meet Dahlia and they arranged it, and she came to the store to meet her and was thrilled. They had a new antiaging product meeting to bring the manager up-to-date about what would be arriving in the coming months, and how to use it.

At least for a few hours, Dahlia put the fires out of her mind. She and Mary left Palo Alto at four. Traffic was heavy and they got back to the hotel at six. Mary Thomas left, and Dahlia thanked her for her help, and went to the concierge desk to ask them to get her a flight out that night. She said she could make a nine o'clock flight, and he shook his head.

"The SFO airport closed an hour ago, and they just closed Oakland and San Jose. The smoke is too heavy to fly safely. The winds are too strong and are blowing the smoke our way."

Dahlia thought about it for a minute. "How long would it take to drive?"

"At least six hours on I-5, on the inside route the truckers use. Eight or nine straight down 101." She was tired and it sounded like too long a night. It was easier just to delay a day and fly out when the airport reopened in a day or so. "I'll wait it out."

"That's what most of the guests have decided. And we're recommending that people not open their windows. The smoke is really bad. We're very sorry." The concierge looked harassed and distracted, and was in a rush.

"It's all right," she said, and went up to her room, took off the suit she'd worn, and lay on her bed. She was exhausted. It was stressful being there, knowing what was happening an hour or two away. So much tragedy and heartbreak.

Dahlia called the rep in L.A. and explained to her that she wouldn't be arriving the next day unless the airports opened. She had her cancel all their meetings for the next day. Dahlia had been planning to take either a late flight that night or an early morning flight the next day and start the meetings at noon.

"I'm not surprised," Lotte Hershey, the L.A. rep, said. "I've been watching the news. It looks terrible up there. We're probably next. We get fires almost as bad every year now. Our forests are so dry they turn into instant firewood by the end of the summer. It's happening early this year."

"We had bad fires in France a few years ago, but nothing like this," Dahlia said.

"Well, stay in your room, wear a mask if you go out. We'll reschedule everything as soon as the airports open. I'll keep an eye on it from here."

"Thank you," Dahlia said. She felt drained by the drama, and after she hung up, she remembered it was the Fourth of July, and all festivities had been canceled. She fell asleep without putting her nightgown on, or ordering dinner. She woke up at six A.M. and turned the news back on. The air quality and the smoke were worse, and there was ash falling on the city that looked like a layer of snow on the cars. The airports were still closed. The wind had shifted. The fires were moving north to wreak new destruction on areas that had been unaffected until then. She was clearly not going to L.A. today.

She checked in with Delphine, told her she was staying in San Francisco until the airports opened, and assured her she was fine.

"I can't believe you've gotten stuck there in that inferno. Do they think the airports will be closed for long?"

"I don't think anyone knows. I can't imagine it'll be more than a day, or two at most. If I have to, I'll get driven to L.A. I just didn't want to deal with it last night. It's a long trip by car. I'd rather fly."

"How was the store in Palo Alto and the new manager?"

"She's doing a great job. I'm glad I went. So far, until now, the trip has been worthwhile. I just don't want to miss L.A. and Dallas. I'd rather not have to come back soon. It's a long way from Paris, a very long flight, and a big time difference, nine hours."

They talked for a few more minutes. Delphine had talked to Alex. "I'm not going to tell her you're delayed in San Francisco. She'll go crazy."

"I'll still be home on time," Dahlia said calmly. "You're right, better not tell her, she'll be calling me day and night about the wedding." And Alex hadn't called to see how her mother was. She just assumed she was fine.

After Dahlia hung up, they ran another clip on TV about the pet rescue center in Napa, asking for donations of pet supplies and for both trained and untrained volunteers: vet students, retired vets, or people with any experience with animals. After she watched it, Dahlia had an idea. She had nothing else to do, and at least she could do something useful. She still had the rented car in the hotel garage.

She ordered a healthy breakfast, since she hadn't eaten the night before, and by eight o'clock she called the concierge and asked them to have her car sent to the front door. She took her mask with her. She wore her running shoes and jeans and a shirt she could get washed afterward, and bought a T-shirt at the gift shop in case she needed a spare. She got the car keys from the doorman and tipped him. The smoke was thick in the air. She put her mask on and got behind the wheel of the rented car. She had jotted down the address of the rescue center and the phone number. They had shown a map on the TV with the exact location, so she had a good idea of where it was, after her visit to Napa on Saturday, but used the GPS anyway. She followed the same route she had taken to leave the city before, down to the water and across the Golden Gate Bridge. There was very little traffic because of the noxious smoke, and the warnings to stay indoors if possible, and she kept her mask on as she drove. She was on the highway leading north twenty minutes after she left the hotel. She had no idea what she could do to be helpful, but she couldn't just sit there watching the disaster on TV anymore. She felt compelled to volunteer to help. She kept her foot on the gas. She felt better being proactive, even if all she could do was help some injured dogs. It was better than spending the day in her room at the hotel. It was something at least, as she drove past landmarks that looked faintly familiar to her now. The sky got darker and more ominous as she drove steadily north. She followed the GPS. It took her an hour and fifteen minutes to get to the southern part of Napa County. Someone had posted a handwritten sign on the road. It said simply "Pet Rescue Center. Please Help." It was what she had come there to do.

Chapter 6

After Dahlia saw the sign for the animal rescue shelter, she followed a rutted dirt road a little distance, and saw a large army surplus tent that had been set up like a field hospital. There were cars parked helter-skelter in a field next to it, so she left her car there and headed toward the tent on foot. As soon as she walked in through the entrance, she saw organized chaos all around her. There was a big man with tousled red hair and a full red beard in a lab coat giving orders. There were exam tables set up; crates and cages for the animals were lined up along one side of the tent. There were men and women of all ages and teenagers in T-shirts and jeans carrying animals with their paws and faces bandaged, and various injuries. Everyone was busy, and for a minute it looked like they all had some kind of animal in their hands. She wasn't sure where to go, and she saw a woman with a clipboard making lists near the entrance. She walked up to her, and the woman smiled.

"Vet? Vet tech? Volunteer?" she asked before Dahlia could ask a question.

"Volunteer."

"Great. Welcome. Thank you. Over there." She pointed to a man with another clipboard. He was writing down names and phone numbers so they could call on them again. Dahlia reported to him. Both his arms were covered with tattoos and his head was shaved. He was someone she would never have met otherwise, but he had a kind face and smiled at her.

"Name? Phone number?" he asked her.

"Dahlia de Beaumont. I don't live here. I'm traveling. But I'm staying at The Ritz-Carlton in San Francisco if you need me while I'm here."

"Thanks for coming. Where are you from?" he asked.

"Paris. France."

"Wow." He pointed to the big burly redheaded man. "Doc Allen can use your help, holding the animals while he bandages them and assesses them. After that, you put them in a cage or a crate over there." He pointed to the wall of cages. There were a lot of empty ones. "Make sure they have kibble and water, and then you can go back to Doc Allen for the next one." There were a dozen people in line, with a technician next to the vet. The people in line were each holding an animal of some kind, mostly dogs. There was a separate line for cats, with another vet and tech. "They'll hand you the animals when you stand in line. We need bandages if you know anyone who wants to donate some." They were standing on dirt, and Dahlia realized they had set up the tent in a field. It was all very rudimentary and rustic, but the tent was full of people wanting to help. "And I'm Hank. Come and find me if you need anything."

"Thank you," she said, impressed by what they were doing, and by how many of them there were. She could guess that there were fifty or sixty volunteers doing various jobs. There was an area for the most seriously injured animals, with a tech tending them.

She got in line with the other volunteers. Some were rough and tough-looking, some were old ladies, there were men and women, all focused on what they could do to help the animals. And then she noticed another group of random people, checking out the animals in the cages, looking for their lost pets. She saw several tearful reunions while she waited her turn in line. There was a kind-looking African American woman with her hair in rows of beautiful brightly colored beads handing out the animals one by one from cages all around her. They were all small dogs. There was a different area for big dogs. Another vet was treating them, and they only wanted experienced people handling them. A vet tech was swabbing down the table with disinfectant after each animal, and there was a shopping cart full of bandages and ointments next to the redheaded vet. Almost all the animals were being treated for burns. There was barking, whining, and yelps of animals in pain throughout the tent.

When Dahlia was next in line, the woman with the beaded hair handed her a small fluff ball with black curly hair and a white patch on his chest. He had floppy ears, and big black eyes with a sad expression. Dahlia could see that all four of his white paws were burned. He was wearing a collar with a tag with a phone number on it, but no owner's name, and no name of the dog. He was shaking in terror as she held him, and he clung to her.

The redheaded vet with the full beard smiled at Dahlia when it was her turn. He told her immediately not to set the dog down on the table; his paws were too badly burned. He cleaned them as gently as he could while she held the dog. He whimpered and buried his head in her chest, as though he didn't want to see the vet. The vet tech standing next to him used a reader, looking for a chip.

"No chip," he said to the vet.

"This is a lesson to everyone to get chips for their dogs, so we can find their owners," the vet said. "All of these dogs belonged to someone," he said to Dahlia. "Almost none of them have chips or licenses, or ID tags so we can locate their owners."

"He's got a tag on his collar with a phone number but no name," she told the vet, as she held the little black dog. He looked like a cross between a poodle and something less fancy. He had a long fluffy tail, and ears like a cocker spaniel. He was a mix and very cute, and small enough to hold.

"He's about two years old, male, I'd say eight pounds. He must have run out of a house in flames the way his feet are burned, and his coat is singed." The vet cleaned the dog's paws gently, put ointment on them, wrapped them in sterile bandages, and told Dahlia she could put him back in a crate, and Mahala would tell her where to put it. The woman with the beaded hair told her to put him in the long row of cages along one side of the tent. A volunteer had put clean pads at the bottom of each crate and cage, and there were two bowls in each for food and water. Dahlia put the little black dog in a crate and taped the paper the tech had written with the vet's assessment to the top of it. She added in red marker to the sheet, "No ID, phone number on collar." Others were making calls to the owners whenever possible.

"Do you have a phone with you?" Mahala asked her, and Dahlia said she did. "Call the number on his collar. Tell them we have their dog. If you get an answer. A lot of the dogs' owners have probably lost their homes and are dealing with bigger problems than their lost pets. Half of these dogs, or more, will never see their owners again," she said seriously. "It happens with every disaster, like floods. The owners are too traumatized themselves to come and claim the animals, and they just let them go." It made Dahlia sad to think of it. The poor little dog she'd been holding was terrified and looked so sad. He hadn't even cried when the vet treated his burned paws.

She put kibble from a huge bag and water from a jug in the bowls in the crate, as the tattooed man named Hank had told her to do. Then she took her cellphone out of her pocket and called the number on the tag. A recording said that the number was no longer in service, so they had no information on the little curly-haired black dog at all. She reached in and petted him, and he whimpered and looked pathetically at her. "I'm sorry, little guy, I've got to go." She walked away and glanced back at him, and he looked tragic sitting in the crate. She wondered what would happen to him, and if his owner would ever show up. What Mahala had told her about most of them getting abandoned made it all seem even worse. They would go to animal shelters to be adopted if no one claimed them. The little curly-haired black dog with the white patch and paws had a long road ahead of him. She tried not to think about it as she walked away, afraid to look back at him again and see his sad face.

She stood in line holding dogs to be treated by the vet for the rest of the day. Others were calling the owners of dogs who had licenses, ID tags, or chips. There were a dozen volunteers working their own phones, and they managed to connect with a number of the owners, who promised to come as soon as they could. But most of the dogs had no ID tags at all, and no chips. There was no way to identify them unless their owners heard about the temporary shelter and showed up. After that they'd have to comb the ASPCA shelters to see if they could find them. Most of the dogs had burns on their paws and on their faces. One had a broken leg. Dahlia noticed that there were a lot of Chihuahuas, but most of the dogs were mutts. There was another long line for cats. Some of them fought like wildcats not to be treated, but the dogs were surprisingly meek, even the big ones.

She stayed until six o'clock and never stopped for lunch. She and Mahala had an interesting conversation. Mahala was a student from Zimbabwe, studying to be a vet at UC Davis, and had come down to help when she saw the notice on TV, and another notice posted on their bulletin board at school. She said other students at Davis had come too.

It was one of the best vet schools in the country. She was specializing in large animals but was happy to help with the animals here.

The vet with the bushy red beard asked Dahlia her name halfway through the day. He could tell that she had no experience, but she had a good heart, which was true of most of the volunteers. A black long-haired Chihuahua tried to bite her, and she didn't seem to mind. He had tiny teeth and weighed about three pounds. He had burns all over his body and a gash on his ear, and Dr. Allen managed to calm him down. And there were so many animals with no identifying tags who would never see their homes and their owners again. The death toll among human victims of the fire had risen shockingly that afternoon.

Some of the big dogs were harder to deal with, and there were several pit bulls that only the real vet techs were allowed to handle. They didn't want well-meaning inexperienced volunteers getting hurt.

A dozen veterinary students had come from the veterinary school in Davis, as Mahala had said. They had brought sleeping bags and camping equipment and were going to spend the night, ministering to the sickest ones who needed medication, and some who were on IVs. They had a hundred and fourteen cats and dogs in Dr. Allen's army tent, all crated, medicated, treated, fed, and watered by the end of the day.

"Thank you for your help," Dr. Allen said to Dahlia as she got ready to leave. "Are you from around here?"

"No, I'm traveling. I saw the story of the rescue tent on TV."

"A lot of people did. Where are you traveling from?"

"France. Paris. I'm just here for a few days."

"It's nice of you to come and volunteer. I have a pet hospital in the city, and a vineyard up here. I figured they needed the help. I did the same thing last time in the fires. I've been to Bordeaux," he said. "You have some amazing vineyards in France." He gazed at her admiringly. He couldn't help but notice how attractive she was. "Are you coming back tomorrow?"

"I'm going to L.A. If the airport opens, I have to leave. If it doesn't, I'll come back," she promised. It had been a heart-warming, rewarding day, and heartbreaking too, seeing how sweet most of the dogs were. They'd been through a terrible trauma, and most of them were facing an unhappy fate. Pets were still being brought in at an alarming rate, some in terrible condition—and some that couldn't be saved. Only the vets and students from Davis took care of them.

"We can use the help. Thanks again." She went to see the little black curly-haired dog again before she left. He wagged his tail frantically when he saw her, and she reached in and petted him, and put some more food in his bowl.

"I'm sorry I have to go," she said to him. "Maybe I'll be back tomorrow, but you're going to be okay. Your owner will probably be back, or someone else is going to love you." He cocked his head and his ears flopped and he whined as she stood up and walked away, and she felt like a monster leaving him.

She drove back to the city and stopped at a pharmacy near the hotel. She bought a shopping cart full of bandages to donate in case she went back the next day. The smoke seemed even thicker that night than it had in the morning. The wind was blowing it all into the city, and when she turned on the news, she saw that the fires still weren't contained. The damage extended over thousands of acres. Firemen were pouring in from other states to volunteer, but so far nothing had stopped the destruction.

She thought of the little black dog with the curly hair and the fluffy tail, and so many others she had handled that day. She was still awake, thinking about them, when Philippe called her at midnight. It was morning for him.

"What did you do in the smoke all day?" he asked her.

"I volunteered at a pet rescue shelter, in an army tent in Napa," she said simply.

"Oh my God. Don't tell me you're volunteering. I can't even imagine it. Why don't you just go to L.A.?"

"It's too long a drive. I'm waiting for the airport to open. And I was happy to help. The poor little dogs were so sad, and so many of them were badly burned. They say that most of them will never see their owners again."

"My darling Dahlia, don't you dare come home with a plane full of stray dogs. The image doesn't suit you at all." He had a very snobbish side to him, and he preferred to think of her as the elegant owner of one of the finest perfume brands in the world.

"I'd bring most of them home with me if I could," she said, thinking of her little curly black friend.

"Thank God you can't. I'm sure they won't let you bring them into France. I think you should go to L.A.—you could be stuck in San Francisco for weeks. Or just come home. You can go to L.A. another time."

"I'll give it a few days and figure it out then," she said, and he laughed at her.

"I wish I'd seen you nursing stray dogs at the shelter. That is *not* the glamorous woman I know."

"It's just another side of me," she said quietly, annoyed by how unfeeling he was about the injured animals.

"One I don't want to know. I love the woman I *do* know. Caviar and champagne and the most spectacular house on the rue de Grenelle. I don't think going to America is good for you. You forget who you are." *Or maybe I remember who I am,* she thought to herself and didn't say to him. He wouldn't have understood.

She liked being many things, not just the glamorous head of an important perfume company. She didn't want to be that all the time. She had liked doing something different that day, helping at the shelter, with people from all walks of life, not just the members of an elite club that excluded everyone else. And she had liked talking to Mahala from Zimbabwe. It added something to one's life to meet different people and she had enjoyed feeling useful in a very simple, basic way. There was no way that Philippe would ever understand. He didn't want to. This snobbish side bothered her at times. His vision of the world was too limited. It always had to be the best and the most important, the richest and the fanciest, a world made up of only people of power.

She had liked meeting the vet who grew grapes too, who owned a vineyard and had been to Bordeaux. The snobbish, pompous side of Philippe made her glad that she wasn't married to him. It was part of why he had never divorced Jacqueline, aside from what it would have cost him. He would have had to admit that he'd made a mistake, that breeding and bloodlines weren't enough, and that he had been married to a woman he didn't love for thirty-five years and had deprived himself of being married to someone real, instead of living as a fraud for more than half his life. It was pathetic. Dahlia would rather admit her mistakes, be open to life, and be real. He loved that about her, but not to be married to. He would rather be with her in secret. It seemed cowardly to her. She had never thought of it that way before, and his terror of loving was part of that lie too. Dahlia was his guilty secret. He thought it was sexy, but it seemed stupid to her, and false. He was wasting the opportunity he had to have something better, and stayed married to Jacqueline because the only thing he respected about her was the fancy family she came from. Dahlia came from a distinguished family too on both sides, but she also worked and was engaged in business, which made her slightly less elite than his aristocratic wife, and Dahlia knew it.

She thought about it when they got off the phone. His loving her to the extent he did, in secret, seemed pathetic to her suddenly. He was too afraid to take a risk. He was more interested in his social standing and bank account than he was in leading an honest life, and preferred to love Dahlia in hiding.

*

The smoke that hung over San Francisco like a curse was even thicker the next morning. The airport stayed closed, so Dahlia left the hotel at eight A.M. and was back at the rescue shelter by nine-thirty. The same faces were there, and even more volunteers had shown up, and many vets from UC Davis. She gave the bandages she was donating to one of the vet techs, and he thanked her profusely. Dr. Allen thanked her himself when he next saw her. He could tell easily from the way she spoke, her good manners, her obvious education, that she was more than a kind person, she was someone important. He didn't know who or what she was, but he could tell that she was someone special.

Mark Hamilton, the head of the ASPCA Board, showed up to acknowledge what Dr. Jeff Allen was doing. And he brought him a big donation check from the ASPCA. They knew each other well from boards they had served on for many years, and Dr. Allen was grateful for the help to fund what he was doing. He would be able to buy all the supplies he needed, and he introduced Mark Hamilton to Dahlia, as she walked by carrying another Chihuahua with burned paws and a gash on her nose. Mark was a tall, distinguished-looking man somewhere in his mid-fifties with dark hair, warm brown eyes, and a kind expression, and he and Dr. Jeff Allen were good friends.

"Jeff says you're passing through from Paris," Mark said

politely, intrigued by her. The vet had hinted to him that he suspected she was someone important or well known, but she gave no confirmation of it when he talked to her. Jeff found her unusually discreet, and willing to work hard, and she was equally kind and gracious to everyone. "What brings you to San Francisco?" Mark asked her, after she put the Chihuahua back in a crate. She was one of the rare dogs they'd seen with a chip and proper dog tags, and they had a good shot at finding her owner. She looked like a well-cared-for dog who had somehow gotten lost during the fires. Mahala had already called her owner and left a message on voicemail.

"I came to do some business. I was supposed to be in L.A. by now, but they closed the airport. And I'd rather be useful here than sitting around my hotel, watching the news, glued to the TV."

"I was supposed to be in court today, but the judge canceled our appearance. He's staying home in the smoke. We should all be doing that," Mark said sensibly. She had taken her mask off to talk to him, and he had his in his hand. And Jeff Allen had been wearing his around his neck for two days. They were hard to breathe with. "Jeff says you live in France. How does that feel as an American?" he asked, and she smiled.

"I'm only half American. My father was American, and I grew up in New York, with summers in France, until I graduated from college. My parents moved to France when I graduated from high school. My mother was French. I've been living in France for thirty-two years, and I'm more French than American by now." Her relationship with Philippe Vernier was ample proof of it, but she couldn't say that to anyone, and certainly not a stranger. It was an arrangement that most American women wouldn't have put up with, and it wasn't ideal for her either. "I went to college in the States, and graduate school. After that, I moved to France."

"Your English is flawless," he complimented her.

"Thanks to my father. I'm really kind of a hybrid. I'm both. French and American. Although I kind of forget the American half until I come to the States, and then it rings old familiar bells and reminds me of my father. But California is a whole different world."

"I grew up in the East too, New York. But I went to law school here, passed the bar here, and stayed. It has its good sides, and some crazy ones. I work in New York too, so maybe that keeps me sane." He smiled at her. She was very beautiful, and he hadn't expected to meet anyone like her in Jeff Allen's pet rescue tent. He had come to deliver the ASPCA check to Jeff himself and see how he was doing. He was very impressed by the efficiency of the operation, which didn't surprise him, knowing Jeff Allen.

The minute Mark spoke to Dahlia, he could see what Jeff meant about her. She was different, and special, and very smart. She had a lovely, gentle, direct way about her. He felt awkward and a little in awe of her just talking to her. She had work to do then and went back to helping with the dogs. He saw her again a little while later, holding a curly-haired little black mutt that had its paws around her neck and was clinging to her.

"See what I mean," Jeff whispered to Mark when he took a break. "I don't know who she is, but I have a feeling she's famous or something, and traveling incognito." Mark laughed at the suggestion. They were like two schoolboys, whispering about the new girl in the class.

"I don't think she's famous," Mark answered him. "I think she's just smart, and from a distinguished background. There's something very aristocratic about her, even in jeans and a T-shirt." He had observed and admired Dahlia's natural elegance. There were no airs about her.

"We should look her up on Google," Jeff said, and Mark laughed again.

"The poor woman just came to help you with your animals, and you want to have her checked out by the FBI. She lives in France, she's on her way to L.A. You're not liable to see her again when she leaves here, so just be glad she showed up and leave it at that."

"I could look her up the next time I go to France," Jeff said hopefully, and Mark rolled his eyes.

"Either you're a hopeless romantic or you're crazy. Besides, for all you know, she's married."

"She's not wearing a wedding band." Jeff had looked.

"A lot of women don't these days. You've been working too hard. You're losing your mind. What happened to that woman you were dating six months ago? The sexy redhead? She was nice."

"She dumped me. She's allergic to dogs, and I have four, two of them long-haired," and Mark knew that one of them was a St. Bernard. He laughed at Jeff again, went to sign some papers for the donation he'd brought him, and then helped out with the dogs himself for a few hours. And at four o'clock that afternoon, the sheriff and fire wardens showed up. The smoke had reached toxic levels, and they told Jeff that he had to close up shop. The air was too unhealthy for the volunteers to be working, and the fires were approaching due to a wind shift. Jeff had been afraid of that, and had already made arrangements to divide up the animals they had between four local pet hospitals, until the toxic air levels came down and it was safer. He warned all the volunteers, and they loaded the animal crates into vans and cars, and an old school bus someone had lent them. It took an hour to clear the tent of all the animals they had. They had a record for each of them taped to each of their crates, in case their owners came looking for them, and when the air improved, Jeff would bring them back to the tent to keep track of them himself. The smoke was so thick by then that you could hardly see through it, and even with their masks on, the volunteers, techs, and vets were all coughing by the time they left. Dahlia was about to get in her car when Mark walked toward her. She realized then how tall he was. He looked very athletic in an old Stanford T-shirt, and he was handsome, even with the cumbersome mask. He felt silly doing it, but he handed her a card with a sheepish grin after he took off his mask for a minute.

"If you ever need a lawyer in San Francisco, give me a call." It was the worst line he could think of and he felt like an idiot saying it, but maybe she'd come back to the city one day and look him up. Or she'd think he was a complete fool, after he said it, and she'd throw the card away. He felt like a schoolboy with her. But so what? Women like her didn't show up in an army surplus tent every day and cross his path. He got the same feeling Jeff did from her. She was special.

"Thank you," she said politely, and shoved his card in the pocket of her jeans. "I work at Louis Lambert Perfumes in Paris," she volunteered, and felt silly doing it too. But there was something about him she liked even if she had hardly spoken to him. There was some kind of strange chemistry between them she couldn't put her finger on. And she thought he was smart too. She liked Jeff Allen as well, although he seemed to be a bit of a bumbler except with the animals. She thought he was great with them, an excellent vet, and had done a fabulous job with the shelter. She had loved working with him for two days. But there was something different about Mark. He was bigger and smoother and deeper all at once. He was the kind of person you'd notice in a crowd, although he was quiet and discreet.

"You'd better put your mask back on before you get sick from the smoke," he told her. She did and got in her car, and he ran to his. He couldn't even see her once he got to his car, and it was only twenty feet away. They all turned their car lights on when they left the field. Driving in the heavy smoke was dangerous and she wondered how long it would take her to get back to the city. Probably a long time.

Dahlia drove out before Mark did, while Jeff stayed until the last animal was in a vehicle. Mark wondered if he'd ever see Dahlia again. It didn't seem likely, but now that he knew where she worked, he was going to do what he had told Jeff not to. He was going to look her up on Google. He was curious about her. There was something unusual and mysterious about her. Jeff had been right about that too. After that, he concentrated on getting on the road without hitting another car. The fire wardens were right to send them home. At five in the afternoon it was like driving in the middle of the night, in the thickest smoke he'd ever seen.

Dahlia crawled along the freeway in her car, unable to see beyond the hood of the car. She drove as slowly as she could, in the right lane, with her high beams on, but they did no good in the thick smoke. She could see headlights in her rearview mirror, but she couldn't tell how close they were. She had her seatbelt on, and was wondering if she should just pull off the road and wait it out, but it was liable to get worse as the fires approached. It was too dangerous to stay in the area. She touched the accelerator just enough to move forward a little faster, and as she did, she was hit from behind with such violent impact that it crushed the whole back end of her car and threw her against the steering wheel. As it did, the force of whatever had hit her catapulted her car into the vehicle in front of her, which she couldn't see, and the front end of her small SUV was crushed too. She was squeezed between the front and back end, in a tiny space, and the air bags didn't deploy. She had gotten a blow on the head, and her chest felt like it was on fire from the blow of the steering wheel. She could smell gas as she passed out, sandwiched between the massive vehicle behind her and the one in front of her. And after she did, her car caught fire from the sparks of the truck that hit her from behind. She was unconscious by then. Her car was burning at both ends, as the men on a fire truck that pulled off the road spotted the blaze starting, and they rushed off the truck to see who was inside and if they were still alive. The remaining space for the passenger was reduced to almost nothing.

Three of the firefighters ran to the eighteen-wheeler tractor-trailer truck behind Dahlia's crushed flaming car. It had flipped on its side after hitting her. The driver was dead, with a broken neck. Two more firefighters ran to Dahlia's SUV, released her seatbelt and pulled her out, noting that the airbags hadn't deployed. One of the firefighters carried her far enough from the burning car in case it exploded and laid her on the ground, while two other men put out the blaze, and two more men from the fire truck ran to the car in front of Dahlia's car and found a woman and a young teenager in the front seats, without seatbelts. They were conscious but injured, with blood on their faces, and paramedics from the fire truck ran to help them. Dahlia was still lying unconscious on the ground, and hadn't regained consciousness even with two paramedics working to revive her. They put her on a stretcher and into an ambulance. The paramedics who tended to her assumed a head injury, and probably much more extensive damage, judging by the condition of the car. The first ambulance sped away with Dahlia, while the second one took the woman from the first car and her thirteen-year-old daughter to the hospital. They were badly banged up, but didn't seem critical, unlike the woman pulled from the burning car. The rescuers feared the worst for her, but she was still alive as the paramedics drove to the hospital as fast as they dared, to try to save her life.

Mark heard the sirens far ahead as he inched his way through the smoke, and he saw the tangled mass of the overturned tractor-trailer and the two cars as he drove by, one of them badly mangled and burned. You couldn't even see what kind of vehicles they were in the opaque smoky darkness. The truck was lying on its side. It was an eighteen-wheeler, and Mark could guess that it was a nasty accident. He wondered if the drivers and passengers had survived, and he continued on his way back to the city, grateful that he got there in one piece and hadn't had an accident, three hours later.

Dahlia was at Marin General by then and was airlifted by helicopter to Zuckerberg SF General Hospital in the city. The crew flew as low as they dared to stay below the worst of the smoke, and all they knew when they got her to the hospital in the city was that she was alive—barely. They suspected internal damage as well as broken bones and the head injury. Her life was hanging by a thread, and it seemed like a miracle that they got her to SF General alive.

Chapter 7

Dahlia woke up in the hospital, speeding down the hall on a gurney on her way to the trauma unit, with nurses and paramedics running along beside her. Zuckerberg had one of the best trauma units in the city, and it was where all the serious accident victims were taken. There were bright lights above her, and voices all around her. They sounded like they were shouting, and her head hurt whenever she tried to open her eyes, so she kept them closed. There was an IV in her arm, and people kept saying her name over and over. All she wanted was to go to sleep, but her head hurt too much. It felt like someone had hit her with a hammer, and she couldn't move her head. She didn't remember the accident, but she wondered if her neck was broken, it hurt so much, and her leg was painful too. She wanted to answer the voices but she couldn't speak. It took too much effort.

She felt them move her onto a table, and she heard people talking about scans, and then everything went black again for what seemed like a long time. She woke up in a room with a nurse talking to her, but everything around them was silent. The nurse wanted Dahlia to answer her, but it was too much work, so she kept her eyes closed and tried to go back to sleep, but the nurse wouldn't let her.

"Open your eyes, Dahlia," the nurse said stubbornly. Finally, Dahlia had no choice but to obey or the woman wouldn't stop talking. She was speaking English, which seemed odd to Dahlia, since she thought she was in France. She had been dreaming about Philippe and wondered where he was, and then she remembered. "He's with Jacqueline," she said out loud in a groggy voice in French. "Do you speak English?" the nurse asked her, and Dahlia opened her eyes again and stared at her.

"Yes," she said, focusing on the woman's face as she began to come out of the anesthetic they had given her.

"That's better. You had an accident, you're in the hospital," the woman explained to her. Dahlia had had her international driving license in the pocket of her jeans. She had left her passport at the hotel. "You have a broken leg and cracked ribs, and you got a nasty bump on the head," the nurse said more gently, "but you're all right, and we're taking care of you. They put you to sleep to set your leg." It explained why Dahlia's head was hurting, and why her leg felt heavy, like it belonged to someone else. She tried to lift her head to look at it, felt a brace on her neck, and saw she had a cast on her leg from her foot to her thigh. "Are you in pain, Dahlia?" the nurse asked her gently. She was in the recovery room after they'd set her leg. Given the condition of the car she'd been in, she was lucky to be alive.

"My head hurts," Dahlia said, laying her head down, and closed her eyes again. The nurse added something for the pain to her IV. They wheeled her to a private room two hours later, but she was sound asleep.

She woke up again at midnight and was more alert. There was a nurse taking her vital signs, and she smiled at Dahlia. "How do you feel?"

"I'm thirsty," Dahlia said in a voice that didn't sound like her own. Everything seemed disconnected and disjointed, and didn't totally make sense yet, as the nurse handed her a glass with ice chips in it, and Dahlia put several of them in her mouth. "Where am I?"

"At Zuckerberg Hospital in San Francisco," the nurse answered. "They brought you in by helicopter from Marin General." Dahlia began remembering the accident then—a tremendous force had hit her, like a building crashing into her from behind, it had launched her forward against the steering wheel, and she hit another car, in front of her, and then everything went black.

"Can I leave?" Dahlia asked her, but she felt woozy and wasn't sure she could stand up. And her ribs hurt a lot.

"Not yet. The doctor will talk to you tomorrow. Try to get some sleep now," the nurse said gently, and a few minutes later, Dahlia was asleep again.

Dahlia woke up the next morning, when the doctor came to examine her and touched her shoulder. She tried to sit up, which made her head and her chest hurt, and there was a throbbing pain in her leg.

"Hello. I'm Dr. Gilbert. I set your leg last night." He looked like he was about her age, in his fifties, and he had a pleasant face, and was wearing hospital scrubs. "It's a clean break, and you should be out of the cast in six or eight weeks. Your ribs will heal on their own. There were no other broken bones, and no internal damage, surprisingly. The police report says that your car was crushed front and rear and caught fire. You were very lucky—they removed you from the car before the flames touched you. You have a concussion, but not a very severe one. You should feel normal in a few weeks, although you may have headaches for two or three months. If they're severe, you should contact your physician. And I don't think you should fly for a few weeks. I understand you're traveling and you don't live here." She had had a key to her hotel room as well as the international license in her pocket when they admitted her to the hospital. "I don't think the leg, the ribs, or the moderate concussion will give you a lot of trouble. And the neck brace was only so you didn't move your head too much last night. You didn't injure your neck. The cast is a nuisance, and you should keep your weight off of it for two weeks. After that, you can put your weight on it. I gave you a walking cast. But you should take it easy for a while until you feel better. You've had a severe trauma."

"Can I go back to my hotel today?" Dahlia asked. She had hated hospitals ever since her parents' deaths.

The doctor hesitated before he answered. "If you promise to take it easy for at least a few days, yes, you can. There's no medical reason to keep you here for long. I'd like to keep you here for twenty-four hours after the accident. So, let's say you can leave at six o'clock tonight, so we can keep an eye on you until then. All things considered, you were very lucky it wasn't worse. The leg and ribs will heal, and the concussion isn't severe since you were wearing your seat-belt."

"Did other people get hurt?"

"I don't know. If they did, they probably went to local

hospitals in Napa. You were the only one from the accident that we admitted here. The police can tell you more about that. I'm sure they'll be in to see you before we release you, to complete their report. They usually show up pretty fast for major accidents. They'll want your account of what happened, as much as you remember." A few minutes later, Dr. Gilbert left the room, after giving her a prescription for pain medication if she needed it for her leg or ribs. The concussion would just take time to heal, there was nothing she could do for it. She lay there, thinking, after he left the room, wondering if she should tell her children. She didn't want to frighten them. And it didn't sound like her injuries were serious. Painful and annoying, but not dangerous. But she couldn't just show up in France with her leg in a cast, having said nothing to them. She did a rapid calculation, and he had said not to fly for a few weeks. The wedding was three weeks away, so she'd get back in time, or Alex would kill her. But on the doctor's timetable, she could still make it, thank God, and at least she wasn't dead, or crippled, or in a coma. It could have been so much worse than a headache, a broken leg, and aching ribs.

She was still debating what to do about telling them, and whether she'd have to cancel her trip to L.A., unless she could manage it on crutches with her leg in a cast, which didn't sound like fun, or very practical. She was mulling over all of it, when two police detectives appeared at the door to her room, knocked, and asked her permission to come in. They were not in uniform, but showed her their badges. They looked serious and apologized for disturbing her. She hadn't even thought of how she looked until then, and it suddenly occurred to her that she must look a fright. Her long hair was tangled, she had no makeup on, and she looked like she'd been through the proverbial wringer.

"I'm sorry, Ms. de Beaumont," the older detective said as he entered the room once she gave him permission to. They stood a few feet from her bed to talk to her and didn't sit down. "We're here about the accident yesterday. We'd like to know your recollection of what happened." She nodded and her head hurt for a minute, as she pointed to the two chairs in her room and they sat down, while the senior detective took out a notepad and a pen.

"Did anyone else get hurt?" she asked him, and he nodded.

"There was a truck involved, an eighteen-wheeler. The truck flipped over, after impact we believe, probably trying to brake and turn too sharply once he saw you. The driver broke his neck and was killed instantly at the scene. The vehicle in front of you was driven by a woman, a Marilyn Nicasio, and her thirteen-year-old daughter Tiffany was in the front passenger seat. Both sustained injuries. Ms.

Nicasio has a broken ankle, a broken arm, and a dislocated shoulder. Her daughter has a broken nose, two broken arms, and bruises to her chin. Neither of them was wearing a seatbelt. Their injuries aren't too severe. The daughter's came from the airbag as much as the impact. Seatbelts would have made a difference. And they both say they have whiplash.

"Ms. de Beaumont, do you recall if the truck hit you, and then you hit Ms. Nicasio's vehicle? Or did you impact her first, and then the truck rear-ended you?" Dahlia didn't hesitate with the answer. It was the one thing she remembered clearly, even if everything after that was vague or she'd been unconscious.

"There's no doubt whatsoever. I didn't know if it was a car or a truck—I never saw it. But it hit me with tremendous force from behind. I felt like my car flew after it hit me. And it threw me into the car in front of me, which I also couldn't see in the smoke, but I felt it. I couldn't stop. But the truck was first, without question. Were there other cars involved?" She felt terrible about the truck driver and sorry for the passengers in the car in front of her. There had been no way she could avoid hitting them.

"No," the senior detective said. "There were only the three vehicles involved. There will have to be an official hearing, and a judge will have to determine if there are any criminal implications, or negligence, since there was loss of life of one of the victims, and three other people were injured. It will have to be determined if there was criminal negligence or not," he said regretfully, but clearly. "Given the circumstances, and the smoke, I can't foresee criminal negligence by Superior Court standards, although the standards are lower civilly, and the Nicasios could sue you." Dahlia looked shocked.

"I couldn't even see the hood of my car and I was crawling along. What would constitute criminal or civil negligence?"

"Drugs or alcohol," the detective said simply, "or other factors. Speed, for instance." None of them could have been speeding in the heavy smoke, or maybe the truck was. Dahlia didn't know, or how they would determine that now. "In the case of an accident of this magnitude, both hospitals involved would have taken blood samples when you were admitted." Dahlia hadn't been drinking so she wasn't worried. "What were you doing in Napa? Did you visit anyone or any wineries?" The area was known for that. She was surprised by the question. The officers obviously were wondering if she was drunk.

"I was volunteering at a pet rescue center that had been set up to treat animals that were lost and had suffered, mostly with burns and other injuries." The detective nodded. The tests would reveal the truth. She seemed like an honest woman, but he was used to people lying to him, sometimes very convincingly. But blood tests didn't lie. "I'd like to ask you not to leave the area until there has been a hearing, and some determination has been made. I'll be asking Ms. Nicasio to do the same. In her case, she lives here, but I understand you're passing through."

"I got stuck here because of the smoke. I was supposed to be in L.A. by now, on business."

"I imagine you'll need some time to convalesce here anyway before you travel. And you may want to consult legal counsel." Dahlia looked stunned when he said that. "Where will we be able to reach you?" he asked her. "The insurance company for the rental car company will also want to interview you. Ms. Nicasio may try to sue them too." In fact, he was almost sure she would. She had mentioned it when they spoke to her.

"I'm staying at The Ritz-Carlton." They left a few minutes later, and Dahlia had a mounting sense of panic. Hearings, insurance companies, police, criminal negligence. The words danced around in her aching head and made her feel worse.

Her phone was on the night table, and she reached for it to call Philippe. She wanted his advice. It was eight o'clock at night for him, a civilized hour to call, and if it was inconvenient, she knew he wouldn't pick up.

It rang three times before he answered, and he sounded a little distant. She suspected he wasn't alone.

"I'm sorry to bother you," she said, fighting back tears, although she usually didn't cry easily. But so much was happening all at once and she was scared and still badly shaken.

"I'm just leaving for dinner. Can I call you later?" he asked, sounding businesslike, obviously not thrilled with the call. He made no explanations to his wife, but he didn't put it in her face either.

"I've had an accident," she blurted out before he could hang up.

"What kind of accident?"

"A car accident. I went back to the animal rescue shelter in the Napa Valley. They evacuated us because the smoke got so much worse, and my car was hit by a truck on the way back. The truck flipped over and the driver was killed. And when he hit me, my car hit the car in front of me. It all happened so fast, and the woman driver and her daughter were injured—broken arms, an ankle, broken nose, nothing fatal. It's a mess. They're in the hospital. I am too." Her voice was shaking.

"Are you all right?" he asked, concerned after hearing what she said.

"I have a concussion, cracked ribs, and a broken leg. I

haven't told my kids yet, so please don't tell them." He never called them, and had no relationship with them, so her warning wasn't necessary, more automatic. "I'm in the hospital, but they're releasing me tonight."

"Oh God, you'd better call a lawyer immediately. You know how Americans are. They're so litigious. Someone will surely sue you, probably the other driver and her daughter, and maybe the car rental company. Have your rep there find you an attorney."

"There's going to be a hearing to determine if there was criminal negligence," she said, as tears welled up in her eyes and rolled down her cheeks. "And the police told me to stay in the area. I can't even go to L.A. now, or come home yet."

"Find a lawyer as soon as we hang up," he said in a stern voice. "Dahlia, this is serious."

"I know it is. I'm scared to death. Can they put me in jail?"

"I doubt it, unless you were drunk or something. But it could cost you millions if they find out who you are." She hadn't even thought of that. She had visions of being accused of murder, even though the truck driver had hit her. Or the mother and daughter might accuse her of negligence. "I'm not a lawyer, but you need one. And I'm not American. But I've heard some ugly stories of lawsuits in the States. Keep me posted. Call me tomorrow when you know something. I have to go now. We're late for dinner." She wanted to ask him who "we" was, he and Jacqueline, or he and his son. She suspected it was most likely his wife. They were always on very cordial terms during their annual vacation in the south with their son. It was the only time they spent together all year, and they were all on their best behavior, pretending to be a happy, normal family, which they weren't.

She hung up feeling worse instead of better, and even more frightened of what might happen next.

She lay in bed crying for a few minutes, and then remembered something. She had put Mark Hamilton's card in the pocket of her jeans. He was an attorney and might be able to recommend someone who handled situations like this. They had cut her jeans off when she was admitted, to access her broken leg, but her lacerated jeans were with the rest of what she'd been wearing, in the closet in her hospital room. It took a lot of maneuvering, but she managed to get out of bed, with her head throbbing and her ribs aching, and hop to the closet on one foot, open the door, grab her jeans and throw them over her shoulder, and hop back to bed, using the crutches they had left at her bedside. She felt dizzy but didn't faint. She lifted her leg with the cast back onto the bed, and reached into the pocket of her jeans. They had destroyed her favorite Chanel jeans, but his card was still in the pocket. She dialed his number as soon as she caught her breath after the challenge of getting to the closet and back. His cellphone number and his office number were on it. She opted for his cell. He answered immediately, puzzled by the number of her French cellphone. He didn't expect a call from her.

"Yes?" he answered in a brusque voice.

"I'm so sorry," she began, trying not to cry. "This is Dahlia de Beaumont. We met at the pet shelter in Napa yesterday. I don't know if you remember me—you gave me your card."

"Of course. How many intriguing French women do you think I meet at a pet shelter in Napa? Did you get back to the city all right? It took me three hours."

"Well, actually, no, I didn't. I had an accident on the way back. Rather a bad one. Someone was killed. I'm in the hospital now, and I'm afraid it could turn out to be a terrible mess. There's going to be a hearing, and I think I need an attorney. I was wondering if you know anyone to recommend who would handle something like this." She sounded breathless when she finished. She had been exceedingly polite, and he was shocked.

"Are you injured?"

"Well, yes," she conceded, "a bit, but not too badly. I have a broken leg, cracked ribs, and a concussion, but I'm all right."

"That doesn't sound all right to me. I'm so sorry to hear it." And then his voice grew more serious. "Was it your fault? Dahlia, I'm an attorney and whatever you say to me is attorney/client privilege. You can tell me the truth."

"No, it wasn't," she said, sounding innocent and childlike. "The truck hit me from the rear, with tremendous force. The truck flipped and the driver was killed. And when he hit me, my car flew into the car in front of me, and I hit that car. The woman driving and her daughter apparently weren't wearing their seatbelts. The daughter was in the front seat and was injured by the airbag. She has a broken nose, and both arms are broken. The mother broke her arm and her ankle, and has a dislocated shoulder, and they both have whiplash."

"That's always debatable," Mark said skeptically. "And why weren't they wearing their seatbelts? How old is the child?" He had visions of an injured three- or five-year-old.

"She's thirteen. The police seem to be focusing on whether the truck hit me before I ran into them, or if I created the accident by rear-ending the car in front, which caused the truck to run into me, in which case maybe I'm responsible for his death."

"Do you remember which it was?" he asked her.

"Definitely. The truck hit me first, without a doubt, and then I hit them. And after that, I passed out."

"I think that'll be the crux of the matter. With the extenuating factor of the smoke, it should be ruled an accident, unless the woman decides to sue you civilly, or tries to claim criminal negligence, but I don't see how she could. She can always try, and technically if you rear-end someone, you're responsible, but if you were rear-ended first, I suspect that's a different story. I'm not a personal injury lawyer, I'm a corporate lawyer, although I'm a litigator, so I'll have to do some checking for you. When can I see you?" She couldn't imagine that he would handle it for her. She was a total stranger, and it wasn't his field of expertise, and she was sure he was busy. She didn't want to impose on him, she didn't even know him. She had just called him for a name. She could have called her rep, but she didn't want to explain the mess she was in to her, and Mark had exuded confidence and was very kind when she met him.

"I don't want to bother you. I'm sure you have much more important things to do."

"I'm happy to help a friend," he said graciously, and she wasn't even that. "I'm so sorry this happened to you, Dahlia. I hope the other driver is an honest woman. Some people try to make money on events like this, big money, especially if the other party has means." Dahlia was well aware of that—it was why Philippe had told her to get a lawyer immediately—and with injuries involved, it could be very costly. "Why don't we get together, and I'll make some notes, and I'll talk to a personal injury lawyer, and see what he says. I'm happy to help you out. Hopefully, we can take care of it quickly, before anyone gets too wound up, and they're talking about enormous settlements." He wanted to protect her, and keep her from harm, and she sounded so shaken and frightened. "When will you be out of the hospital?"

"The doctor said at six o'clock tonight. They just want to be sure my head is okay and I can manage on the crutches. I haven't mastered that yet, but I don't want to stay here. I want to go back to the hotel."

"Is it too soon if I come to the hotel at eight or eight-thirty tonight? I think we should get on this quickly, before it gets blown out of proportion."

"Are you sure you don't mind? I feel awful bothering you." She was incredibly grateful to him.

"I feel terrible knowing it happened to you. I should have followed you to the city. I didn't even think of it. None of us knew how bad the road would get. The smoke was really grim." And it was no better that day, a day later. If anything, it was worse, and the air quality was for sure. "Call me if you need more time, or if you're too worn out when you get back to the hotel. I could come tomorrow too, if that's better for you." He wanted to help her. She was far from home and injured, with no one to protect her. He was happy to do so.

"I'm really grateful, Mark. I was panicked after I met with the police."

"Don't do that again," he warned her, "unless you have an attorney with you. You have a right not to answer some of their questions. They might try to trap you into saying something you shouldn't that isn't true. You've been through a lot in the last twenty-four hours, you could easily make a mistake, and remember something inaccurately that they could use against you. I'll see you tonight. And don't talk to anyone about the accident in the meantime. The insurance people will want to talk to you very soon. If they show up, tell them you have a headache and can't talk. They're going to want to get rid of this quickly, even if they have to pay a big settlement. They're used to it. The last thing they want is an expensive trial. I doubt it will come to that. But we don't want you to have to go through a trial, even a civil one. I want to do all I can to avoid that for you, if the other driver is reasonable. See you tonight." The calm and confidence in his voice reassured her. It was a big deal, which he didn't deny, but he didn't sound panicked. She was taking her cues from him. And oddly, when she left Napa the day before, she thought she'd never see him again, and now she had reached out to him. She had no one else.

She didn't want to call a total stranger. At least she'd met him and liked him.

Dahlia told him which hotel she was staying at, and after they hung up, Mark did what he had told Jeff he shouldn't do. He looked Dahlia up on Google, both her name and the firm she had mentioned to him the day before, Louis Lambert Perfumes. And he was impressed to see she was the CEO and owner, when she only told him she worked there. She was definitely modest and discreet, as well as beautiful. He was fascinated by the firm's history, and liked the fact that it was a real family firm and two of her children worked there.

It was clear from everything written about her and the firm that it was an enormous and impressively successful enterprise, and she ran it all. And there was something wonderfully exotic about perfumes, which the firm had supplied for five generations, and yet had added modern cosmetic lines. On the personal side, she was much less visible, but there were a number of photographs of her at major Parisian social events with her very handsome children, including one who was wearing Doc Martens boots and had pink hair, while the three others were conservative in their dress. Dahlia looked elegant in every photo and nothing like the way she had looked the day before in jeans and T-shirt at the makeshift shelter. She was a very interesting woman of many facets and apparently immense talent and success in her field. He loved the contrasts in her life, combining both family and business, and he wanted to do everything he could to help her get out of the jam she was in, so she could go back to Paris in peace.

He was sure he was going to find a reasonable way to do it, unless the other driver was greedy and dishonest. He was thinking about it as he left his apartment in the Millennium Tower on Mission Street. He had sold his Pacific Heights house to buy it when his daughters had grown up and rarely came to visit anymore. They lived in the East, and one was married with children. He had a guest wing for both of them in the apartment for visits, and it was the ultimate bachelor pad, with a spectacular view of all of San Francisco and both bridges from the fifty-seventh floor.

He drove to The Ritz-Carlton, remembering the photographs he'd seen on Google. Dahlia de Beaumont was a very interesting woman. The biographical piece he'd read said she was a widow and had run the business alone for twenty-six years, and her husband had been an aristocrat, an extraordinary athlete, a champion skier and alpinist who had met his death in the French Alps. There were some other photographs of her with a very attractive older man in black tie at some openings and social events. They made a handsome couple, and it mentioned that he was the CEO of a major luxury brand Mark recognized. He wondered if the man listed as Philippe Vernier was her boyfriend, but they could have been just friends judging by the slightly distant way they stood together. There was a lot about Dahlia he wanted to know, although he knew it would do him no good since she lived in Paris. But first, he had to help her with the fallout from the accident. And one thing he was almost sure of—if the driver of the car in front of her, Marilyn Nicasio, got wind of who Dahlia was in a much bigger world, she was probably going to try to get millions from her. Mark wasn't going to let that happen, if there was anything he could do about it.

He left his car with the doorman at the Ritz, thinking that Jeff Allen's instincts about Dahlia were right. She was famous, and kind of a star after all.

Chapter 8

Getting from the hospital to the hotel when they released her at six o'clock proved to be more complicated than Dahlia had expected. She had the hotel send a car and driver for her, and a nurse had shown her how to manage on her crutches without putting her weight down on her right leg. She left the hospital in a wheelchair, holding the crutches, and it took an orderly and the driver to help slide her into the car and put the wheelchair she'd rented in the trunk.

She looked pale with dark circles under her eyes after the accident, and once they got to the hotel, a bellboy took her upstairs in the wheelchair to her suite. She sat, looking around the room, feeling as though she'd left a month before and not the previous day. She hadn't watched the news in two days, and her driver had told her the fires in Napa had gotten worse. That didn't seem possible—the smoke seemed to have cleared a little, and there was less of a haze hanging over the city—but he had told her that the wind had changed direction and was blowing it all toward the East Bay. It seemed to shift around the area but didn't dissipate.

She eased out of the wheelchair and lay down on the couch for a few minutes, trying to get up the energy to put on decent clothes for her meeting with Mark Hamilton. She had returned from the hospital in hospital scrubs that looked like pajamas, with her sliced-open jeans and T-shirt in a plastic bag. Her Hermès sneakers had come off in the accident and disappeared with the mangled car when they put it on a truck and took it to the police lot for further examination. She was wearing hospital slippers, and when she saw herself in the mirror in the suite, she almost screamed. She looked like she'd been shipwrecked or had been sick for a year.

"Oh my God," she said out loud. She was sorry she'd agreed to let Mark see her, but she needed his help.

She ordered tea from room service and felt better after a cup, and then she went to the bathroom, perched on her crutches, and washed as best she could. She was afraid of falling in the luxurious marble bathroom, which was now a hazard for her. The nurses had shown her how to shower with a garbage bag on her leg, but she was too tired to try it, and she realized she'd have to ask one of the maids to help her. She didn't want a nurse, but it was a challenge managing alone.

She put a red sweater on. The room was cool with the air conditioning. She got into a short denim skirt and slipped a flat red sandal on one foot. She washed her face, brushed her hair, and put on a bright red Lambert lipstick. Everything was a chore with her cracked ribs, but by seven-thirty, she looked better than she felt, and she looked human again in real clothes. She was too tired to eat, and she still had the headache she'd had since she'd woken up after the anesthetic. They told her it would take several days to recover from the shock of the accident. It had been a major trauma to her system.

She tried to look and act normal when she opened the door to Mark on her crutches. He arrived promptly at eight, and was both worried and relieved when he saw her. At first glance, she looked fresh and beautiful, with her long blond hair pulled back, and the bright lipstick. Her one good leg looked great in the short denim skirt, but when he looked more closely, past the polite smile, he could see how tired and in pain she was, and how shaken up by what had happened. She lowered herself onto the couch, and he took a chair across from her, and stretched out his long legs. He was wearing impeccable jeans, a crisp, perfectly starched white shirt, and dark blue leather Hermès loafers with no socks. He looked more New York than San Francisco.

"Help yourself to whatever you want from the bar." She pointed to where it was hidden in a handsome upright antique desk. "I'm not much of a hostess." He wondered if they should have done the meeting by phone, but he wanted to see her, and not entirely for professional reasons. He was grateful for the opportunity but very sorry she was hurt.

"Are you feeling well enough for me to be here?" he asked her honestly, and she smiled.

"It'll cheer me up. It's a little weird having gone through all that far from home. I'm trying to figure out how to take a shower without killing myself. I'll manage, and at least I can call for help if I need it. Thank you for coming to see me. I'm so sorry to bother you with this mess. I didn't know who to call, and having your card was providential."

"I want to help you," he said sincerely. "And I was thinking on the way over, if you'll allow me to, I want to hire a private investigator."

She looked puzzled by the suggestion.

"Because we don't know how honest the other woman is. She may be genuinely hurt just as she says, or she may be out for money. She clearly wasn't careful if she had her daughter in the front seat and they weren't wearing seatbelts in all that smoke. And now she may want to make you pay for it."

"I didn't check the box for extra insurance," she confessed mournfully, as he poured himself a glass of chilled white wine and brought her a glass of water and a can of nuts. She was too tired and stressed to eat, or to drink wine.

"Can I get you something else?" he offered, and she shook her head.

"The insurance company is going to pay all her expenses, you can be sure of it, and her daughter's, and they'll add a nice amount to it. And if she sounds like she's going to make trouble, they'll start offering her larger amounts. It will be a negotiation, and she'll probably hire a personal injury lawyer who'll take full advantage of the situation." He sighed then, wanting to be honest with her.

"After you called me from the hospital, I looked you up on Google. I wanted to see what she would find, just entering your name on a computer. I found you easily, and your family history is fascinating, but if she looks at those photographs and sees you wearing evening gowns and jewelry, she's liable to want some of that too. That's why I'm not a big fan of the internet. I think it creates more problems than it solves. If she's a greedy woman, and wants to make money from this, her lawyer is going to have a field day with you. 'Rich French business mogul rear-ends single mom,' if that's what she is, and 'injures her and her thirteen-year-old daughter.' And when you go back, 'flees to Paris to shirk her responsibilities.' You can see the potential there, and that would only be the beginning. It could be a lot worse, with them swathed in bandages from head to foot, and a picture of you in an evening gown and diamonds."

"Those pictures you saw are old, by the way."

"They won't care. Once they see that, they'll know you're having fun in the photo, you're wealthy and successful, and she'll want whatever you have. Do I have your permission to hire a private investigator? I want to see what he turns up about this woman. I want her to be squeaky clean like the Virgin Mary, so we know she won't try to discredit you." Dahlia liked the way Mark wanted to protect her and thought of everything.

"What'll I do about their not letting me leave town? I just canceled my meetings in L.A. today. My local rep isn't happy, but it would be too hard trying to do all that on crutches. And I told her to cancel Dallas too. I'll have to make a separate trip to cover those cities, and maybe add a few others. I haven't told my kids about the accident. I'll do it tomorrow, I don't want to upset them, and I'll be fine. I'm just very worried about the legalities, the police investigation, and if this woman is going to try and blame me for something I couldn't help and had no control over." Mark was worried about it too. Personal injury cases attracted dishonest people, both clients and attorneys, like bees to honey.

"I think it will all be fine," he said reassuringly, but he recognized the possibility that the other driver might try and take full advantage of Dahlia, if she was less than honest. He asked Dahlia a few questions and made some notes, and after that he told her how intrigued he was by her business.

"Some of the most famous women of France wore our perfumes," she said proudly. "Movie stars, and presidents' wives. I love the historical aspect of it, but at the same time we try to keep it contemporary. My daughter Delphine has made some great New Age contributions to the brand." She looked proud when she said it. "My mother was never interested in the business. Her generation thought it was vulgar for women to engage in commerce. But I fell in love with it as a child, when my grandfather explained it all to me, and taught me about how they make perfume and how important perfume is to French history. I used to love going to the factory, and I've tried to share that with my children."

"Are they all involved in the business?" he asked her.

"No, two out of four, which isn't bad. One of my daughters

is a television producer, and the youngest is an artist. But my son Charles and my daughter Delphine are very engaged in it. The TV producer is getting married in three and a half weeks. She'll have my head if I don't make it home in time. She was worried about the trip. Who could have foreseen this?" She looked dismayed, and he could tell that her children were an important part of her life, in an active way. "Do you have children?" she asked him, curious about him too. It was such serendipity that they had met, and now he was helping her with a major problem.

"Two daughters. One lives in Washington, D.C. She's an attorney, specializing in international trade, and the other one lives in Virginia, on a horse farm her parents-in-law own. They're twenty-seven and twenty-nine, and they don't come out here very often anymore. I go to visit them when I want to see them. Their mother and I divorced when they were very young. She moved back to New York and remarried. It makes it hard to stay current in children's lives when you only see them for school holidays and summer vacations. Maybe I should have moved back too, to see more of them, but I had a growing law practice here, and I didn't want to live in New York again. We get along well, but I wasn't around for every day and weekends. Distance takes a toll." He looked like he regretted it, and showed her a photo of his daughters on his phone. They were both beautiful, and one of them looked like him with dark hair and brown eyes. The other one was blonde and blue-eyed, and Dahlia guessed looked more like his ex-wife.

"You never remarried?" she asked him.

"The first one wasn't a great experience. Other than my daughters, nothing about it made me want to try again. I got very comfortable with being single, and stayed away from serious relationships for a long time, and I got set in my ways. I had my kids for vacations, and I dated interesting women, but no one I wanted to be married to or stay with long-term. One of them is a senator now. She almost got the vice presidential nomination in the last election. She was in love with her political career, not with me. It suited me for about five years, and then we both moved on." He didn't look like he regretted it. "I didn't want to take a chance on another marriage that didn't work out. My ex-wife and I are good friends now, at a distance, but we were both very unhappy while we were married. She hated California. She thought San Francisco was too provincial, and she wanted to go back to New York. I didn't. I never missed it. The life here suited me, and when I want big city excitement, I go to New York or London for a visit. I have several clients there. But none in Paris." He smiled at her. "My French is terrible. I studied it in high school and never got past *'bonjour.'* I'm impressed with the way you speak

English. I thought you were totally American when I met you."

"I grew up as both at home, so it was easy."

"And you never remarried either?"

She shook her head. "When I was young, I never met anyone as exciting as my husband. He was a wild risk-taker, which I thought was terrific then. It would terrify me now. I was never as daring as he was. I was widowed at thirty, with four children under five. I didn't want an outsider involved with them when they were growing up, and between the family business to run, and four children—they're the same age as yours—I didn't have time for anyone. I didn't want to remarry, and then once they grew up, it felt like too late, and by then all the men I knew were married. Frenchmen don't usually get divorced. If they're unhappily married, they just work around it, and have an 'understanding' with their wife, and discreet arrangements with other women. And unhappily married Frenchwomen aren't faithful either as a rule. Most Americans are much more clean-cut and aboveboard about it. If the marriage fails, they get divorced and move on. In France, they move on, but they forget to sever the ties with their wife, and continue living with each other, even if they hardly see each other. That wasn't what I wanted. Jean-Luc and I had a real marriage, although it was very brief."

"The French system seems too complicated to me, although I know men who've done that here too. I could never see the point of marrying someone in order to cheat on them." She laughed at the way he described it.

"Most of the good men in France are married and stay married. Sometimes you have to make your peace with it," she said, thinking of Philippe. "I don't want to be alone forever, and grow old without companionship, but I don't want to marry again either."

"It sounds like you have a lot on your plate," he said, looking at her. She had beautiful green eyes that were almost emerald.

"The business keeps me busy." From what he had read online, it was huge.

"It's interesting that you haven't taken it public."

She laughed at the suggestion. "My grandfather would come out of his grave and haunt me if I did. He believed in family-owned businesses. There are still a number of important firms in France that are privately held. Maybe my children will take our business public one day. But I won't. I prefer to honor our traditions. That must sound very old-fashioned to you."

"It sounds very noble in a way. I like the idea of traditions being respected, but family-owned enterprises aren't easy to run, with a lot of personalities involved."

"It's probably a blessing that only two of them work for me, and they're both very easy to get along with. My son is very conservative, involved in the financial end, and my daughter Delphine is very innovative. She keeps us fresh and modern and ahead of the trends. We all bring something to it."

"I'll have to wander in the next time I see one of your stores. I've seen them all around the world, but I've never been in one. They look very elegant."

"Thank you. We have men's products too." She made a mental note to send him some, as a courtesy. She had thought of sending some as a gift to Jeff Allen, but she didn't think he would use them. He looked like a natural man who would rather have a good bottle of French wine. "Do you have brothers and sisters?" she asked him, and he shook his head.

"No, I'm an only child."

"So am I," she said. "It's both harder and easier. No competition when you're a child, but my parents died young, and I missed them terribly. The only family I have are my children." It explained a little why she was so close to them, and he could tell she was. Much closer than he was to his daughters.

He loved talking to her, but he was afraid to wear her out, after what she'd been through. She was enjoying talking to him too. She couldn't resist asking him where he'd gone to college, and he said he'd gone to Yale undergraduate and Stanford Law School. His father had been a lawyer too, senior partner of a well-known New York law firm, as Mark was in San Francisco.

"And you?" he asked her.

"Columbia, and Wharton for business school. My father insisted on it. With the company to run one day, he thought I should be prepared. It served me well. My daughter Delphine went to college in the States too. She loved it and then she got married after she graduated and came back to Paris. Her husband is French. The others all went to university in France."

"I'm the only member of my family who moved to the West. All the others preferred the East, and my daughters did too," he volunteered. "When I decided to stay in San Francisco, my parents thought I was crazy. My wife thought so too. She studied law but never practiced, which seemed like a waste to me." He respected Dahlia for the career she had, and how actively she pursued it, but he also knew she paid a price for that. He could see why she'd never remarried. She didn't have time, between the business and her family.

They had strayed far from his reason for coming to see her and he had enjoyed it thoroughly.

"So do you agree to hiring a private investigator, to find out what we can about the Nicasio woman?" he confirmed, and she nodded.

"I hate to be so cynical, but it seems like a smart thing to do." She was a businesswoman after all, and realistic about people's motives. Other people's greed was not new to her.

"I'll take care of it tomorrow and get him started. I think we should get some information on her quickly. Have the police given you any idea of when a hearing might be?"

"No, they said they'd be in touch. I was still feeling pretty rough when they came to see me in the hospital this morning. The main thing they wanted to know was who had hit who first."

"If you hit her car first, before the truck hit you, you could be held responsible for the accident," he said.

"No, I'm sure the truck hit me first—I remember the impact distinctly—and then I hit her." She was certain of it.

"The insurance people are going to want to see you soon too. Let me know when you hear from them. I'll come with you."

"I feel terrible taking up your time. If you want to assign the case to someone else, I'd understand."

"I want to see this through for you," he said with a serious expression. In the wrong hands, he knew it could turn into a nightmare for her and he didn't want that to happen. Living it had been bad enough, and he was glad she hadn't been injured more severely. She could have ended up dead, like the driver of the truck. She really had been lucky it wasn't worse.

It was eleven o'clock when he left, and she was tired, but she felt better mentally. Talking to him had reassured her, and made everything seem more normal and not so terrifying. She could sense that she'd be in good hands if he handled the legal aspects for her. It was kind of him to do so. She expected him to bill her for it, but he could have handed her off to someone else and he hadn't so far, and it didn't seem like he was going to.

After he had gone, she sent an email to the local rep and told her she was staying in San Francisco for a while, but didn't tell her why, just that she wouldn't be working. She didn't want to make a big fuss about the accident, and thought it was best to keep quiet, so it wouldn't wind up in the press and feed any interest in it.

She turned on the news and saw that the fires had gotten worse. The air quality in San Francisco now was equal to that of Beijing. Then she did what Mark had done before he came to see her. She googled his name, and his biographical and professional information came up immediately. He was fifty-eight years old, the senior partner of his own law firm, with twenty-five other lawyers who were partners of the firm. His clients were some of the biggest corporations nationally and in the West, and it listed some of his most illustrious clients. And he had won lawsuits against some mammoth corporations. He was a star in his own field and very impressive. There was very little personal information on it. He had shared much more with her while they talked. And one thing was for sure, if he handled the legal aspects of her situation, she would be in excellent hands.

After she had read about him on Google, she decided to call Philippe. She somehow felt that the accident gave her the right to call him, despite his family vacation, and his wife's presence. Dahlia had promised to let him know what was happening. The time difference had been wrong to reach him when she left the hospital and got back to the hotel. It was the middle of the night in France. She waited until midnight to call him, which was nine A.M. for him.

He answered the call immediately, and sounded cool when he did.

"I'm just leaving to play tennis with a friend," he informed her in a businesslike voice. She could tell he wasn't alone.

"I found a lawyer. He's the head of a big firm, but he's doing it to help me."

"Good, you need one."

"And I'm back at the hotel."

"Thank you for keeping me informed," he said. "Stay in touch." He was off the line before she could tell him anything else, and she realized when he ended the call that he had never asked her how she felt. His wife was obviously nearby. It was the disadvantage of having a clandestine affair with a married man. She felt rejected after he hung up. She decided to call Delphine then. She knew nothing about the accident, just about the fires. And Dahlia had to explain why she wasn't in L.A.

Delphine had just gotten to the office and was organizing her day when her mother called. She was happy to hear Dahlia's voice. She missed her—she had been gone for two weeks, and it was beginning to seem long.

"Are you in L.A. now?" Delphine asked her, sounding cheerful. Dahlia didn't want to frighten her about the accident, but she needed to say something to explain her change of plans.

"Actually, I'm still in San Francisco," Dahlia said blithely.

"The airport's still closed? Shouldn't you go by car now? You're going to throw off your whole schedule in Dallas and L.A."

"I had to cancel that part of the trip," Dahlia said calmly, as though it was a minor decision. "I ran into a problem. It sounds worse than it is. I had a small accident. I got rear-ended, and I broke my leg. It's ridiculous and a nuisance, but I'm fine. The cast will be off in six weeks."

"Oh my God, Mom, how awful. Are you sure you're okay? Are you coming home now?" Delphine was instantly worried about her.

"No, I need to sort it out with the insurance people and the car rental company. I hired a lawyer to take care of it. I'll come home as soon as it's taken care of. It's just administrative details," Dahlia said, underplaying it.

"That's awful. And it's a shame about L.A."

"I'll come back another time," Dahlia said, minimizing it as much as she could.

"It must have been quite an accident if you broke your leg."

"It wasn't pleasant, but I'm fine. The cast is a bit of a bother." She didn't mention the concussion at all, nor the cracked ribs.

"When do you think you'll come home?"

"As soon as I sort it out. They need to determine who was at fault. The other driver got injured too. She wasn't wearing a seatbelt."

"Do you think she'll sue you?" It was always a concern, particularly in the States.

"Hopefully not, but in the U.S. you never know. That's why I stayed, to get all of that worked out before I leave, so I'm not dealing with it long distance. It's much simpler to deal with it while I'm here. I'll still be home on time. But maybe you could go to Alex's dress fittings with her."

"Maman, are you sure you're all right?" Delphine was suspicious. She knew her mother never liked to cause them concern, and she was sounding very light and breezy for a woman with a broken leg. Delphine used her childhood name for her, which was a sign that she was worried.

"I'm positive. They're just sticklers here for all the legalities. And it takes a little time to sort out. I'm not going to tell Alex, or she'll be hysterical about the wedding. Do you mind doing the fittings with her?"

"Of course I mind, she'll be a monster at the fittings. The diva unleashed. But I'll do it for you. Just take care of yourself and come home when you can. I have a meeting in five minutes so I have to go. I'm so sorry about your leg."

"I'm fine, darling, and thank you." Delphine got off a minute later to get to her meeting, and Dahlia let out a sigh. She knew Delphine would worry anyway, but at least now she knew about the accident, in a sanitized version that didn't sound too bad. She didn't want to tell her that she was worried about a lawsuit, and even charges of negligence. Delphine didn't need to know any of that. Dahlia knew she would tell Charles, but not Alex or Emma, neither of whom needed to know. Alex would drive her crazy, and

Emma would be scared for her. It would just make things harder for Dahlia if they knew. Delphine could handle things at home. She was competent to handle any situation that came up.

After the call, Dahlia struggled out of her clothes with the cumbersome cast and lay in bed, thinking about all of it. It was a relief to finally get to bed. In the past two days, she'd been in a horrifying accident that had killed a man, been injured herself, and spent a night in a hospital and an evening with her new lawyer who had the potential to become a friend. She was facing a hearing about the accident, possible charges of negligence, and hopefully not a lawsuit, but it could happen. She had told her daughter about the accident, and had talked to Philippe, who acted like it was a call from a business associate or an acquaintance because his wife was obviously within hearing distance. It made her wonder what she was doing with her life and if she was on the right track or making terrible mistakes. She was always trying to protect her children from reality and soften life's blows for them. She never told them when she was weak or scared, hurt or felt vulnerable.

She had been involved with a man for six years whose whole life was a lie, and she was lying with him and enabling him. And now she had to face lawyers, judges, and courtrooms for an accident she didn't cause, and because she pretended to everyone that she was always strong, she would be facing it alone. It was a lot to manage, and sometimes she wondered if it was worth it. She had no one to lean on except herself, no one to stand beside her when things went wrong, or protect her.

She had chosen a hard path after Jean-Luc died, and she was still on it, carrying everything alone, protecting them all, while no one protected her, and all to prove how capable and efficient she was, and how she could keep all the balls in the air for all of them. What if she couldn't? What if she dropped one, or wasn't strong for once? Would their world come to an end if she didn't solve every problem for them? And would hers end if they didn't need her quite so much?

She didn't have the answers to the questions, as she fell into a deep sleep, her leg in the cast propped up on pillows, and her head still hurting from the accident. Sometimes it all seemed like too much. It would have been nice not to always have to prove to all of them how strong she was. What if she wasn't? And somewhere in the darkness, the fires were still raging out of control, and the world was burning.

Chapter 9

After she struggled out of bed in the morning, turned on the TV to watch the news, and had a cup of coffee and some toast, Dahlia called housekeeping for a garbage bag to wrap her leg, so she could take a shower. The news of the fire was depressing. It seemed to be roaming freely, devouring homes and small towns all over Napa County. Most vineyards didn't burn, but everything else did. Thousands of acres of the beautiful Napa Valley had been destroyed. It had looked so perfect the first time she saw it on the first of July, and now only a week later, everything was charred black and unrecognizable. The tragedy worsened day by day, and so far nothing had stopped it.

She tackled the shower, which proved to be more complicated than anticipated, balancing on one leg, and getting out on the marble floor. She nearly fell once, and sat down on a chair breathless afterward, with her ribs aching, and put on one of the terrycloth robes the hotel provided with her initials on it. She felt victorious when she got her underwear on and brushed her hair. Nothing was easy with the cast, unable to put her weight on it, and her head felt better but she still had a mild headache. She kept reminding herself that she was lucky to be alive. Mark called her right after she put a ruffled white skirt on and was buttoning her blouse. She felt as though she had climbed Mount Everest since breakfast.

"Good morning," he said, with a deep cheerful voice. He sounded like a man of action who had everything in full control, which was the exact opposite of how she was feeling. She felt as though she had been in a free fall since the night of the accident, with the ground rushing toward her at full speed, and her parachute refusing to open. "How do you feel today?"

"Like I lost a heavyweight championship two days ago. I'm still a little punchy, but my headache is better. I watched the fires this morning on the news. It looks just terrible." The wind had shifted and they'd gotten worse during the night. Four more important wineries had been burned to the ground.

"It happens nearly every year now, but these are the

worst we've had yet." They were called complex fires, because they started as separate fires, which eventually joined up with greater force than ever. "I'm afraid you're not seeing San Francisco at its best. Our investigator started at eight o'clock this morning, and he has an update on the Nicasios. They've both been released by the hospital. The mother has more injuries than the daughter. It sounds like all of the daughter's were from the airbag. But none of their injuries are permanent or liable to cause lasting damage," which was Dahlia's situation too. "There were a lot of accidents on the road that night. The insurance company must be swamped. You may not hear from them for a few days. The investigator is going to do some background checking on Marilyn Nicasio, to give us an idea of what kind of person she is. Criminal record, credit rating, where they live, what kind of tenant she is, things like that. It should give us an idea of what we have in store for us." He was fully on her side, and made it sound as though they were a team, and Dahlia was touched.

"I'm sorry to cause you all this trouble."

"I'm happy to help." She was a woman alone and he had the feeling that she needed protection. Her success and her career didn't suggest that, but he had gotten that sense when he spoke to her the night before, and even when he met her in Napa. She seemed so strong, but he sensed that behind the façade she was fragile, more than just from a broken leg, and he wasn't wrong. She felt out of her element, disoriented by the accident, and far from home. She was used to dealing from strength in a familiar world, on home turf, and suddenly she felt lost in the woods, which was entirely foreign to her. "What are you doing today?" he asked her. He wanted to invite her to lunch, but doubted she was up to it, although she sounded strong and upbeat when she talked to him. His self-assurance and optimistic outlook were contagious.

"I don't know yet. I just took a shower, which was like qualifying for an Olympic event, on one leg, with a marble floor. Being in a cast is humbling," she commented.

"Be careful with the marble floor. Maybe you should have one of the maids help you."

"I was going to, but I decided I could do it myself. I'll do better next time." She wasn't easily daunted.

"You should take it easy, and don't be afraid to ask for help. Do you want a nurse?" he asked her.

"God, no. It's just a broken leg, like a skiing accident. And the doctor said I'd feel better in a few days. I already do feel better than yesterday."

"Good. And if I can do anything to help, just call me. My office isn't far from the hotel," he offered, and she smiled.

"You're already doing more than enough, for a total stranger. I'd be lost without you right now." They hung up a few minutes later. She looked out the windows. There was still a heavy haze over the city, and she couldn't see the bridge or the bay. She checked her computer and saw that she had an email from the insurance company for the rental car agency. They wanted to see her that afternoon. She called Mark back immediately.

"They want to see me today, at my earliest convenience. Is that okay? Should I just see them?"

"Not without legal counsel present. In the long run your interests may be counter to theirs. I have a meeting I can't cancel at two this afternoon. Why don't you see if they can do it at four, and I could be there with you," he said.

"Are you sure you have time?"

"I do, and I don't want you seeing them alone. They may want to put pressure on you to see how you'll react. They want to know how good a case Nicasio has before they start making settlement offers. It's standard stuff. I know it doesn't feel like it, but it's all proceeding normally so far. We just want to be sure it doesn't go off the rails later, so what you say now is important. It could all go against you if we're not careful or the police decide you're responsible. That's what we need to be prepared for, and where the private investigator could be useful. And your position as

CEO of a highly successful company could complicate things if Nicasio is after big money."

"I can't even wear decent clothes for the meeting," Dahlia lamented. "I brought mostly pantsuits and slacks I can't get over my cast," but fortunately she'd brought a few summer dresses for L.A.

"They're just insurance appraisers. Keep it simple."

"I'll let you know what they say about the meeting." She sent them a short email after they spoke, and they responded within minutes. Four o'clock at her hotel was fine for them. And at least they could see that she wasn't trying to avoid them. She had nothing to hide and had told the police the truth right from the beginning, when she saw them in the hospital.

Mark sent her an email as soon as he got hers and said that he'd be there a few minutes before four to prep her, and was looking forward to seeing her then.

He sat thoughtfully at his desk for a minute after he sent it to her. He was questioning his own motives and had to admit that offering his help wasn't entirely altruistic. Every time he saw her, he wanted to get to know her better. Jeff Allen had been right. She was a very unusual woman, and he liked her modesty and discretion as well as her fine mind and beauty. She had everything going for her except geography. He was intrigued by a woman who lived six thousand miles away in a world entirely different from his. And anything he wanted to develop or pursue with her had no future to it. But it didn't seem to stop him, although he knew better. Dahlia intrigued him, and he had never met anyone like her. She was as much a mother as a CEO, she was internationally known and yet seemed to live well below the radar of celebrity. He knew she must run her company with a hand of iron, but she seemed like a gentle person. She was strong and feminine, probably rich but didn't show off. She was willing to work at a shelter rescuing injured animals when she could have been getting a manicure and her hair done. She was beautiful but didn't make a big deal of it. She could have been a snob, and even had reason to be, and instead she was warm and gracious to everyone. In so many ways, she seemed like an ideal woman to him, after dating so many others who weren't, others who were fraudulent in some way, and one of her qualities he liked best was that she was real. There was nothing phony or boastful about her. She wasn't a show-off, wasn't in competition with him, and didn't have an agenda. He hadn't met anyone he was as eager to spend time with in years, and because of who she was, he didn't know how to do it, or approach her.

Helping her avoid a lawsuit was enough for the moment. The worst part was that no matter what he did, once the problem was solved she would go back to Paris. He couldn't even pretend to himself that there was a future to it. He hadn't dared be close to any woman in years and didn't want to be, but Dahlia de Beaumont had gotten under his skin. He felt bewitched by her, and he knew he couldn't show it. She didn't even suspect it, which was what he wanted for now. They had work to do together, and complicating things would only make it harder.

Dahlia was wearing a light blue summer dress when she opened the door to him at three forty-five. She looked pretty and fresh and young, like one of her own daughters. She was using her crutches and not the wheelchair. The wheelchair only made sense if someone pushed it.

He walked in looking busy and purposeful and like a man in command of his surroundings and any situation he confronted. He was wearing a dark gray summer-weight business suit with a white shirt she recognized as Hermès and a dark blue tie. He looked like a successful businessman from New York, with the stylish air of men of power in that city. He was no small-town boy or ordinary lawyer.

She offered him a glass of wine, which he declined.

"I'm working, remember," he reminded her gently with a smile. "If I represent you while falling down drunk, it may not make a great impression."

He briefed her before the insurance people arrived and told her to try to relax and be herself, and to answer them honestly, and if she didn't remember something, just say it. He had been preparing witnesses to take the stand for three decades, and he assured her that honesty was always best, and would reassure the insurance people that she would be a solid witness if it came to that. And they'd be meeting with Marilyn Nicasio too, if they hadn't already. They'd want to see if their stories matched up, or if there was any divergence.

Dahlia seemed very calm to him by the time the doorbell of the suite rang. He went to the door for her so she didn't have to get up and do it on crutches. Two men and a woman walked in, wearing proper business attire, looking very serious. Dahlia stood up to greet them to show them some respect. She didn't want them to think her haughty because she hadn't gotten off the couch.

She offered them coffee or tea, which they declined, and after a few minimal polite words, they got down to business, while Mark watched them carefully. He could tell two things right at the beginning of the meeting, in the first few minutes. They were impressed with Dahlia, and they knew who she was. They asked her to describe the circumstances of the accident, and precisely how it happened, if she remembered. She did as she was asked and told them in minute detail what had happened. She described each moment like a film on pause as she went from one memory, fact, and impression to the next. The woman looked particularly touched by her, and the men looked moved by her recital too.

"You're absolutely sure that the first impact was from the truck behind you?" one of the men asked her pointedly when she was finished. And Mark was impressed too by how clearly and calmly she had described it.

"Completely," she said without wavering. "He hit me so hard, I thought I was going to fly through the windshield, but my seatbelt kept that from happening. I still managed to hit my head on something. The sun visor, I think. The car I was driving wasn't very big." It was a compact SUV, and the interior hadn't been large. "He hit me with incredible force, and I felt like my car was lifted off the ground and thrown forward more than just pushed into the car in front of me. I hit the car in front pretty hard, but not as hard as he hit me, I think." It had been a truck after all, a very big one. "And as soon as I felt the impact of hitting the other car, I passed out, and I didn't wake up until I was in the hospital. But I remember both moments of impact distinctly, the one behind me, and seconds later, the one in front. I must have hit my head when I hit her, so I passed out then. But I was wide awake when he hit me, and when I hit her."

"The police think it's possible that he was going faster than he should have in the heavy smoke. The visibility was almost nonexistent in the smoke, and he probably didn't see you, and when he did, it was too late. He hit the brakes as hard as he could, so he jackknifed and flipped over after he hit you, but he couldn't avoid hitting you," one of the men said. "It's amazing you survived it, given the size of the vehicle," he added. "We can see from the car you were driving how hard the impact was, which is why you hit the car in front of you. You couldn't avoid it."

The female insurance appraiser then interjected, "Ms. Nicasio says you hit her first, and she heard the truck hit you *after* you ran into her. We saw her this morning, and she's very definite about it." All three of the insurance appraisers were expressionless when she said it.

"That's not how I remember it," Dahlia said simply. "And I know I didn't hit my head when he hit me. I hit my head when my car impacted the one in front of me. And then I passed out."

"According to the paramedics' report, your car caught fire after both impacts, one of the firefighters told them. You were unconscious when they pulled you out of the car. They just managed to get you out without needing heavy machinery to do it, and laid you down on the side of the road, far enough from the burning car in case it blew up.

Their report says you remained unconscious throughout the procedure and didn't regain consciousness until after they air-lifted you to Zuckerberg in the city." Dahlia looked shaken after they explained it to her, and glanced at Mark. He looked stricken by the report too. She could easily have died at any point during the accident or after.

"I don't think it's a negligible detail," Mark said to them, "that the other driver is not going to get the kind of settlement from the insurer of the truck," which was an unknown local company with low rates for trucks, "that she can hope to get from you, from an internationally known rental car company. If Ms. Nicasio can claim that Ms. de Beaumont was the initiator of the accident, making you responsible for it as world-class insurers, it will be a lot better for her financially than if the truck was initially responsible—from a small supermarket chain, carrying tomatoes from L.A., insured by a much smaller insurer. Let's be honest, you have the deep pockets here, and so does Ms. de Beaumont, if Ms. Nicasio sees that as an opportunity." Their faces looked pinched for a minute before they answered. They were well aware of it too, and Mark knew it and shone a bright light on it immediately. It was the key issue here, or one of them.

"The truck's insurer is answerable for the death of the driver, and we don't know yet what kind of condition the truck was in mechanically, like how good the brakes were.

We're investigating that now, and we may have a suit against them, but we think the policy may have been limited. It's a small company. And we are prepared to make a sizable settlement to Ms. Nicasio, dependent on the medical reports. She told us that her daughter has been deeply affected by the trauma and won't be able to go to school for several months, possibly not even in September after the vacation, with both arms broken, and Ms. Nicasio can't go to work either. And she has to stay home now to care for her daughter."

"They should have been wearing seatbelts, especially in the existing conditions with that kind of poor visibility from the smoke," Mark said coldly, and Dahlia was surprised by his tone. It didn't sound like him, even as little as she knew him. She was getting an advance look at Mark Hamilton, the famous litigator. It wasn't lost on the insurers either.

"A number of factors will weigh in on the settlement we offer. We still have the court hearing to get through to determine who was in fact responsible, and if there was criminal negligence involved on anyone's part. And we're waiting for medical reports on the deceased truck driver." There could have been drugs involved, or medical issues, or a number of other factors, if he'd been driving for too long and could have fallen asleep at the wheel. Mark knew that anything was possible, and so did they.

They stood up then, satisfied that they had heard Dahlia's version of the story. It was in direct conflict with what Marilyn Nicasio had told them, and none of them knew if she was an honest woman or had her eye on a prize she might never have a chance at otherwise.

"There are likely to be civil suits resulting from this as well," the lead insurance appraiser said as they stood up.

"We're well aware of that," Mark responded.

"She got Ms. de Beaumont's name from the police," the appraiser said, looking uncomfortable, "and we believe she's done some research." It was what Mark had feared for Dahlia, but there was nothing they could do about it. Dahlia was who she was, and she was a big target. If the Nicasio woman was greedy and dishonest, she was going to have a field day.

"Thank you for the warning," Mark said quietly. They all shook hands and the three insurers left a minute later. Dahlia had walked them to the door on her crutches, and she and Mark went back to the sitting area after they left and looked at each other.

"Well," she asked him, "what do you think?"

"I think you were terrific, and everything you say is solid and rings true."

"Because it is," she said quietly, and he nodded.

"But I smell trouble from the Nicasio woman. I think she's

going to give it a shot, and I'm sure she'll find some sleazy contingency lawyer to help her do it. You're an irresistible target," he told her, and she understood that too. It was why she was worried. "We have to take this one step at a time. First the hearing, to determine if there are criminal implications. It could be that the truck driver was on substances, or guilty of something illegal. But we need to determine if he was responsible, or you are. The Nicasio woman wants you to be, so she can go after you. The trucker's side of it won't be nearly as lucrative for her as going after the rental car company, and you civilly. She won't have a shot at it, if the courts decide, or a jury, that you're not responsible. That's the key here." The hearing was set for a month away, and Mark was using all his connections to get it moved earlier. The whole thing could be deemed an accident, and there would be no criminal implications. Mark wanted to know that as soon as possible. Or it could go all the way to the end, with Marilyn Nicasio sticking to her story, and it would wind up as a civil jury trial, at her insistence, which would be long, painful, and expensive for Dahlia. He wanted to spare her that if he could, and he had made several calls that morning about the hearing date but hadn't heard back yet.

"You did very well," he told Dahlia again. "You'll make a fantastic witness. I just hope we don't have to demonstrate that."

"Do you think they believed me?"

"To a point. They may think that you're trying to protect yourself financially. They probably don't know who to believe right now. And Ms. Nicasio is probably very convincing. She has a lot riding on it. Maybe she's an honest woman, but if she's done 'research' on you, as he put it, I strongly doubt that she's honest. I believe you, Dahlia, now we just have to convince everyone else. It will all fall into place. But it will take time."

"I have to be back in Paris in three weeks," she said, looking desperate, "for my daughter's wedding."

"Let's see if we can get the whole thing dismissed at the hearing, but with one man dead, and three people injured, dismissal may not be possible. I want to be honest with you." She nodded. She was sure he was doing his best, in difficult circumstances, and she fully realized how lucky she was to have met him, and that he was helping her.

He left shortly after the insurers. He said he had a lot of work to do, and promised to be in touch if he had any news. And she thanked him again for his support.

Dahlia slept a lot for the next two days, which helped her head and ribs feel better. The headache was almost gone, but getting around with the cast was annoying. Mark called her two days after she'd last seen him, and he sounded pleased. A judge he knew had helped him get the initial hearing moved, to determine if the matter would be dismissed as an accident or if there was any question of negligence. In either case, Marilyn Nicasio could still sue Dahlia civilly and accuse her of negligence and demand a civil jury trial, which would be lengthy and costly. The attorneys would try to negotiate a settlement, up until the trial date. But Dahlia's life would return to normal for a while. Right now, everything was hanging, waiting for the hearing. And the police had told her not to leave town.

"Who ever said that golf wasn't a useful game? I play golf with two Superior Court judges once a month, and one of them just gave us a hand. He beat me last week, so I think was sorry for me." Mark had actually told the judge the truth, and was sorry for Dahlia. "He spoke to the judge assigned to our hearing, and he agreed to move it up by three weeks. It's set now for next Monday. Everyone's been notified. I hope we have a decent chance to get it dismissed. We need to get that hearing behind us so we know where we stand."

Dahlia was relieved to hear it and nervous too. If it went badly, the implications were serious, she could be stuck in San Francisco for a long time, pending trial. The ramifications of going to trial would be considerable, not to mention Alex's wedding, which would have to be postponed, or Alex would have to get married without her, which would upset

Dahlia profoundly, and the bride. She hoped it wouldn't come to that. So the early hearing was great news.

She thanked Mark profusely, and he called her back the next day. He said he had more good news. Their investigator had some early reports on Marilyn Nicasio, and they confirmed Mark's suspicions that she might not be an innocent. The investigator had discovered that she was a receptionist at a low salary, living in a seedy apartment building on the fringes of the Tenderloin, an unwholesome area filled with drug addicts and alcoholics lying on the street, and not a pleasant place to live, but the rent was low. Ms. Nicasio had no criminal record, but her credit rating was a disaster. She was in credit card debt up to her ears. And she had previously sued both a landlord and a boss. She didn't win against the landlord, and owed him a year's back rent, but she had successfully sued an employer for sexual discrimination because she was a woman and was passed over for a promotion. She had been awarded twenty-five thousand dollars and had been unemployed for six months afterward because no one would hire her after the suit.

None of it proved that she was dishonest, but she certainly hadn't had an easy life, and anything she could get in a settlement now would be a windfall for her. It was the kind of opportunity that would be hard to turn down, particularly if she wasn't honest. And she was sticking to her story, which Dahlia knew wasn't true, that she had hit the car in front first, before the truck hit her. That technicality made Dahlia responsible for any damage to Marilyn Nicasio and her daughter.

What the investigator had unearthed about Ms. Nicasio gave them some information about her that suggested a profile of someone in need who didn't hesitate to go after others to improve her situation. Dahlia felt sorry for her, for her hard life and her injuries, but she wasn't willing to be a sacrificial lamb for her. If it had been her fault, Dahlia would have paid damages willingly. But it wasn't—they had all suffered injuries, and the truck driver death, as the result of forces they couldn't control and had all been the victims of, with no one person to blame.

When Mark called her about the new hearing date, and information about Marilyn Nicasio, he surprised her with an invitation.

"Jeff Allen is back in business again. The winds shifted and they set up the rescue tent in the same place. We're giving him another check from the ASPCA, and I prefer to deliver them hand to hand. I'm going up on Saturday to give it to him. Would you like to come? I don't know if you'd be comfortable riding in the car, and there's a different route we can take to get there, through the East Bay, so you won't have to go past where the accident happened." He didn't want to traumatize her for the sake of a Saturday afternoon drive.

With the smoke still in the air, and Dahlia still adjusting to crutches, with some residual pain, he knew she was staying in the hotel most of the time. It was smoky in Napa too, but for now the wind was from a different direction, and when Mark had spoken to him, Jeff had said you could actually breathe up there, for now.

Dahlia hesitated for a moment, thinking about it. She liked the idea of seeing Mark, and Jeff again, and Mahala and the others she had volunteered with briefly. She was just passing time, waiting for the hearing. Agnes was sending materials for her to work on by email, but she was lonely at the hotel. The rep had come by to have tea with her once, but for the most part, she was alone, and liked the idea of going to Napa with Mark. She wondered if the little black dog with the white patch was still there. She was sure that either his owners had come for him by now, or he had been adopted. He was too cute to stay there long.

"Actually, I'd like that," she said to Mark. "And taking a different route sounds like a good idea," she said gratefully. It was thoughtful of him to suggest it, and even consider it. He was a compassionate person. And she didn't want to have flashbacks of the accident. She'd had nightmares at night ever since, but her headache lessened every day. She only noticed it now when she was tired at the end of the day. "It'll be fun to see them all. I wish I could volunteer again, but I think I'd be more of a burden than an asset with my cast."

He promised to pick her up at ten o'clock on Saturday morning. They could have lunch with Jeff if he had time and wasn't too busy. She was looking forward to it. And in the interim, she kept in close touch with her office, spoke to Agnes every day for messages, and talked to Delphine regularly. She had another big project in mind that she wanted to discuss with her mother when she got home. They were busy in Paris.

Charles called her a few times too, about financial matters. He was concerned about her accident, but more so about a potential lawsuit, although they could afford it, but he wasn't pleased at the prospect, nor was Dahlia.

The day before her plan to go to Napa with Mark, the police visited her in preparation for the hearing. They asked her to go over her version of the accident again, and her story was consistent, because it was the truth. They asked her if there was anything she would like to change, and she said there wasn't. It was her precise recollection of the event. She didn't remember anything more or less now than she did the day after it happened. They hadn't warned her of their visit, and she called Mark when they left.

"You did the right thing seeing them. They're looking for inconsistencies, or to see if you changed your mind about what you told them before."

"I didn't. I don't remember anything differently. And I was unconscious almost the minute I hit her car. I don't remember anything after that until I woke up on a gurney in a hallway at Zuckerberg. I don't remember the helicopter ride at all." He was glad she didn't. She would have been in excruciating pain with the broken leg, cracked ribs, and head injury. It was a mercy that she had passed out.

"I'll see you tomorrow," he said, sounding upbeat. He knew she was nervous about the hearing on Monday; he wanted to distract her and knew they'd be happy to see her at the animal rescue tent. Everyone who had met her liked her and said she was a pleasure to work with.

"Do you think it'll be smoky up there? Should I take my mask?"

"Probably. It doesn't hurt to take it. Jeff says the air is better up there right now, but that could change in minutes." Living with the fires nearby was becoming a way of life. And seeing the devastation on the news every night was like watching the reportage of a war, with the death toll mounting, as exhausted firefighters took greater risks, desperate to put out the fires that instead spread farther every day. They were in three counties now, with Napa at the hub of it, and the fires only four percent contained. It felt like Armageddon. The end of the world. Paris had never seemed farther away.

For no particular reason, she called Philippe on Friday night. She was tired and homesick. She missed her children, and him. She felt useless sitting in San Francisco, unable to go to her office in Paris every day, and waiting for hearings, for the other shoe to fall, for a lawsuit or charges against her, or a settlement of some kind.

She called Philippe at one in the morning for her on Friday night, ten A.M. for him on Saturday morning, on a glorious sunny day in Saint-Jean-Cap-Ferrat on the Riviera.

"Are you busy?" she asked him.

"No, I'm sitting in the sun, having breakfast. It's a gorgeous day." She could hear the birds chirping in the background to prove it. "Why did you call?"

"I just missed you," she said simply. It was true. She hadn't seen him in almost three weeks, and she was due back soon. But she couldn't go now, at least not until after the hearing. The police had reminded her again not to leave town. But a day trip to Napa didn't count. It was an hour from the city.

"You know it's not a good idea to call here. She's out, so it doesn't matter this time. She went to some farmer's market she heard about. When are you coming home?"

"Soon. There's a hearing about the accident on Monday, where a judge will decide if there was negligence involved. I can't leave before that."

"That's absurd. They're treating you like a criminal. You should just get on a plane and come home. There's no extradition from France. Once you're in France, they can't touch you. Use your French passport to come home." It was a clever idea but with long-term consequences, she knew, if she fled the country before the hearing. And it would make her seem guilty.

"If I do that, I can never come back to the States."

"That's ridiculous, over an accident that's not your fault."

"They're not sure if it's my fault or not. That's what the hearing is for. And the woman is lying, which is what makes it so difficult. We have two different stories, so the judge may send it to trial." She'd gone over it again and again with Mark. He kept reminding her that she was innocent. She hoped the judge agreed with him.

"I think you should just leave," Philippe sounded bored. "How are you feeling, by the way?"

"Better. The cast is a nuisance though."

"I'm playing golf today. We're going to a big party in

Monaco Friday night, at Jimmy'z." It was a popular disco in Monte-Carlo. She went there sometimes too in the summer with her kids. It felt like a lifetime away. He was having a fun summer, while hers was a nightmare.

"It sounds like everything is going smoothly there," Dahlia said, more jealous than she wanted to be.

"We're civilized people, and it's good for Julien to have both his parents here. He says he loves it." It didn't sound like an adequate reason to her, to stay married to a woman he admitted he had never loved.

"I'm going back to Napa tomorrow, to the animal rescue," she said, to have something to say.

"It sounds like a deadly dull town."

"It is, but it's very pretty and geographically spectacular, with mountains and beaches nearby."

"I'd rather be here," Philippe said. He sounded cold. He thought she should just come home and leave the mess to the lawyers to work out. He wasn't warm or reassuring.

"So would I," she responded. "I always feel like a fish out of water in America. I've been gone for too long to feel any connection to it. And I never really felt American."

"You aren't. There's nothing American about you. They take everything too seriously. Look at the fuss they're making. It's a car accident, for God's sake. You didn't shoot the president. And they're treating you like a criminal." She couldn't disagree, but she almost forgave them for it. It was a serious matter after all, with injuries and a man's death.

"Hopefully not, after Monday," she said, missing him, and not even sure why. He wasn't being affectionate, and he hadn't been overly sympathetic about the accident. He kept their time together on a regular schedule, and he was careful never to get too close. It was all very regulated and controlled on his terms. By now, it would have been nice to have more, but she wasn't sure if she was ready for it either. They each had their freedom and separate lives, and their time together twice a week, and went to big events together, while Jacqueline turned a blind eye, like a good French wife. At fifty-six, Dahlia wanted more out of life, but she didn't want to take the risk to have it, and neither did he. Their relationship suited him, and by default it suited her. They had sacrificed passion for an "arrangement" that originally suited both of them, and now seemed more to his advantage than hers. It was tailor-made for him. And in the summer, he could still go on vacation with his family. He was risking nothing for her and had never pretended that he would. And she wasn't risking anything either. They were playing it safe, keeping love at a distance, and one day, it would be over when they were too old to bother or care, when twice-a-week sex by appointment was no longer of interest. There would be no companionship in her old age, no hand to hold in the dark, no comfort for their final years together. They would never have more than they did now. She had finally understood that. And when she was alone in her old age, he would still be married to Jacqueline and spending summers with her in Saint-Jean-Cap-Ferrat, out of habit, if nothing else.

He wished her luck at the hearing when they hung up. He didn't tell her he loved her, in case someone overheard. He only said that in bed after they made love, if he was feeling tender. He didn't sound tender now, he seemed very remote. She didn't know why she'd called him, except that she had no one else to call. It hadn't brought her comfort, it had just made her sad, and reminded her of the inadequacies in their "arrangement." A situation like hers at the moment made them stand out in sharp relief. She was injured and in a bad situation far from home, and Philippe was keeping his distance, and on vacation with his wife. The realization wasn't lost on her.

Chapter 10

Mark picked Dahlia up on Saturday morning at the hotel at ten o'clock. She was standing in front of the hotel on her crutches to get some air. The smoke was still hanging over the city, and there was a haze on the bay but the smell wasn't as strong as the fires moved away, carried north on the wind. The fires were just as fierce and as dangerous, but they weren't as close to the city as they had been for days. It allowed one to believe things were getting better, but they weren't. Nothing had changed except the direction of the wind. The fires were still raging out of control. It was a catastrophic event.

"What do you do on weekends in Paris?" Mark asked her as they headed east across the Bay Bridge. They would head north after that. He drove an Aston Martin, and had fit her crutches in behind her. Getting into his car was an acrobatic feat which took both of them to get her into her seat. "I'm sorry, I should have brought my SUV. I thought this would be more fun." He drove smoothly through the traffic, and obviously enjoyed driving.

"It depends," she said in response to his question. "I go to the country sometimes with friends. I don't have a country house near Paris anymore. I sold it when the children grew up—it was too lonely being there alone. If I'm in the city, I have dinner with friends, go to galleries. A lot of the time, I bring work home on the weekends." She never saw Philippe on weekends, only Monday and Thursday nights, or on other days if they had an event or a party to go to together. "What do you do?"

"The same thing you do. I catch up on work or have dinner out. I have a house at a place called Stinson Beach. It's a long, beautiful beach of white sand. I love going there, sometimes just for the day. It's half an hour out of the city on a winding road. Driving there is fun, and walking on the beach. The weather usually isn't great. It's cold and windy a lot, but it's a special place. I'll take you there when you can walk in the sand or sit on the deck in the sun. San Francisco isn't known for its warm, sunny weather. Summers are usually windy and cold. You can always spot the tourists. They're the ones shivering in their T-shirts and shorts, wishing they'd brought a coat. In the winter, I go to Lake Tahoe to ski, my favorite sport. We had a house in Vermont when I was a kid. We spent Christmases there."

"I used to ski with my kids. I haven't done that in a long time." He was impressed by how much of her life was interwoven with her children, unusually so, given how old they were.

"I get the feeling that you spent a lot of time with your kids when they were growing up and still do."

"That's true. My youngest still lives at home, that's more common in Europe than here. I hardly see her. She's always busy, at a gallery show, or an art class, or in her studio painting. I visit my grandchildren sometimes on the weekend too, but not often. Since their mother works with me, I don't like to intrude on her on the weekends. It's hard to know when to let go." She smiled at him. "I'm not good at it. Probably because I didn't remarry. So, I filled my time with them. I'm still solving their problems, doing errands for them, more than I should. But they're used to it now and so am I. I'm trying to learn how to let go, not too successfully," she confessed.

"I never got to spend that much time with my girls, except in the summer, since they didn't live in the same city, but I enjoy them now, as adults." He seemed as though he led a very grown-up life, and spent most of his time working, as she did. He looked at her cautiously then and asked her a question she didn't expect. "Is there someone waiting for you in Paris?" he asked her. "Is there someone in your life?"

"Sort of. In a way. On a very limited basis. It's a very French arrangement. He's not interested in being very close, and that suited me too. I have my work and my kids. I've been seeing him for six years. It's not a passion or a great love, it's more of a friendship. And to be honest, he's married. I never wanted to be involved with a married man. It's comfortable companionship some of the time. But I know it's not right, and it's not enough. It works better for him. He's not 'waiting for me' as you put it. He's on holiday with his wife and son in the south of France. He has a bad marriage, and I'm the solution. I add color to his life, and he adds some warmth to mine, and a distraction from work." She was painfully honest about it, with Mark and herself.

Mark nodded, thinking about it. "You're right. It does sound very French. There are situations like that here too, but probably more so in Europe. Americans usually just get divorced when the marriage doesn't work. Europeans don't seem to. They seem to work around it and get involved with other people. There are other ways not to get close." He smiled at her. "I've had serially monogamous relationships for twenty years. And when they get too close, I find a reason to end it. I think I like my freedom more than a partnership that doesn't work. I've been seeing someone for the last few months. It's not right, it's a dead end, and we both know it. We just haven't said it yet. It is such a chore to be with the wrong person," he said, and she smiled.

"That's so true, but it's hard to say it. I didn't have time for serious relationships when the kids were young, and I didn't want that around them. Now I work almost all the time to fill the void they left."

"And relationships are so risky," Mark added. "I've been risk-averse ever since my marriage. It wasn't terrible, but it was bad enough and it wasn't fun. Short-term mismatches seem to work well for me to avoid serious involvement," he said, and she laughed.

"I think I might be in that category too, although I've been in my current mismatch for six years, which isn't short-term."

"No, it's not. That's actually a long time," Mark agreed.

"It's familiar," she said, thinking of Philippe. "Sometimes it's enough, even if it's not right. And you're correct about that. You have to be willing to take a risk for love, and be vulnerable, to go with your whole heart. I haven't been willing to do that since my husband. And that was thirty years ago. That was real love, but we were young. It's harder to get it right when you're older. You're not as motivated to try. Somewhere along the way, cowardice sets in. And habit takes precedence over finding the right relationship." Knowing she was leaving soon made it easier to be honest with him, they could be friends.

"That sounds like me," he said, and didn't seem to regret it. But he hadn't met anyone like Dahlia in years, if ever.

They chatted amicably as he crossed over from the East Bay to Napa. They arrived by a completely different route than the road where she'd had the accident, and the big army surplus tent, Jeff Allen's pet rescue field hospital, came into view an hour and a half after they'd left the city. It had been a very pleasant ride, chatting with him about their lives and their children, their college days and their work. It was nice getting to know him. They had similar ideas about a lot of things. And she joked about being a mother hen. She didn't deny it.

He parked in the field where they'd parked before, next to the tent, and he went looking for Jeff, who was at the far end of the tent with a vanload of new dogs that had been rescued and brought in from the fires farther north, near Calistoga. And Dahlia went looking for her little black friend in the long row of crates. She thought he was gone, and then found him in the last one.

"What are you doing all the way down here?" she asked him, and he went crazy when he saw her, wagging his tail and barking to be let out of the crate. She bent down awkwardly with her crutches and her sensitive ribs, sat down on the ground next to the crate, let him out and he ran circles around her, and then climbed into her lap and kissed her face. She was still holding him and they were still having a lovefest when Mark and Jeff came to find her. Jeff had been stunned when Mark said he'd brought her with him.

"How did you pull that off?" Jeff had asked him.

"She had a car accident on the way back to the city the last time she was here. That big mess with the eighteen-wheeler that flipped over when you got evacuated. The driver ran into her and she hit another car and broke her leg. She needed an attorney, so she called me. I had given her my card."

"You are smooth, man," Jeff said, half admiring and half jealous. "I should have thought of that. Maybe she could have used a vet."

"There's a hearing on Monday about the accident, and she's nervous about it. I thought coming up here to see you would be good for her." Mark sounded protective as he said it.

"Are you her lawyer now? Personal injury?" Jeff looked surprised.

"I'm just helping her out. I'm hoping we can get the whole

thing worked out and dismissed on Monday. The driver of the car she hit is telling a different story about what happened and causing a problem."

"I hope it comes out okay. She seems like a good person."

"Yes, she is," Mark agreed.

"Where is she?" Jeff asked. "I want to say hello and warn her what a slick operator you are."

They were both grinning when they found her sitting on the ground with the dog, with her crutches next to her.

"Hey there, Dahlia. I heard about your broken leg. Couldn't you find a decent lawyer, so you wouldn't have to use this guy? He doesn't know squat about personal injury. All he knows about is big corporations." She laughed and put the little dog back in his crate and he whimpered and barked to be let out. Mark helped her stand and handed her the crutches.

"Hi, Jeff. I'm sorry I haven't been back."

"We miss you. Mahala's going to be sad she wasn't working today. Why don't you adopt that little guy? I don't think his owner is going to show up, if he hasn't by now. The family may have lost their home and can't deal with a dog, or they'd be looking for him. We have him on the ASPCA site and no one's asked."

"I'd have to take him back to Paris with me," she said.

"I can think of worse fates for a mutt from the Napa

Valley. You can take me instead. Do you guys want lunch? There's a deli down the road that's not bad." Mark had already given him the check, and Dahlia navigated the uneven ground to the opening of the tent as best she could, with Mark ready to catch her if she stumbled.

"Sure." She looked questioningly at Mark, and he nodded. He and Jeff had dinner together from time to time in normal life. Jeff had been on the ASPCA board too, which was how they'd met.

They drove the short distance in Jeff's van, which was a mess with crates, boxes of dog food, and cartons of medicine and bandages everywhere. Dahlia sat behind the two men, and they had a good lunch at the deli, and Jeff drove them back to Mark's car. Dahlia didn't go back to see the dog. She didn't want to upset him when she left. Jeff gave her a hug and wished her luck on Monday, and patted Mark's shoulder firmly. The two men exchanged a knowing look and Mark laughed with a guilty smile. Jeff had reminded him earlier that he had seen Dahlia first and been too much of a gentleman to hit on her, and Mark got lucky because of her accident. But he said he was just being friendly. He wasn't pursuing her. He said as much to Jeff, who hooted at him and didn't believe a word of it.

"I may look dumb, but I'm not," he said to him, and then they joined Dahlia and the comments had ended.

"Come back and visit," he said to them, as he lumbered back to work. They were still getting a steady flow of lost injured pets, and some wildlife that was harder to deal with. Jeff had set the leg of a young deer the day before, and had transported several horses to local vets in horse trailers people had lent them.

Jeff was still smiling when he went back to work. He liked Mark a lot, and he still thought Dahlia was special. He wondered if anything would come of it, even for a short time before she went back to Paris. Stranger things had happened, and he wished them both luck as he thought about them. They seemed good together, and very compatible. He liked the well-bred ladylike quality she had, without ever seeming snobbish or arrogant. She was nice to everyone.

They drove back to the city the way they had come, via the East Bay and the Bay Bridge, and he drove her back to the hotel around four o'clock.

"What are you doing for dinner tonight?" he asked her.

"The usual," she said, grinning. "Room service and TV. I lead a very glamorous life here."

"Do you like Chinese food? There are some great Chinese restaurants right below your hotel. Can I tempt you?" It sounded like fun, and she'd had a nice day with him.

"That sounds wonderful."

"Pick you up at seven-thirty? You can rest your leg before that. You gave it a workout in the tent. I was afraid you'd fall."

"Me too," she admitted. "I'm getting better at this, and it will be a lot easier when I can put weight on it. And thank you for the dinner plan." She swung into the hotel on her crutches. Mark was smiling as he watched her disappear. It had been a great day. And it wasn't over yet.

Dinner with Mark at the Golden Monkey was fun that night. They ordered too many dishes, some of which were real delicacies, and tried all of them. They talked for a long time about issues that interested them, and he questioned her about the perfume business. She had a good time, and was happy when she went back to the hotel at eleven. They were among the last people in the restaurant. She asked him if he wanted to come up for a drink.

"I think you've seen enough of me for one day. I'll take a rain check, if you'll give me one."

"With pleasure. Thank you, Mark, I had a wonderful evening. And I don't think I've ever eaten so much in my life."

"We'll do it again soon," he promised, and helped her out of the car. He walked her to the door of the hotel and left her there, and then drove back to his apartment and stood looking at the view from his terrace, thinking about her. She was an amazing woman, and it was an irony of life that he had met a woman as remarkable as she was, and she was only going to be in his life for days or weeks, and then she would go back to Paris, and they might never see each other again. It made each moment more precious, and he wanted to spend every minute he could with her, without seeming ridiculous about it.

He was still thinking about her on Sunday, when he went to Chrissy Field in the Marina for a run and looked at the smoke-streaked sky farther north. The fires were still burning in the distance. The smell of smoke was a constant now. He cooked dinner for himself that night and called Dahlia, to encourage her for the hearing the next day. He told her he thought it would go well. It was set for eleven A.M. in a courtroom at City Hall.

"Get a good night's sleep for tomorrow," he told her. He wondered if she would leave for Paris the next day if the case was dismissed. He didn't want her to, but there was nothing he could do to stop her. That was where she belonged.

Dahlia lay awake in bed for a long time, thinking of what was ahead of her the next day. It would be the first time she would see Marilyn Nicasio, who was determined to blame her for the accident. She hoped that justice would prevail.

She got up early the next morning, so she'd have time to compose herself. It was only ten o'clock at night in France when she got up and she was tempted to call Philippe, but she didn't want to have another stilted conversation with him, when he tried to make it sound like a business associate was calling at that hour. She sat quietly trying to mentally prepare for the hearing, and her phone rang just after nine A.M. It was Mark. She was happy to hear his voice. He sounded serious.

"I just heard from our private detective. Marilyn filed a civil lawsuit ten minutes ago. She's suing for five million dollars for negligence, damages, and emotional damage inflicted on her and her daughter. I'm sure she knows exactly who you are, and now we know why she's in this. I assume she's going to ask the car rental company for the same amount or more. She's out to win on a lottery ticket. That was her lucky day when you hit the back of her car, if she wins this."

"Do you think she will?" Dahlia asked him in a subdued voice.

"No, I don't. Even if we win at the hearing today, there's nothing to stop her from suing you. But no jury and no court is going to give her five million dollars for a broken arm and a broken ankle. This is all a ploy for a big settlement. She probably wants a million from you, and another million from the car company. She'll be lucky if she gets fifty thousand. It was an accident, however you look at it. You didn't run her down with your car, trying to kill her. We'll see where it goes today. Don't let this shake you up, Dahlia, it's just noise. I'm sorry to tell you before the hearing, but I didn't want someone else to broadside you with it and shock you. I'm not impressed," he said. "I'll meet you at the courthouse as planned, at a quarter to eleven."

She was wearing the black linen suit she had worn in New York. It had a skirt so she could wear it with her cast. She looked elegant and serious when she left her hotel room and went downstairs to the car and driver the concierge had gotten her. It was ten-thirty, and she felt emotionally prepared to deal with the hearing. Her nerves calmed immediately when she saw Mark waiting for her on the sidewalk.

He helped her out of the car and up the ramp on her crutches. He looked as distinguished as she did in a dark suit, light blue shirt, and light blue tie. They made a handsome couple, with his dark hair with very little gray, and her blonde hair in a neat bun, like a ballerina, and simple pearl earrings on her ears. She had to wear a flat black shoe, for her crutches.

They took an elevator to the second floor, and Dahlia walked into the courtroom with him. The previous hearing was just finishing, and there had been couples downstairs, waiting to get married.

The courts were overbooked, and they had been assigned one of the old courtrooms at City Hall. The judge was one of a list of retired judges the city hired and jokingly called "Rent-a-Judge," but they were competent, experienced Superior Court judges with years of trial experience behind them.

Dahlia's back was straight and her head held high, as she took her place next to Mark at the defendant's table and saw Marilyn Nicasio walk in. She was wearing a tight white dress that outlined her figure, and a silver sneaker. Her ankle was in an orthopedic boot, which looked incongruous with her dress, and her arm was in a sling. Her hair was long and curly, dyed a reddish brown. She gave Dahlia a victorious look, as though she'd already won. She wanted to unnerve her. Dahlia looked unmoved when she saw her. She looked calm and businesslike seated next to Mark.

The judge disappeared from the bench for a few minutes, and the clerk announced him when he returned. Everyone stood up, and court was in session. Dahlia recognized the two police detectives who had interviewed her, and the rental car company's three insurers. The judge respectfully called the senior detective as his first witness, to read the police reports of the accident. Copies of the documents were handed to the judge. He had already seen them and thanked the officer.

The conclusion of the police was that at the moment it was impossible to determine in what order the two vehicles had been impacted, because of the contradictory statements of the two victims, which were in direct opposition to each other, although the logical order of events would have been that the truck hit Dahlia first, but there was no way to prove it.

Dahlia was then called as the next witness. She was calm, clear, coherent, polite, and sure of her testimony. She said there was no doubt in her mind that her car had been hit first, and then she hit the car in front of her. Her testimony appeared to be honest, and was convincing. The judge asked her a few questions, and then thanked her and dismissed her. He smiled as she left the stand, which Mark thought was a good sign.

Marilyn's testimony was emotional and argumentative, and nearly hysterical at times. She said how her daughter had been suffering from the trauma, the nightmares she was having. She burst into tears when the judge asked why neither of them were wearing seatbelts on a night when they couldn't see beyond their windshield because the smoke was so thick, and amid sobs, she never answered the question of why they weren't. Without actually saying it, she did everything to convince the court that Dahlia was lying and behaving irresponsibly, trying to avoid paying a settlement to her and her daughter, when the subject of settlements hadn't been raised yet, but it was clearly foremost on her mind. She was still sobbing when she left the stand and gave Dahlia an evil look, which Dahlia ignored, looking straight ahead at the judge.

The testimony took a little over an hour, and the judge spoke to the assembled group in the courtroom in a calm, clear voice. He seemed young to be retired, and was respectful to both sides.

The judge explained to them that from the evidence there was no way for him to determine whose car had been impacted first. And he reminded them that the purpose of the hearing was to determine if Dahlia was guilty of criminal negligence. The question did not arise for Marilyn Nicasio since her car was first in line and had hit no one, although he admonished her for not wearing a seatbelt, nor her daughter, in such dangerous conditions. Her face turned bright red when he said it.

But he said that whoever had been impacted first, it was clear to him that Dahlia was in no way guilty of criminal negligence and was certainly not responsible for the trucker's death. His only mission in court that day was solely to determine if there was *criminal* negligence on Dahlia de Beaumont's part, and he was confident there was not. She met none of the criteria for criminal negligence. He had the lab report from when she was admitted to the hospital, and there had been neither alcohol nor substances in her blood at the time. She had taken no undue risks and had done nothing reckless. She was a victim of the accident, just as Ms. Nicasio and the driver of the truck had been, with none of the criteria for criminal negligence met on Dahlia's part. And which car had been impacted first would have to be determined in civil, not criminal, court, by a jury trial, since that was the plaintiff's right to request, which she had in the lawsuit she had filed in civil court that morning. The decision of the criminal court was that Dahlia was not guilty of criminal negligence. He rapped his gavel sharply after he said it, stood up, and left the courtroom, as Mark smiled at Dahlia and Marilyn Nicasio glared at her and rushed out of the courtroom. Her civil suit would have been almost a sure win if Dahlia had been charged with criminal negligence. Dahlia looked at Mark with relief, and one of the insurers approached them and asked to speak to Mark. He stepped into the aisle to confer with him in whispers. Mark nodded, and after ten minutes, returned to Dahlia.

"What did he say?" she asked him with a worried look.

"You're free to go now. The risk of criminal charges is no

longer an issue, but they'd like you to stick around for the next few weeks, to see if they can settle the case with you here, and they want to depose you while you're here in case there is a trial. There won't be, but it probably won't settle till hours before the trial date."

"How long would I have to stay?" Dahlia looked worried.

"At a guess, three to six weeks. I'm going to make a motion for a speedy trial, on the basis that you have to get back to Europe."

"Mark, I can't stay—my daughter is getting married in two weeks."

He already knew that and looked concerned. "I think it's important that you stay and cooperate with them, to settle it out of court. It'll happen faster and probably better if you're here, rather than letting it drag out by dealing with it long distance."

They walked out of the courtroom together then. They had cleared the first hurdle but now there were others to deal with, and Alex was going to go crazy if her mother didn't go home for her wedding, or if she had to postpone it.

"There will be a mediation hearing," Mark explained to her at the top of the steps of City Hall, "and you'll need to be here for that. I'll try to get it set as soon as I can, when I ask for a speedy trial."

He helped her down the ramp then, back to her car. She barely had time to celebrate being relieved of any criminal charges when she had the next steps to worry about.

She went back to the hotel, and Mark went to his office, to start making calls.

He called her at the hotel that afternoon. He knew the judge they'd been assigned to for the pretrial hearing and had requested a meeting in his chambers the next day.

"What if I leave for the wedding and come back the day after?" she asked Mark on the phone.

"Technically, legally you can leave now, but let's see what date the judge gives us for the mediation hearing. You need to be here for that."

Mark was meeting him in chambers at nine o'clock the next morning. Dahlia worried about it all night.

Mark called her at exactly ten o'clock the next morning. He had thought about it all night too. And had called in every favor he had to get the meeting in chambers with the pretrial judge. He knew him slightly, and he explained Dahlia's circumstances to him as compassionately as he could, the trauma of the accident she'd been through, her injuries, a business that depended on her in Paris. He didn't mention the wedding, because it sounded frivolous. By some miracle, he convinced the judge to give them a speedy trial, and an early mediation date.

"Plaintiff's attorney will have to agree to the dates," the judge told Mark, which Mark already knew. "It'll never get to trial anyway. The insurers will settle," he said cynically.

"I'm sure you're right, Your Honor," Mark said respectfully. The case was a blatant shakedown for money from the car rental company and Dahlia. The judge saw cases like it every day. They very rarely went to trial and this one wouldn't either.

"The judge is a decent guy," Mark told Dahlia when he called her. "He granted us the speedy trial so you can get back to France. He set mediation for August third, and the trial to begin on August twentieth. That's the best I could get. Nicasio's attorney will have to agree to it, but if he's a contingency lawyer, he'll like it, and so will she, because they'd get the settlement money soon. That means the trial is in five weeks. And Dahlia, I'm sorry about the wedding. I hope your daughter will understand that you need to take care of this and get it behind you before you go home. I'm glad he granted us the speedy trial." So was she, and she was grateful to Mark, but dealing with Alex would be another story. The word "reasonable" was not in her vocabulary. The wedding would have to be postponed, or she'd have to get married without her mother there. Dahlia wasn't sure which she would do. Alex was hard to predict, and whatever she did, it would include some form of punishment for her mother for the change. She was punitive and could hold a grudge longer than anyone on earth. In Alex's mind, Dahlia would be entirely to blame.

Mark assured her that the trial would take five days. So presumably, if there was a trial, she could leave San Francisco around the twenty-sixth or twenty-eighth of August, after the verdict. The wedding would have to be postponed by a month if Alex wanted her mother there. She felt sick thinking about it.

"Can I come to the hotel for lunch and we can talk about it?" Mark asked her.

"Of course," she said, grateful for all the time he was spending with her to help her.

He came at noon and they ordered club sandwiches, which were good at the hotel. She knew the room service menu by heart now, but it was peaceful talking to him in her suite.

The bottom line was that she had to stay in San Francisco for the next six weeks, till the end of the trial, for her deposition, mediation, and all the meetings required to negotiate a settlement or prepare for trial, if there was one. If they reached a settlement before that, she could go home sooner, but it wasn't likely.

"You'll be back in France by the end of August," he assured her while they ate lunch. She would be missing her annual vacation with her children in Saint-Paul-de-Vence, but they could all go to the house without her. The problem was Alex and the wedding.

"She's not my most reasonable child," she explained to Mark. From his perspective, if Alex was getting married she wasn't a child, and her mother was facing a trial and possibly punitive damages. The wedding could wait.

"Fortunately, there won't be a lot of evidence to gather to prepare for the trial. It's your word against hers, and it will all boil down to what the jury believes and which of you is most credible. I would cast my vote for you, particularly after what I saw of her on the stand yesterday. She was openly hostile to you, and she marched down the steps of City Hall like a soldier. She claims she's too injured to work and can hardly stand up, but she looked like she could do jumping jacks in that boot. You're going to get the sympathy vote at the trial. You're a lot more respectable than she is, to say the least, and when they see the photographs of the car you were driving, after the accident, no one is going to believe a word she says, if they're crazy enough to go to trial. Her lawyer is suicidal if he does, or they're both blinded by greed. This is all about the biggest settlement she can get, not justice or truth. They're going to hope we won't want to take it to trial. I would love to get my teeth into her on the witness stand," he said, and

Dahlia smiled. Then he turned to her with a gentler look. "Are you very upset about being stuck here for another six weeks? You can be on the next plane after the verdict."

"I'm very grateful they didn't charge me with criminal negligence." They hadn't even had a chance to celebrate their victory yet. "But I am upset to have to tell my daughter she has to postpone her wedding. It's not going to go over well."

"How old is she?"

"Twenty-nine. But she's difficult, and its a big deal." He nodded. He understood by now how hard she tried to please her children and make them happy.

"It's not your fault, Dahlia," he said gently.

"Thank you for doing such a good job for me and getting the judge to set the trial in August," she said gratefully. "No one in France does business in August, so my being here won't have an impact on my work. And I would have been away anyway." When they finished lunch, he went back to his office. It was after two o'clock by then, after eleven P.M. in France, and too late to tackle Alex then. She'd have to wait until the morning in Paris to tell her.

Mark had wanted to invite Dahlia to dinner, but decided to let her deal with her family dramas. They could have dinner another time. The judge had given him a six-week reprieve. Dahlia was going to be in San Francisco for another six weeks, until the end of the trial. He knew it made no sense, and it was crazy, but privately he was thrilled. He had six more weeks to spend time with her and get to know her before they had to say goodbye.

Chapter 11

Dahlia spent the evening in her hotel room, thinking and making notes and tentative plans. She sent Mark an email thanking him again for doing such a good job, and telling him how grateful she was.

She waited until ten P.M. to call Delphine, which was seven in the morning for her, and she knew that she'd be up, taking care of her daughters. Their nanny didn't come to work till eight A.M., when Delphine left for work. And on weekends, she took care of them herself. She could hear the two little girls squealing and laughing in the background when Delphine answered.

"Do you have a few minutes to talk?" her mother asked her.

"Is something wrong? Are you all right?" It had already

been a worrisome trip with her mother having an accident and breaking her leg. "Francois can watch the girls." She signaled to him and he took over, and she left the room so they could talk.

"I'm fine, but I have a problem," Dahlia said seriously. "We had the hearing yesterday, for the accident, to determine if there was any criminal negligence on my part, and the judge ruled that there wasn't, which was good news. But the woman in the other car is suing me civilly for negligence and damages. My lawyer was able to get something called a 'speedy trial.' The trial is set for August twentieth, with an important court mediation on August third, and I need to be here to prepare for it. I'm stuck here for another six weeks. It probably won't even go to trial. It will settle before, but not until the last minute."

"Oh no . . ." Delphine said, understanding immediately what the problem was, just as Dahlia had when she heard the words from Mark. "Oh my God. Alex."

"Precisely. I've been thinking about it for hours, and there are only two options. You all go ahead with the wedding without me, if that's what she wants, and I'll agree to it if that's her wish. Or she has to postpone it till sometime between September first and fifteenth, so I can be there, or later, if she wants. It's really up to her."

"She's going to have a total fit," Delphine said in a horrified voice.

"Yes, she is," Dahlia agreed. "But there isn't a damn thing I can do about it. I have to respect those dates. And my lawyer is right. I need to take care of this and finish it before I leave, or it could drag on for months or years."

"It's so unfair. You were a victim of the accident too," Delphine said angrily.

"She seems to be after money. A lot of money."

"Poor Maman." Delphine felt genuinely sorry for her mother. And she knew how hard Alex would be on her.

"I feel terrible for Alex. No one wants to postpone their wedding, but she might have to," Dahlia said sadly.

"She won't want to get married without you," Delphine said with certainty.

"She might. Even as pure revenge. She's capable of it, and I'll respect her wishes."

"You're a good sport. When are you going to tell her?"

"Now. I wanted to call you first and see what you think and give you a heads-up."

"She was a monster at the dress fitting, and rude to everyone. I knew she would be. She's having them make a million last-minute changes to the dress, which they'll never have time for. They were frantic."

"Well, now they will have time. We're giving them the

gift of another month to finish everything. I just hope all the suppliers and the venue will be available a month later if she agrees to move it. I'll get Agnes working on it as soon as Alex gives me the green light, if she does. This won't be easy, especially getting her to agree to it. If she doesn't, then so be it. You can set up some kind of high-tech video system so I can at least see her get married." Delphine was always impressed by the degree to which her mother would go to accommodate her children and make them happy, something which Alex never appreciated, and she always had something to complain about and blame her mother for. It infuriated Delphine whenever she did it. She had been that way all her life. She blamed their mother for their not having a living father, which was absurd. Dahlia had more than compensated for their father's absence for all their lives.

"By the way, I wanted to talk to you all last week, and I haven't had time. I was going to talk to you this week when you got back, and now you're not. I have an idea for a fantastic new line. A cosmetic line for young girls, young women, with a medicated component if they want it, for those with troubled skin, and a line of younger perfumes to go with it. We could be the beauty advisors to a whole new generation and add an important element to our demographics. I'm thinking sixteen to twenty-five, with younger salespeople trained in the cosmetic needs of that age group.

It will cost a fortune to develop it, but it would be worth it in the long run, we'll make a fortune from it. I really want to explore the youth market. What do you think?"

Dahlia smiled as she listened to her, and the excitement in her voice.

"We could even do pop-up stores just for them all over France, and worldwide later," Delphine added.

"You're a genius. When did you come up with this? Driving your kids to nursery school, or while helping your husband on his latest project, or on the weekend when you're cooking for your family, or when you're doing my work too because I'm stuck in California and can't come home? My darling girl, you are a marvel. I think it's a brilliant idea."

"Will you green-light it?"

"Yes, I will. You can get to work on it right away. It's going to take time to develop it and get it right, particularly if some of it is medical. We can't make mistakes with that."

"Oh my God, Mother, you're incredible. You're the genius. Thank you for letting me do it. Charles thinks it's crazy and too expensive. And he thinks sixteen-year-olds are too young to wear makeup, but they steal their mothers' makeup anyway."

"He's too conservative, and it will be expensive, but I agree with you, it will pay off in the end."

"Thank you, Maman, for being so modern and open-minded and forward-thinking. That's why Lambert is so successful, because of you."

"And because of you, now. We're a good team," Dahlia said happily. As always, Delphine had cheered her up. She was great for the business. She added a whole new element that would carry them into the future. She was their future.

"Can I do anything to help you with Alex?"

"No, I have to do it myself. I should call her now before she goes to work. You'll probably hear the screams from your apartment. And by the way, I want you all to go to Saint-Paul-de-Vence without me. There's no reason to spoil the vacation because I can't be there." Delphine had wondered but didn't want to ask. It seemed so greedy to want their summer holiday if their mother couldn't come. It was so like her to give it to them anyway. "You can have it for the whole month now. I'll try to come for the last weekend before the wedding, if she moves it to September, so we can all be together. But go down there on the first of August, as always."

"Thank you, Maman. Let me know how it goes with her."

"I have no doubt you'll hear immediately. I did think of one thing, though," Dahlia said. "We should re-invite her whole original guest list. She lost a lot of people because they had summer plans. She may get a much bigger turnout in September, if we can work out the rest."

"You're right," Delphine agreed. "But she won't admit it."

As soon as she hung up, Dahlia called Alex's number. It was almost eight in the morning, and she'd be up. She answered immediately and launched into a diatribe with her first words.

"Oh my God, Mother, the fitting was a nightmare. They got everything wrong; the front of the dress is too long, the veil is too short, and Delphine has no idea what she's talking about. She kept confusing them with suggestions. You really should have been there," she said reproachfully.

"She was trying to help since I couldn't be there," Dahlia said calmly.

"She may know about perfume, but she knows nothing about fashion. And when are you coming home?" Alex was talking a mile a minute, and the conversation was off to a bumpy start. Dahlia knew it was going to get considerably worse.

"I need to talk to you seriously about something," Dahlia said, trying to sound serene. "I had a problem in San Francisco, and had to cancel my plans in L.A. I had a car accident and broke my leg. I'm fine now, but it threw a monkey wrench into everything."

"Why didn't you tell me?" Alex sounded insulted more than concerned.

"I didn't want to worry you. But it's gotten complicated.

There were three vehicles involved, a truck and two cars. I rear-ended the other car when the truck hit me, and there's a debate now about who hit who first. It's complicated to explain, but Alex, to put it simply, I have a hearing here in San Francisco on August third, and there might be a trial on the twentieth."

"That's not a problem," Alex said blithely, "you can fly back there the day after the wedding."

"Actually, I can't," Dahlia said, lighting the match to the fuse of dynamite. "They need me here for mediation meetings, my deposition, and settlement conferences. I can't leave responsibly while this is pending. I have to stay in San Francisco to deal with it. She's suing me for five million dollars."

"What are you saying to me?" Alex sounded like she'd just been hit by a bolt of lightning.

"I'm saying what I was hoping not to have to say to you. I can't be back on the first. You can get married without me, or we can postpone it to the first two weeks in September. There's nothing I can do about it. I'm so sorry."

"Are you *insane*?" Alex shrieked at her. "I've been planning this wedding for a year and you're not coming home for it?"

"Darling, I can't. I can't leave. I want to be there, but this is a huge mess here." Alex hadn't commented even once on her broken leg.

"What did you do, *kill* somebody?"

"No, it's about money. The driver of the other car is suing me for damages and lying about it. I think it's all a ploy and she wants a big settlement. We have to fight it out in court."

"Did you maim her children? What did you do?"

"She has a broken arm and ankle, and her daughter broke her nose and both arms. They weren't wearing seatbelts."

"I can't believe this. What am I supposed to do?" Alex sounded as panicked and hysterical as Dahlia knew she would.

"I know this is a terrible disappointment. We can move the wedding forward a month, or you can go ahead. I want to be there, but I'll understand if you don't want to wait for me. I don't want to miss your wedding, and we can set up video screens so I can see it."

"I don't want video screens at my wedding. Come home!"

"I can't. Alex, I need you to be reasonable." Dahlia was fighting to stay calm, in the face of Alex's fury. "I could fly home on the twenty-fifth or -sixth of August, after the verdict, but not before, unless they cancel the trial, which they won't. It won't be a long trial but I have to be here." She felt sick just saying it.

"I'm taping my show all month after the fifth of September, and Paul will be on location in Australia. I don't want to postpone my wedding." Alex started to cry, and Dahlia felt as though someone was ripping her heart out of her chest. It broke her heart to hear Alex crying. She kept repeating how sorry she was, which Alex didn't want to hear. "You don't care about me. You never did. It's always about Delphine and Charlie because they work in the fucking business with you, and I tried to do something on my own, not controlled by you. So you're punishing me for it and ruining my wedding. You only care about them."

"I love you, Alex. This is because I had an accident, not because I don't love you. And I'm not trying to control you. I'm proud of what you do."

"You don't want me to be happy. You always ruin everything for me. It's all about you, and the fucking perfume. I hate it, it makes me sick when I smell it, because it reminds me of you."

"Alex, let's try to figure this out together, if you want to wait and postpone it, or go ahead."

"It's in two weeks. And if we postpone it, it can't be later than September first," Alex said angrily.

"I can be home by then," Dahlia said, trying to stay calm, and ignoring the insults her daughter heaped on her.

"What if no one can come, or we can't get the château?"

"I can have Agnes check all the suppliers today. She can let us know where it stands by the end of the day. I'll do everything I can to make it work either way. The last thing I want to do is miss your wedding, but if you decide to stick to August first, you can do that. Actually, more people might come in September, because they won't be away for the summer. We can re-invite your whole original guest list."

"I can't believe you're doing this to me. Are you happy you're ruining my wedding? That's what you want, isn't it? You don't like Paul. You only like Francois, because he's Delphine's husband. Miss Perfect who can do no wrong and is your little minion in the business."

"Your sister isn't my minion, Alex," Dahlia said in a taut voice. Alex was pushing her to her limits.

"That's why you hate me, because I don't want to be your monkey on a chain."

"I've never tried to force you into the business. I respect what you do."

"No, you don't. All you care about is the business and the ones who work for you."

"This is about your wedding. You don't have to tear everyone to shreds to make this decision. I know it's disappointing, but we can make it work if you postpone it, either way."

"This is for your convenience. Everything is always about you. Well, this isn't about you. It's my wedding, not yours."

"It's about an accident I had, Alex, and a trial for damages. I don't make the rules."

"How did you get in an accident? Were you drunk?"

"Of course not. There were fires here, and a lot of smoke, and my car got hit by a truck." Alex was quiet for a minute, mulling it over. She never asked how her mother was or about her broken leg. Dahlia was used to it. Alex was a narcissist to the core.

"I have to ask Paul what he wants to do," she said harshly.

"Just let me know, and I'll get Agnes on it immediately. I'll wait to hear from you. I love you, please know that. I love you very much and I want your wedding to be perfect for you," Dahlia said with tears rolling down her cheeks, and Alex answered in an ice-cold voice.

"No, you don't," she said, and hung up, as Dahlia sat staring at her phone. She had a rock on her heart after everything Alex said. It was all hateful, but Dahlia had been there before with her, whenever Alex didn't get her way. Planning the wedding with her had been difficult too.

She couldn't go to bed and sleep after that. She walked around the room on her crutches, thinking of what her daughter had said to her, and knowing she meant it. Half an hour later, her phone rang and she saw Delphine's number come up, and she answered. She hoped it would be Alex to apologize, but she never did.

"How did it go?" Delphine asked her.

"As expected. The usual abuse. She's furious and she hates me."

"Did she get that you can't help it and it's not your fault?"

"No, and she doesn't care. She thinks I'm trying to ruin her wedding."

"She'll get over it."

"No, she won't," Dahlia said, and blew her nose. "She never does. She'll never forgive me for making her postpone her wedding. If I could be there, I would."

"I know that, Maman," Delphine said gently. She hated what Alex did to everyone whenever she felt like it, especially their mother. She spewed venom like a volcano, and she was just as hard on Delphine when it suited her, especially since she and their mother were close.

Dahlia stared at the TV blindly for a while after she talked to Delphine, and she finally went to bed, thinking about all of Alex's accusations. They weren't true, but Dahlia could never convince her of it.

She woke up at ten o'clock, and the headache was back. She saw that she had a message on her phone and looked at it. It was from Alex. "Fine. September first. I'll never forget what you are doing to my wedding. Alex."

Dahlia sent an email to Agnes then, explaining everything, and telling her to check all the suppliers before she postponed and canceled the August date. And she told Agnes to call her if any of them couldn't switch to September first. And then Agnes would have to send emails to all the guests, announcing the change, inviting them on the new date and requesting rapid answers. There were a million details to think of and remember, and they'd go over it together for the next six weeks, to make sure everything was in place and perfect. Dahlia answered her daughter's text then in the simplest terms. "Thank you for changing the date. I love you. I want to be there and we'll make it beautiful. I love you, Maman." Alex didn't respond, and she never apologized for the hurtful things she said when she was angry. She meant them. She wanted to wound her mother as much as she could—and she had. It was a character flaw in Alex. She had been like that since she was thirteen. Life-and-death battles peppered with insults, vicious attacks, and unjustified accusations. Dahlia had the scars of thousands of those battles on her heart, and this one was only slightly worse than the other attacks Alex had launched at her before. She always felt mortally wounded afterward, which was what Alex wanted, to hurt the other person as deeply as she could. She soothed her own pain and disappointments by wounding others, and her mother was always her prime target.

Dahlia felt sick, it was so painful, and halfway through

the afternoon, trying to recover from the blows, she had an idea. It wouldn't change anything or make Alex like her any more, but it might make Dahlia feel better. She was at the bottom of the emotional barrel, as she always was after Alex's attacks. This was the worst one yet.

She called the concierge for a car and driver, an SUV. It was at the front of the hotel in twenty minutes. Dahlia went downstairs when the concierge called her, and the doorman directed her to it. She got in, thinking about Alex, realizing that it was late night in Paris now, and Alex hadn't texted her all day. Maybe it was a blessing not to hear from her. Dahlia knew that she would punish her forever for having to postpone her wedding. But there was no other choice if she wanted her mother there. It was up to her. Dahlia just hoped that the venue and the suppliers could adapt to the change despite the short notice, and that Alex would adjust in the end.

The hotel driver followed the traditional route to Napa. She wondered if she was crazy, but she had thought of it before and she needed something to put balm on the gaping wound Alex had left her with. That was always her intention, to inflict pain, in order to relieve her own. She did it so well. She was a master of the art, slashing and burning and hurting those who loved her. She just wanted to injure them, as viciously and cruelly as she could.

They made the trip to Napa in record time, and she knew now where the accident had happened and was solemn as they drove past it. A man had died there, after all. After that, she directed the driver to the right turnoff, and the old dirt road that led to Jeff's rescue tent. She hopped in slowly on her crutches, and she saw that Jeff was there, and Mahala. It was almost six o'clock by then and they were wrapping up. The air quality was still red that day, and most of the volunteers were wearing masks. She had forgotten hers at the hotel.

Jeff saw her hop in unsteadily with her crutches and came toward her. "What are you doing here?" he asked, surprised. "Is Mark with you?"

"No. I came to see a friend."

"A volunteer?" She shook her head and Mahala waved to her. She was carrying two small dogs, taking them back to their crates. She came to join Jeff and Dahlia a minute later. The two women hugged.

"Did you just come to visit?" Mahala asked her.

"No, I came for an adoption," she said solemnly. "My little curly black friend with the white patch on his chest." Jeff grinned when she said it.

"It's about time. He's waited almost two weeks for you. I'm happy to see you taking him home. His people never came for him." But she knew that they would keep his information, a photo of him and the identity of his new owners, as a record. If his original owners showed up, they'd have to work it out. He would be in Paris with her. "I'll give him a rabies shot in case his shots aren't current. We've got food for you. He's got a collar and Mahala can give you a leash." A pet shop in Yountville had donated bowls and harnesses, collars and leashes and dog food, and the ASPCA donations had paid for medicines, vaccinations, and blankets for the old and sick dogs, and donated crates and cages for animals of all sizes.

Dahlia walked back to where the little dog was in a crate, and he started barking as soon as he saw her. "I'll take him to the car with you so he doesn't trip you on your crutches. Be careful," Mahala warned her. She got him out of the crate and put him on the leash, and they took him over to one of the exam tables so Jeff could give him the rabies shot. He filled out a certificate and handed it to her, and she put it in her pocket. She looked at Jeff with a happy smile, and handed him a check with a healthy donation. The dog was panting and yelping and dancing with excitement. He knew something major was happening. His time had finally come.

Dahlia had tears in her eyes as she looked at him, her heart warming after all the unkind things Alex had said to her. She always knew how to wound her. The echo of her words was haunting and stayed with her although she always forgave her and she had this time too, with unconditional motherly love.

"What's his name?" Jeff asked her, and she thought for a minute and smiled.

"Francisco. It will remind me of all of you when I go home to Paris."

"Good one," Jeff said, and walked to the car with her, with Mahala holding Francisco on the leash, keeping him away from Dahlia's crutches and her one solid foot. Jeff patted him, and helped Dahlia into the car, and Mahala handed the dog to her. His fluffy tail was wagging frantically like a victory flag. Jeff closed the door, and she opened the window, with Francisco on her lap. "Come back and visit us," he reminded her.

"We will," she promised, and waved as the driver rolled slowly out of the field onto the rutted dirt road. Francisco turned and licked Dahlia's face then, as tears rolled down her cheeks. They were tears of happiness over her new dog, and of sorrow over the damage her daughter had done. Francisco licked her tears away and she held him close, beaming. Francisco was finally going home.

Chapter 12

Dahlia had the driver stop at a pet supply store that was still open when they got back to the city. It was a huge place with everything one could need for any kind of pet. Dahlia found the dog section and bought Francisco a bed. It was a cozy little blue igloo with teddy bears on it, and plush fur inside. She bought him red and blue dog bowls, some toys, chew bones, and a nicer collar and leash than the one he was wearing, and a carrier for him to travel in when she went back to Paris. He was fully equipped for his new adventure, and a boy at the checkout stand carried it all to the car for her. She noticed that Francisco was steering clear of her crutches, either because he was afraid of them, or sensed that he had to be careful for her. His tail was wagging the entire time. She had bought some dog treats too, and when she got in the car she opened the package and gave him one. He gobbled it up immediately and sat waiting for more, and handed her a paw.

"You know tricks too?" she said with a grin, and he politely shook her hand. Someone had obviously cared about him, and he looked healthy and well fed. She was sad for the owners who had lost him, but it was obviously a match that was meant to be. He trotted into the hotel next to her, as though he felt entirely worthy of his fancy new home. And the minute she let him off the leash in the suite, he ran from room to room in ecstasy, and rolled on his back on the soft carpet, and then jumped on a chair to reach the bed and barked at her once he was on the bed.

"Are you supposed to be up there?" she asked him, and he cocked his head again and dove under the pillows and peeked out at her. She laughed as she watched him. He was exactly what she needed. He was the antidote to misery and pain, physical or emotional. She hadn't had a dog since she was a child, since Charles was allergic to them, and had had asthma as a child. But she could have one now. The girls had always wanted one, but they couldn't because of Charles.

She fed Francisco and put water in one of his new bowls,

and when she turned the TV on to watch the news, he jumped onto her lap and stared at the television intently. He had obviously done that before with his previous owner. A little while later, she asked for a bellman to come upstairs and take him for a walk, since she couldn't do it herself. She put his leash on, and he hesitated with a worried look, she gave him a treat, and he trotted out on his fancy new black leather leash. She had gotten him a red collar and replaced his old one. And he went crazy when he saw her again when they came back. He was ecstatic that she was still there. He dove into his pile of toys then, and dragged them all over the room, hid a small squeaky toy under a pillow, and then brought her a ball, looking expectantly at her. She threw it and he brought it back and put it at her feet to throw again. She was playing with him when Mark called to see how she was.

"I'm sorry I didn't call earlier. I had a long day playing catch-up. How are you?" he asked with concern. She'd been through a lot with the hearing and now the trial looming.

"Very happy," she said with a light tone. "I have a new friend." He was surprised to hear it, but relieved that she wasn't too depressed about their going to trial and getting stuck in San Francisco. He had worried about her all day and wanted to call, but he hadn't had five free minutes to call. "Do you want to come for a drink and meet him?" It sounded like a slightly odd invitation, and he wondered if she'd been drinking. He had no idea who she was entertaining. But she was a beautiful woman and might have met someone at the hotel.

"I can stop by for a few minutes on my way home." He was curious who was with her. It was a side of her he hadn't seen before, but he hardly knew her, so anything was possible. "I'm just leaving now."

"Terrific, see you soon," she said, and hung up.

She and Francisco continued playing. He loved his new ball and the other toys, and ten minutes later, the doorbell of her suite rang and she went to open it. She was smiling when Mark saw her poised on her crutches, holding a ball and an elephant toy, with Francisco standing next to her, wagging his tail, as though he remembered Mark. Mark laughed as soon as he saw them and the toys all over the room as he followed her in.

"Is this your new friend?" he asked her, relieved that there wasn't some strange man sitting on the couch, drinking a martini.

"Of course. This is Francisco de Beaumont. I couldn't resist. I went to get him this afternoon. I've wanted him since I first saw him. And Jeff says hello." Francisco dropped his ball at Mark's feet and he threw it, and Francisco brought it back. "Would you like a drink? He plays ball and he shakes hands, and he likes to watch TV," she said, and it made Mark happy just seeing how elated she was. The little dog was sweet, and about to have an extremely nice life with his new owner, who was visibly enamored with him. He jumped up on her bed then, and lay on his back, suddenly exhausted by all the new excitement in his life. It was a long way from being cooped up in a crate in Napa in the rescue shelter. He had won the lottery that day.

Mark sat down on the couch, and Dahlia sat next to him and left her crutches on the floor at her feet. "Help yourself to a drink," she said, still smiling. Francisco had turned the day around from one of sorrow to one of joy. "Do you want something to eat?" she asked Mark, as he opened a bottle of wine from the minibar.

"To be honest, I haven't had time to eat all day. I'm starving. Have you eaten?"

"I've been too busy playing with Francisco. Do you want to order something from room service? It'll be faster and easier than going out."

"That sounds fantastic." They ordered burgers and he poured Dahlia a glass of wine too, as he relaxed and took off his jacket. It was nice seeing her at the end of a long day. He hadn't seen her or talked to her since he came for a sandwich the day before to discuss the trial schedule. She'd obviously been busy, if she'd gone to Napa to get the dog. "Was that a spur-of-the-moment decision?" he asked her. "Or had you planned it?"

"He was the first dog I helped bandage when I volunteered there. I fell in love with him. It was love at first sight." His paws were already healed. "I haven't had a dog since I was a little kid. My mother had a pug, but it died years ago. And my son is allergic to dogs, so we never could have one."

"He's going to be the most spoiled dog in Paris from what I can see." His bowls, bed, and toys were all over her suite, and it warmed his heart to see her happy. She was going through a hard time, and she deserved some pleasure in her life. Mark's face grew serious then. "Did you talk to your children yesterday about having to stay for the trial?"

"Yes, two of them," she said, with a sad look in her eyes.

"What did they say? Especially the daughter who's getting married."

"She reacted as I expected her to," she said quietly. "I talked to Delphine first, who works with me. She was wonderful and sensible and helpful as always. She manages two children, a husband, a big job, her employees at home, and my staff, and does it all with grace. She wants to introduce a new product line for a younger market, which is brilliant. She told me about it yesterday. She's going to run Lambert beautifully one day."

"She sounds like you," he smiled at her.

"She's better than I am. She has more contemporary ideas and is always looking for ways to expand. I try to improve on what we have. She always comes up with something new I never thought of. She is a great asset to the business. And then I spoke to my other daughter, Alex, the future bride, and predictably, she went crazy. Insults, accusations, anger, raging at me. She blames me for everything wrong in her life. She acts as though I do it to her on purpose if something goes wrong. I explained to her about the trial and what's at stake here. She doesn't care. It's all about her. She doesn't give a damn what happens to me, or how I feel. I gave her the choice of postponing the wedding or doing it without me. She'll have my blessing either way. After a great many nasty accusations and insults, she hung up on me, and she sent me a text later. She's going to postpone, but *only* until September first. It's inconvenient for her after that. You said the trial would take five days, so if it starts on August twentieth, it should be over by the twenty-fifth. That gives me exactly a week to get home and be at the wedding. It's tight but it should work." He nodded, listening carefully to what she was saying and feeling sorry for her. It sounded like her about-to-be-married daughter did everything she could to make her mother's life difficult, in already hard circumstances for her.

"She doesn't give you much of a break," he said cautiously.

"She never has—she blames me for anything that goes wrong in her life, whether my fault or not." And in this case it certainly wasn't Dahlia's fault. "She's always blamed me for her not having a living father. I didn't kill him. Her list of grievances is endless—this is just one more, the list is long." She hated airing their family's dirty laundry and giving Mark such a negative description of one of her children, but it was true, and she had no one else to talk to, except Delphine, and she didn't want to burden her any more than she already was, with a very full plate and a million balls in the air at work and at home. "I'm sorry to tell you all this. It isn't very gracious of me. She's hard to deal with sometimes, and she ran over me like a bus yesterday. She never apologizes, and she always does it again. At the first opportunity, she throws everything at me that she hates about me or thinks I've done wrong. It's impossible to win with her, and this is a huge deal to her, having to postpone her wedding. It would be to anyone, but she manages to make it worse by attacking me. My secretary and I will get everything done as seamlessly as we can, but her attack yesterday was a little too much on top of everything else happening here." She sighed wistfully. "Francisco was the only antidote I could think of. And he did a very good job of cheering me up."

"I'm glad he did," Mark said gently, wishing he could be the one to comfort her.

"It's odd how children can grow up in the same house, with the same parents, only a year apart, and be so totally different. Delphine is always there to help me and can't do enough for everyone. Alex does whatever she can to make it harder and hurt me. I always hope that will change, if she's happy in her own life, but it hasn't happened yet. Maybe it never will. If her wedding turns out well now, she'll forget all the awful things she said to me, and go on, leaving all the damage she causes in her wake."

"Some people are that way," he said quietly, "they're unhappy, so they want everyone else to be too. Can you really manage the wedding from here?" He didn't see how she could, but he didn't know her and what a tornado she was when she had to be. She was efficiency personified, and her assistant was a huge help.

"Yes, I can. My secretary in Paris is a miracle worker, and I can do a lot from here. If the suppliers and venue are available, we can pull it off with ease." And they had an end point now, as to when Dahlia would be going back to Paris, in about six weeks. It was good to know, and a reminder to Mark, that she wasn't there to stay. She was going home, and had major responsibilities there, to her business and her family.

"By the way, Nicasio's lawyer accepted the trial date today, and the mediation. I was sure he would. It means fast money for them if they win." But it was a relief to know the schedule was set now, and the car rental firm wanted to put it behind them quickly too.

Their dinner arrived then, and the room service waiter set it up on the dining table in the suite. Francisco greeted him and followed the good smells from the rolling table to the dining room, and sat down expectantly next to Mark and Dahlia. Their burgers looked delicious.

She mentioned while they were eating that she felt sorry for Tiffany Nicasio, the plaintiff's daughter, with her broken nose and arms.

"It must have been a terrible trauma for her too. They talk a lot more about her mother's injuries than hers."

"Because her injuries are directly her mother's fault, since she didn't make her wear a seatbelt."

"I wondered if I should send the girl something to cheer her up," Dahlia said, thinking about it, and Mark stopped her immediately.

"Absolutely not. It's a sweet thought, but you can't. They would use it to imply that you feel guilty. You have to stay away from both of them." He was emphatic about it, and Dahlia nodded.

"I understand," she said quietly, as they ate their burgers.

Francisco was sitting right below them, hoping for manna to fall from the sky. He seemed to be no stranger to table scraps, a habit Dahlia didn't want to encourage, so she just patted his head under the table.

"You can't mother everyone," Mark said gently. "You seem to be very generous about solving all your children's problems, but you can't fix things for everyone."

"Sometimes not even for my own children," she said sadly.

"It sounds like you're going to do everything you can for Alex. You have nothing to reproach yourself for. She's a grown woman. What is she doing to help you?" Mark asked her.

"Nothing. That's not her style." He didn't like what he was hearing about her.

"I was thinking about something. If it's not too smoky in the area on Saturday, would you like to go to my beach house for the day? It's such a peaceful place. You can't walk on the beach with your leg, but you can sit on the deck. If we're lucky, it might even be sunny. I like it even when it's windy and cold. It's beautiful there, and very rugged. You could bring Francisco." He smiled at her.

"I'd like that. I'm going to miss the beach entirely this summer. I told them to go to the south of France without me." It struck him again that she was always thinking about others, particularly her children. She never seemed to think about herself.

He left at midnight, which was late for him on a work night, but he always had a hard time tearing himself away from her. There was always more to talk about, discover, and share. He told her too that the private investigator would be working to find out more about Marilyn Nicasio before the mediation hearing, which might affect any settlement they ultimately made. For the moment, Nicasio was shooting for the moon, and had her sights set high, based on what she guessed Dahlia could pay, not on the size of her "crime," if there was one, which remained to be determined at trial if they didn't settle before.

He said he had busy days for the rest of the week, but they agreed on their plan for Saturday. They were going to his house in Stinson for the day, for a picnic lunch. It sounded wonderful to her.

As soon as Mark left, Dahlia called her office in Paris, to speak to Agnes. It was nine A.M. there, and they discussed the wedding at length, everything that needed to be handled for the postponement. Dahlia had made a list, and so had Agnes, and she promised to check in at the end of her workday once she knew more about the venue and suppliers.

"I'm so sorry that you've been delayed," Agnes told her. "Is your leg okay?"

"It will be." And her ribs were slowly healing too. She could breathe more easily now, but laughing or coughing still hurt.

"How did Alex take the postponement?" she asked her, and Dahlia sighed.

"As you can imagine. You know how she is." Agnes certainly did, firsthand, having been the target of Alex's rages and her razor-edged tongue more than once. She felt sorry for Dahlia, imagining what it had been like. Agnes spent an inordinate amount of time trying to protect her employer and help her in every way she could. It infuriated her when her family didn't do the same, weighed on her, expected too much, or actively made her miserable, like Alex. It was so unfair and Dahlia didn't deserve it.

By the end of the conversation, they had matters in hand, and everything they needed to do mapped out. And as efficient as they both were, Agnes had no doubt that they could pull it off.

Dahlia got ready for bed then, and Francisco watched her and jumped onto the bed, via his usual chair. He gave her a quizzical look, as though to ask if it was okay, and she smiled and patted the bed next to her. He lay down beside her with a little sigh, and then sidled up and put his head on the pillow next to her, and rolled over on his back, which made her smile. He was snoring a few minutes later, and then she fell asleep. Adopting him had been the best thing she'd done in years.

She slept later than usual, and called Agnes while Francisco went for a walk with one of the bellmen. They were going to walk him four times a day since she couldn't do it herself. It was seven P.M. in Paris by then, only ten A.M. in San Francisco, and true to form, Agnes had all the answers they needed. The château was free on September first, which was essential, and so were the caterers, the photographer, the videographer, the hair and makeup people, the car parkers, the wedding cake baker, the florist. Every one of the suppliers was able to make a switch. It was a miracle.

"Then it's a go. Will you send Alex an email and let her know? We need to send emails to all the guests, so you need to clear it with her." Dahlia was still smarting from the blows Alex had inflicted on her, and she wanted to keep her distance for a while, while making sure that everything was locked in. "She can make her own appointments for the final fittings of the dress, and this gives her time to get it just right," Dahlia said.

"She's a lucky girl," Agnes said in a terse tone, and Dahlia didn't disagree. Luckier than she deserved sometimes, but she was her daughter after all, and Dahlia loved her, no matter what.

Mark came to pick Dahlia up on Saturday in the SUV. He thought she'd be more comfortable on the drive; she had Francisco with her and there were a lot of hairpin turns on the road to Stinson. He loved driving it in his Aston Martin, and felt like a racecar driver, but for her first visit, he didn't want to scare her, or the dog.

As he had promised, the drive took thirty-five minutes, and it was early. There was still a haze over the city from the fires, but there was a brisk wind, which kept the air cleaner than it had been in weeks, and they didn't have to wear masks.

She was surprised by how quickly the drive became rugged and there were no houses except in small clusters on cliffs, with fantastic views of the ocean ahead of them, and the skyline of the city behind them. Just driving there felt peaceful.

"Sorry about the winding turns," he said.

"I love it." Francisco was asleep in the backseat.

They drove through a small village with half a dozen tiny shops, a grocery store, and a sleepy little restaurant, and a few miles down the road, there was a gated community. A guard let them in, and they drove down a road to a neat-looking white house with hedges around it. The smell of the ocean was strong, the air was brisk, and seagulls were calling to each other. Everything about it felt peaceful as Mark stopped the car, and Francisco woke up, stretched, and sat up to look around. Mark had brought a few groceries with him for lunch, and he had warned Dahlia to wear jeans and bring a sweater in case it got chilly.

She followed him to the front door on her crutches, while Francisco checked out the sandy garden, and they went inside. The décor was simple and tasteful. The paintings were mostly beach scenes or large Richard Mizrach photographs of the ocean. The furniture was inviting in beige and white fabrics. Everything about it was peaceful and appealing. The living room was large with a perfect view of the ocean and the beach, and there was a bigger-than-life driftwood-and-bronze sculpture of a horse by Deborah Butterfield. Mark said it was his favorite piece. The kitchen was simple and modern. There was a long dining table in the living room, and a wide handsome deck with the same splendid view. The master suite was on one side of the house, and four guest rooms on the other for when his daughters visited. And there was a big cozy fireplace where he lit a fire on chilly afternoons and evenings.

Dahlia looked around with admiration. It was the perfect

beach house, and she could see why he loved it and went there often. It was completely different from her house in Saint-Paul-de-Vence, which was so typically French, with a mixture of antiques and bright colors, and she loved filling it with flowers. Everything about Mark's universe at the beach was pale and soothing. It suited him, and made her feel calm, just being there.

"I love it," she said warmly, and he looked pleased. "And I love the Mizrach photos." There was one of a beach that was almost as large as the picture window. His living room was floor-to-ceiling glass, and it was almost like being on the beach, with sliding doors that opened the whole room to the deck for warm days.

"It's my refuge from a chaotic world when I get too busy with stressful cases. It's the best part of my life in San Francisco. I love my apartment, but it has a whole different feeling, up in the sky above the world. I love the way this house makes me feel as though I'm lying on the beach with my feet in the ocean." It was the perfect way to describe it. Just being there was calming, with the sound of the ocean outside. And then they both laughed as they saw Francisco on the deck, leaping into the air trying to catch a seagull who had just squawked at him and flew by, while he had a fit barking at it. "That'll keep him busy," Mark said, smiling at her. "I wish you could walk on the beach. It's three miles long. It always clears my head." But there was no way she could with her cast and crutches. He took a heavy beige cashmere blanket out of a concealed cupboard and set it up for her on a deck chair. The air was decidedly cool even though it was July, and the sun was dimmed by the haze from the fires, although the ocean breeze swept most of it away. It was a relief not to smell smoke in the air.

He put the groceries in the kitchen and came to sit with her on the deck. The sun was warm, what there was of it. "This is my perfect hideaway when I want to be alone," he said, "but I like sharing it with you. It's like showing you my secret place. I feel safe here, from all the pressures in my life." It was obvious being there that he had kept a distance between himself and the world for a long time. Dahlia had the sense that he was inviting her into his private world. She led a much more populated life than he did, with four adult children she was close to. His lived far away, and he admitted that they seldom visited him in California. He went to visit them. She kept "outsiders" at arm's length. Even she and Philippe didn't have a close relationship. They had one that was easy for both of them, at a safe distance. And Mark had already admitted that he wasn't close to the women he went out with, and his romantic relationships didn't last long. There was always some valid reason to end them before they got too close.

They sat on the deck together, talking for a while, and then Mark whistled to Francisco, who came running, and took him down on the beach where she could see them. He threw some sticks for the dog and let him chase the birds. He took his running shoes off, rolled up his jeans, and waded into the water with him. When he came back to Dahlia, who had enjoyed watching them, Francisco sprawled out on the deck in the sun, exhausted. It was hard work chasing birds and fetching sticks. Mark handed her a perfect sand dollar and she smiled up at him.

"I wish I could walk on the beach with you," she said, and he sat down on the deck chair, next to her broken leg.

"If you get your cast off before you leave, we will," he said, and looked out to sea, at the fishing boats in the distance. "We get sharks here sometimes, attracted by the chum off the fishing boats, and the water is ice-cold. I wear a wetsuit when I swim here." It was all so different from the Mediterranean that she was used to. It was a whole way of life there that was hot and lively, and sunny in the south of France, with lots of people all around. It didn't have this quiet, peaceful feeling that Mark's beach did. There were a few people walking on the beach, but not many. He reached over and took her hand as their eyes met when she looked at him. There was something very deep there. He was usually uneasy with the women he went out with, protecting himself, and careful to keep his distance. With Dahlia he wanted to throw the doors open wide and let her in. “Thank you for coming here,” he said softly. She saw a whole different side to him here from the tough successful lawyer dealing with major corporations every day. The time he spent at the beach gave him the inner strength to fight his battles. He was a man of interesting contrasts, both warm and distant, just as she was strong and vulnerable. As he sat there with her, he leaned toward her and kissed her. She didn’t expect it, but she was irresistibly drawn to him, as though they fit together perfectly, and he was what had been missing in her life and she didn’t know it.

“You make me want to throw caution to the winds,” he said in a deeply moved voice. “I don’t think I’ve ever felt that way before.”

“What are you afraid of?” she asked him gently.

“Myself . . . getting too close,” he said, honest with her.

“Me too,” she admitted, but she wasn’t afraid of him, and wondered if she should be. Something about him reminded her of Jean-Luc so many years ago, and how devastated she had been when he died. She had guarded herself against those feelings ever since then. “Maybe love isn’t possible unless you’re willing to take a risk,” she said softly, as she looked at him. “Maybe that’s what makes it worthwhile.

You can't love someone unless you put all the cards on the table, and all the chips, and you're all in."

"That sounds terrifying," he said, but he didn't look terrified. He looked happy and he kissed her again, and she responded. Afterward, he smiled. "This is very unprofessional. I could be disbarred for this," he said, and she laughed.

"I promise I won't tell," she whispered, kissed him again, and made room for him next to her on the wide deck chair. He lay next to her, with an arm around her, feeling her warmth next to him, and breathing in the faint scent of her perfume, which was delicate and exotic at the same time. "What is it?" he asked her, and she smiled.

"It's one of mine. They make it specially for me, so no one else has it. They just call it 814, which is the reference number. It doesn't have a name."

"I love it. And I think I agree with you about risk. It's what I've been afraid of all my life. I pick women who aren't challenging for me because I know I won't love them. The trouble is I married one of them," and now he had met Dahlia and she was everything he had feared all his life, a woman he could love, and was already falling in love with. And she was leaving in six weeks and lived halfway around the world.

They sat on the deck chair together for a long time, and then went to make lunch when they were hungry. He had brought enough food to make sandwiches, and some cheese and foie gras. It made a very adequate lunch they took back out to the deck to eat. Francisco followed them, and then went back to chasing birds for a while and digging in the sand.

At the end of the day, Mark looked at Dahlia. It had been perfect being there together, and they had opened a door they had both been afraid of. He held her most of the time and they couldn't stop kissing. And they had dozed off to sleep in each other's arms for a while, and nestled closer when they woke up.

"How dangerous could this be?" he said, looking at her. "You're leaving in six weeks. We know when this has to end, and we can't do anything about it. How risky is that? We can't get in too deep in six weeks. Why not seize the moment while we have the opportunity? This time will never come again. This moment belongs to us. You're alone here. We can savor every minute of it and remember it forever when you leave. Are you willing to risk six weeks of your life? That's all it's going to cost either of us. It doesn't sound that dangerous to me," he said, trying to convince himself as well as her.

"And when I leave?" she asked him. "Then what?" It was an honest question, as she thought about what he'd said.

"We kiss goodbye, we cherish the memory, and it's over,

but we live it fully for those six weeks, and no one gets hurt in the end. There's no risk, no danger, no expectations, no disappointment, no reproaches or broken hearts later."

"Are you sure you can measure out love that way?" she asked skeptically. "I'm not sure human hearts open and close like that." It was how he had always lived before, to a much lesser degree, since he was never in love with the women he dated, was attracted to, amused by, or infatuated with briefly. He had loved by drops before. Dahlia was like a flood to his senses, and he was underestimating the force of the tide rushing in, and confident that he would know when to stop it. What he was offering was tempting, to seize these six weeks fully, and then go home and cherish the memory, put it in a box with the scent of summer, to dry silently like shells when they left each other.

He kissed her again, hoping to convince her. It was a searing kiss and what he was offering was too intoxicating to decline. She nodded assent, and gave him a kiss he would long remember, with her whole heart and soul, and then he helped her out of the deck chair. She took her crutches and smiled at him. There was mischief in her eyes, ready to accept the challenge.

"You're a dangerous man, Mr. Hamilton," she said, in a soft, sensual voice. They had much to look forward to. They had six weeks. No one would ever know. He had not expected to propose that to her when he brought her there. He just wanted to show her his beach house. But he had shown her a great deal more. He had let her peek into the depths of his soul, and after what she'd seen, there was no way she could resist him, and didn't want to.

Chapter 13

The drive back to the city was exhilarating on the winding road, as they watched dusk fall over the ocean and the sun set. They had stayed at the beach longer than they meant to. Dahlia couldn't wait to go back again. It was their secret place, their refuge, just as it had been his until now.

They stopped for an early dinner at the Zuni Café and ate oysters and pasta. They talked about some of the big cases he had worked on, both for and against major corporations. He came to life when he talked about them. He loved his work, just as she did hers. They were a powerful force together. The dinner was delicious, and the atmosphere was lively and fun and very San Francisco.

"You're practically a native now. I come here a lot when

I'm not at the beach." The restaurant was a straight shot up Market Street from where he lived on Mission Street, which had previously been a bad neighborhood and had been turned into a cluster of extravagantly expensive apartment buildings and offices. And after dinner, he drove her back to the hotel. She turned to him with an invitation in her eyes.

"Do you want to come up?" she asked him. He nodded, and left his car with the doorman. Francisco looked happy to go home to his toys and soft bed, and fancy new digs. He had waited in the car while they had dinner, and they brought him some boiled chicken, which he thoroughly enjoyed. He had come up in the world since his lucky adoption.

She let them into the suite, where the maids had already turned down the bed. The rooms were invitingly lit, and it felt like coming home. He stopped her before she sat down, and gently took off her jacket and unbuttoned her shirt, and shed his own at the same time. They walked into the bedroom together, with their agreement to live fully and treat the next six weeks they had as a gift. The lights were dim in the bedroom, and Dahlia got onto the bed and Mark followed her, and they sealed their agreement with hours of lovemaking, while Francisco lay snoring on the couch in the other room, having sensed that he wasn't welcome. It was everything they had both avoided for years, lovemaking that was worthy of the name, not just sex that was a satisfying athletic adventure, born of experience but devoid of sentiment or passion. Mark spent the night with Dahlia, which was something he rarely did, but it was all permissible in the next six weeks. Mark already realized that it would be his first and last venture into love, and he didn't want to miss a minute of it. They made love again before they fell asleep, and in the morning as the sun came up. He stayed for breakfast, and then left her and promised to come back later to pick her up. They were going to walk in Golden Gate Park, as far as she could, and he wanted to drive her past some of the prettier spots in the city and take her to his apartment and cook dinner together.

He could barely bring himself to leave her, but he wanted to change clothes, and he had some calls to make, one in particular. The woman he'd been seeing once a week for the past three months was another dead end he already knew would go nowhere, but she was intelligent and being with her helped pass the time. She was also a lawyer. He felt honor-bound to tell her now that something had come up, and that there was no point pursuing what they both knew but hadn't said was a waste of time for both of them. She was no more in love with him than he was with her. He wanted to make the call now, before his involvement with Dahlia went any further. He wanted to do things cleanly with Dahlia for the next six weeks.

After he left, Dahlia had a long conversation with Francisco, who had climbed back into bed with her after Mark left, and she found herself thinking of Philippe, and the contrast between the two men. Mark was everything that Philippe wasn't. He was free and open and loving and made love to her with emotion and abandon, not technical precision and skills he had honed over a long history of sexual exploits independent of his wife. She knew little of Mark, but what they had was honest and clean. What she shared with Philippe never had been. Everything about Mark was genuine and real. He said he was afraid to love, and yet every look, every gesture, every kiss brought them closer, dangerously so. She felt like she was cheating on Philippe. He had history and the priority, and in six weeks she'd be back in Paris, and Mark would be out of her life. Almost as though she had conjured him, Philippe called her. It was one in the morning for him, and Mark had just left her bed. She felt instantly guilty when she heard Philippe's voice.

"Are you all right? Why are you calling so late?" she asked him, feeling strange, as though he could guess what she'd been doing.

"Jacqueline went to a wedding in Brittany this weekend. I'm alone so I thought I'd call you. What are you up to?" She told him about the trial coming up and about postponing Alex's wedding. She'd been meaning to let him know, but she hadn't yet. "So, when are you coming back?" he asked her.

"Right after the trial if there is one. The last week in August. I'll meet up with the children in Saint-Paul-de-Vence for their last week there. I'm letting them have the house for the whole month since I'm in California."

"I want to see you when you get back." He sounded bored, but not like a man who loved her. He never had been. He loved no one, except maybe himself, she remembered now. And he wasn't there to help her. He wasn't calling her regularly to check on her or ask how she was. He called her when he felt like it. Mark was reminding her of what love could be like, but their relationship was finite, set to expire in six weeks. It was a short-term love affair, and she had been with Philippe for six years. Both men had their merits, and both situations. She had longevity with Philippe, on his terms, but they were her terms too, she had agreed to them, and didn't hope for more with him. Her flame with Mark would burn white-hot and then be extinguished when she left, by their mutual agreement. He was going to show her all that love could be, and then be gone, when she left, so she could miss him forever. She wasn't sure which situation was better, except that Mark was honest, and Philippe wasn't. Maybe that made all the difference. Philippe was a liar, and she was a liar with him. So why did she feel like she was cheating on him? Habit maybe.

"I wish you were here with me," he said. But only until Monday when Jacqueline returned. He was comfortable just the way things were, and Dahlia wasn't. She didn't know if she would ever feel the same way again about their arrangement. It wasn't clean, but it was all he had to offer, and he never pretended to offer more.

"Oh, I got a dog, by the way," she said, laughing.

"Why would you do that?" He sounded puzzled.

"I fell in love with him."

"Ah. Good. Then you won't fall in love with anyone else. Keep the dog."

"I intend to," she said quietly and firmly, thinking of Mark too. She had no intention of giving him up for a married man who was spending the summer with his wife, even though he said he didn't love her. But he didn't love Dahlia either, and suddenly what he was offering wasn't enough. She had something to compare it to now, and it didn't compare favorably.

"See you when you're back," he said. It was only weeks away, although she and Mark had just begun. And already she could feel the rush of the sand in the hourglass pouring down.

She sat thinking after they hung up. Philippe didn't know what had happened, but suddenly everything was different. She had changed.

When she saw Mark that afternoon, Philippe slipped out of her head and disappeared into the mists. Mark said he'd made some calls, checked his emails, and talked to his daughters.

"And I called the woman I've been seeing for the past few months that I told you about. It wasn't working and never would. She knew it too. And I wanted a clean slate with you," he said honestly, as they walked slowly around Golden Gate Park, near where the buffalo were grazing.

Dahlia looked surprised and impressed. "Did you tell her about me?"

"No. It wasn't working before I met you. I was just being lazy about it. I wanted to be clean with her." It was something Philippe never had been. Dahlia didn't mention the call from him. She hadn't figured out how to deal with him yet, and didn't want to make promises to Mark she couldn't keep. She didn't want to lie to him. Not even once.

They spent the afternoon in the park with Francisco, and then they went to his apartment. She was stunned by the view. It was in sharp contrast to the beach house. It was serious, sophisticated, and elegant. It looked like an English gentlemen's club perched in the sky, with a panoramic view of the city. She loved his taste, and his treasures. He had a beautiful collection of old books and antique silver he'd inherited from his parents, and wonderful paintings and family portraits. It had the same ancestral feeling to it as her house in Paris, except her decorating was more feminine. It felt like a miracle that they had found each other.

They cooked dinner together that night and wound up in his big comfortable bed that embraced her just as he did, and made her feel safe. Whereas other men she'd met had felt dangerous to her, even Philippe, Mark made her feel that she was safe from the world, without making her feel invaded or suffocated. They were there by choice. Not by default, but as a privilege. They were equally impressed by each other. And she didn't frighten him as other women had, because he knew when it would end. And how attached could you get in six weeks? He kept telling himself that in six weeks, they'd both be ready to let go. Dahlia wanted to believe him, and that there would be no pain involved. It wouldn't be the shocking agony of Jean-Luc dying. Their letting go would be expected and natural. The perfect summer romance in a foreign country, and then she'd go home, and they'd each lead their lives and go on.

In the meantime, the meshing of their bodies was extraordinary, beyond what either of them could have imagined or hoped.

Mark had early meetings the next day, so he took Dahlia and Francisco back to the hotel and hated leaving her there. He almost changed his mind and stayed, but he had a seven A.M. conference call with New York, and needed to be at his desk in his office.

Dahlia played with Francisco when she was back at the hotel. He had been very well behaved all weekend, and at Mark's apartment. And at midnight, she called Agnes at her office. Everything was falling into place for the wedding, and the guests had been notified of the postponement. As she had hoped, they were getting more acceptances than they'd had before. After she answered all of Agnes's questions, she had her connect her to Delphine.

"Hi, darling, how was your weekend?" Dahlia asked her.

"Busy. How was yours? You're not too lonely there waiting for your meetings and hearings?"

"No, I adopted a dog," Dahlia said, and Delphine sounded surprised.

"How's your leg?"

"Better. I can start to put weight on it now. That'll be easier." She didn't say a word about Mark. That was a private side of her life her children didn't need to know. She wanted her two worlds kept separate.

"Has Alex apologized?" Delphine asked, still upset about how she treated their mother.

"Of course not. She never does. And she won't this time." Dahlia didn't expect it. Alex's style was to burn the village to the ground, kill all the locals, and move on, without apology.

"Do you want me to talk to her?" Delphine offered. She was the peacemaker.

"No, you have too much on your plate as it is. I'm all right."

"How's the wedding shaping up? The postponement," Delphine asked her.

"Agnes has it all in control. Thank God we did the civil ceremony in May. It would be hard to do both now." With the division of church and state, French weddings happened in two parts: a civil ceremony at the mayor's office in each arrondissement, usually attended by family and close friends, with a luncheon afterward, and on a separate date, sometimes months apart, the official church wedding, in full regalia, with bridal gown, officiated by a priest. They'd had Alex and Paul's civil wedding, with a lunch at the Salon César Ritz at the Ritz Paris and in the garden, with fifty people present. It had been perfect. So technically, they were already married, with the big hoopla to come on September first now, with the Dior dress Alex was in love with.

"How's Emma doing?" Dahlia asked Delphine about her younger sister. She was so quiet that the others rarely mentioned her. "I've had some text messages, but not many."

"I've called her a few times to make sure she was okay with you away. She says she's painting like crazy. I haven't seen her," Delphine said, feeling guilty. Her mother was the one who kept them all in line, bonded and together. Without her presence, they got busy on their own paths, and lost track of each other, except for Delphine and Charles because they saw each other at work every day.

Charles walked into her office seconds after Delphine had hung up. He had a question about the expenses of one of her projects, which Dahlia had approved before she left.

"Have you called her since she left, by the way?" Delphine asked him about their mother.

He looked vague and slightly embarrassed before he answered. "Yes, sure, of course."

"For business or to ask her how she is?" Delphine asked him pointedly.

"Both. Do I have to make separate calls? Why? Did she complain?"

"She never complains about any of us and sometimes she should. She's stuck in California with a broken leg, which must be painful, threatened with a massive lawsuit, and possibly a trial, far from home and from all of us. The least we can do is call her and make her feel supported."

"I do. Well, actually, I usually text her," he admitted.

"That's not the same. She's not going to tell you in a text that she's lonely or scared, or her leg hurts. You should call her once in a while, just to say hello."

"I've been busy with Catherine," he said vaguely. "And I talked to Mom about the potential lawsuit. I didn't know about a trial. She didn't tell me."

"That's why Alex's wedding is being postponed. The trial is to determine if there was negligence, and to award the other woman damages. Apparently, the woman in the car Maman hit is lying and trying to make her look responsible, so she can get a big settlement. And Maman can't leave San Francisco until the trial in order to prepare for it and possibly reach a reasonable settlement."

"I thought the wedding was postponed because the dress wasn't ready or something. You know how Alex is."

"Yes, I do. And she was awful to Mom when she called her."

"That's not new." Charles wasn't impressed or surprised by his sister's behavior.

"No, but it's incredibly mean of her, and selfish. And I'm sure Emma hasn't called her either, she's too busy painting.

She forgets everything else when she is. We should make an effort till Maman gets home."

"Okay, I'll try, I'm sorry. So, what about that creative bill I got for mock-ups?" he asked her, and they spent the next half hour talking business, which Charles preferred.

In the morning, when she stepped out of the shower, Dahlia got a call from her youngest daughter out of the blue. Emma was elated when Dahlia answered.

"I just got a gallery! I'm going to have a show!"

"That's fantastic!" Dahlia said, smiling broadly. She loved hearing from her children. She felt so disconnected stuck in California. It was as though she was on another planet, far from Paris. She'd only been gone for a month, but it felt like a century. And she was particularly pleased for Emma, and proud of her. She worked very hard on her paintings, and she had wanted a gallery for a long time.

"And it's a good gallery, Mom. They love my work."

"That's so exciting." They talked for about twenty minutes and Dahlia loved connecting with her. She was still smiling when Mark called her to tell her that the car rental's insurance company wanted to take her deposition before the trial.

"When?" she asked him, instantly nervous about it.

"This week or next, as soon as possible. It's normal for

them to do that. They want to know what they're up against, and what kind of witness you'll make. You'll be fine. And I'll be with you. They'll want to depose Ms. Nicasio too."

"At the same time?" she asked, with a knot in her stomach. Her romance with Mark was wonderful, but the rest of what she was facing, and the reason she was there, wouldn't be. Mark was just a bonus, but the main event was unnerving. And she had the mediation hearing ahead of her too.

"We'll go over the deposition carefully beforehand. And I can object to what their lawyers ask you." It was run-of-the-mill to him, but not to her. She had never been in a lawsuit, nor been deposed. "How are you, by the way?" She could hear the smile in his voice when he asked her.

"I was better before I heard about the deposition," she said honestly.

"I promise you'll be fine. I'll set the date with them today. Do you want to go out to dinner tonight?"

"I'd love it." It made her realize that without him, she'd be sitting in her room, worrying, waiting for the days to pass. Mark added a whole exciting other dimension to her life. She had something to look forward to every day now. It was an odd contrast of terrible times and wonderful times all blended in together. It made the time with him even more special.

*

He called her back that afternoon with the date for the deposition. It was set for two o'clock on Friday afternoon.

"Why don't we leave for Stinson after that? We can go straight from the deposition, and spend the weekend, as long as it's not smoky." It startled her to be reminded of the fires again. Every time the direction of the wind changed, the smoke covered the city or dissipated, but the fires were continuing to burn. It had been two and a half weeks, and the fires were still only five percent contained, with hundreds of thousands of acres burning north and east of the city. It had begun to seem unreal. It was on the news every night and looked like a rerun of the night before. Nothing changed except the air quality in the city, from orange to red to magenta and back again.

Their dinner that night was relaxed and pleasant. Mark talked about his day, to the extent he could, and she told him about her conversations with Delphine and Emma, and about her gallery show.

"It feels so strange. I feel so cut off here. I can't go to the office. I'm barely working. I can't see my children or do anything to help them. It's like I'm dead. I feel useless. I haven't had this much time on my hands since I was a kid. And all I can do is wait for the deposition, the mediation hearing, and the trial. And thank you for taking me out. I know the room service menu by heart now. And with this damn leg, I can't even exercise." She was used to being active, going at full speed, and she was living a waiting game now, under stressful conditions, with a lot at stake. Mark was sympathetic to the situation she was in and wanted to help make the time pleasant and easier for her, and he loved seeing her. He'd been looking forward to it all day.

They spent a long time over dinner, and she relaxed being with him, and then they went back to the hotel, and as soon as they walked into her suite, Mark put his arms around her, and she forgot everything except him. They were floating in a universe all of their own. Afterward they sat on the couch in the thick terrycloth hotel robes, and ate chocolate-covered strawberries, and he opened a bottle of champagne. He felt like celebrating every time he was with her. She smiled when he said it to her.

"Maybe we'll be celebrating my going to jail for negligence," she said nervously.

"You're not going to jail. We're trying to keep you from paying an exorbitant settlement unjustly. No jury is going to convict you of negligence, Dahlia, and it will never get that far. This is all a game of chicken, a poker game, of seeing how far they can push you until you crack and start coughing money. I'm not going to let that happen, and

I have a strong feeling that there's fraud involved. Their injuries are not excessive, yet she claims she can't work and her daughter can't go back to school in September. Our investigator is very good, and if she's lying, it'll come out, and I don't think her lawyer will push this all the way to trial. These things usually die on the courthouse steps. It's unnerving, but we just have to stick it out, and they'll get reasonable at the eleventh hour. We're not going to give her five million dollars, and a jury won't either. She didn't lose her legs or her life or her daughter. This all hinges on a technicality of who hit who first, and I believe your story and not hers. Aside from the fact that you're more credible and I trust you, your version makes more sense. It's going to come out right in the end. Trust me." He put an arm around her and pulled her close, and she smiled up at him.

"I don't know why I got lucky enough to meet you at the pet rescue. I got you and Francisco out of it," she said.

"I'm not sure if I should be flattered or insulted by that." Francisco looked up at them and wagged his tail, and Mark patted him. He was falling in love with him too.

They went back to bed and made love again, and eventually fell asleep watching TV.

Mark got up early the next morning. She ordered breakfast for him, and after that he went home to change and go to work. He grinned at her as he left her suite.

"It's been years since I did the walk of shame in the morning before I go to the office. I kind of like it. It makes me feel young again." She laughed and kissed him, and he left with a wave. "See you tonight." It was crazy. She was fifty-six years old, and he was fifty-eight, and they were having a passionate love affair. It certainly improved the situation she was in.

She walked carefully from the door across the room, putting her weight gingerly on her cast. She could put her weight on it now. It had been nearly three weeks since the accident. Nearly three weeks since she and Mark had met, and nearly three weeks since her whole life had changed. It was almost as though her life in Paris didn't exist for the moment and had been put on pause, while she led this parallel life with a man she hardly knew and had fallen in love with. It was the strangest thing that had ever happened to her, and she loved it.

Mark was smiling as he let himself into his apartment, thinking that he had six more weeks of this to look forward to. The sweetest weeks of his life so far. And then she would fly away. He couldn't think of that now, he was too happy to care. And her leaving didn't seem real to either of them yet. They were savoring every moment they had.

Chapter 14

Mark had prepared Dahlia carefully the night before for the deposition on Friday. He had gone over the expected questions the car rental business's insurance company and their lawyers would ask her, and the curves they would probably throw her. Her simplest answer to everything was the truth, and Mark was confident she would handle it with intelligence, honesty, and grace. The insurance company was bringing three lawyers with them, and only one would handle the deposition itself. There would be a stenographer in the room to record it. Marilyn Nicasio would be there with her attorney and Mark was bringing one of his lawyers, mostly for appearances. He didn't need the help. This wouldn't have been a major case if it weren't for who Dahlia was, and the obscene amount of money Marilyn Nicasio was asking for. She had now added to her claim that she was suffering extreme pain from the whiplash, resulting in migraine headaches, alleged fevers at night, and post-traumatic stress, and that her daughter was supposedly showing evidence of psychological damage. And Ms. Nicasio was unable to work—she was caring for all her daughter's needs herself. And she was suing both the car rental company and Dahlia personally. Meanwhile, Dahlia had a broken leg and really did have headaches and nightmares, and wasn't suing anybody. Mark was filing a claim for her with the trucker's insurance company, but Dahlia would only let him ask for medical expenses, and she didn't even want that, and no damages.

"This is only about greed and a big settlement," Mark reminded her again as he drove her to the deposition. He was convinced that there was an element of fraud and was counting on his investigator to uncover it.

The deposition was being held in the insurance company's offices downtown, in their conference room. Mark and Dahlia were met by an assistant when they arrived, found the young lawyer from Mark's law firm already waiting for them in the lobby, and went upstairs to the floor where the conference room was. There were pitchers of water the length of the table, and glasses at each seat, and soft drinks on a side table. The insurance company's three lawyers were waiting, and two minutes after Mark and Dahlia, Marilyn Nicasio arrived with her bearded lawyer in a shiny gray suit that looked like silk. She was wearing a turquoise bodysuit with the sling they'd seen before, and a shoe with rhinestones on it and the boot on her ankle. She gave Dahlia and Mark a dark look and sat down, whispering to her lawyer.

"May we begin?" Herb Mayer, the chief counsel for the insurance company, asked the assembled group, and they all agreed. They wanted Dahlia to go first, and she walked up to the seat they indicated at the far end of the table, using her crutches, and sat down next to the stenographer, who was typing on a small black machine. Everything appeared to be in order. Mayer was a large, portly, bald man who had been defending the company against claims for thirty years. Mark had never met any of them before, since this wasn't his specialty, and he sat down close to Dahlia so he could confer with her or stop her from answering an inappropriate question they had no right to ask her.

She gave her name, home address in Paris, and waited for the first question, which came quickly. All of the questions were about the night of the accident, what she had been doing before, had she imbibed any alcohol, or taken any medication, was she supposed to be wearing glasses and wasn't. And they got to the key question very quickly, about the order of when she'd been hit, and when she hit the car in front of her. Her testimony was consistent and solid, and they didn't throw her any curves. Mark was satisfied. And, quite correctly, she said she didn't recall anything after she hit Ms. Nicasio's car because she'd been unconscious. They also asked her about the injuries she'd sustained, which she reported matter-of-factly, without drama.

They took a break then, and Marilyn Nicasio took the witness seat when they came back. She had been whispering frantically to her lawyer in the shiny gray suit in the hall, and as he walked past, Mark noticed he had a diamond stud in his ear. He looked like everything other lawyers said about personal injury lawyers, and Mark looked right through him as he walked past. Mark's reputation in his own specialty of corporate defense law was legendary and everyone in the room knew who he was. Herb Mayer was very respectful of him. He was well aware that Dahlia had made no claim against the insurance company although the airbags in her car had never opened, and she had a valid claim against them if she chose to enforce it. She had refused to do so, so far, but she still could.

To the list they already knew, Marilyn Nicasio added that Dahlia had been driving too close to her for some time.

They stopped and asked Dahlia about it, and she said that she couldn't see the end of the hood of her car, so she wasn't aware of it, and didn't see any lights in front of her in the smoke. Mark was sure it was a fraudulent addition. He thought Marilyn Nicasio was lying through her teeth. It was useful for Mark to see how the Nicasio woman performed, her attitude and her aggressive looks at Dahlia, and she cried when she spoke of her daughter's injuries and her own, and said she was on pain medication. When they had asked Dahlia the same question, she said she wasn't, and hadn't taken any since her release from the hospital, despite the headaches she still had occasionally from the concussion, which they had told her at the hospital were to be expected.

Marilyn Nicasio offered no explanation as to why neither she nor her daughter had been wearing seatbelts. She said she thought her daughter's was broken, but wasn't sure.

Dahlia came across as a dignified, respectful, not hysterical woman who reported the facts, and if anything, played them down. Marilyn Nicasio was milking it for all it was worth. Everyone in the room knew who Dahlia was, and Mark was sure that they had all googled her and read the estimates of her worth, which was colossal by normal standards. The company alone was worth a fortune. Marilyn had stars in her eyes as a result, enough so to lie and enhance her testimony about her injuries to get the five million dollars she wanted. He was sure that her sleazy-looking lawyer had helped her pick the amount, guessing that they'd wind up with one million if they asked for five. And another million from the rental car company.

The insurance lawyers thanked them for their cooperation, and they all left the building at six o'clock. It had been a long four hours and Dahlia felt drained.

"How are you doing?" he asked her, as they drove to the hotel to pick up the dog.

"I'm exhausted," she said honestly. "My God, that woman is awful. She's so blatant, and she looks so cheap," she said, and he smiled.

"What did you expect? I particularly liked her attorney's suit. I'll have to find out who his tailor is," he said with a grin, and she laughed.

"The trial is going to be so ugly."

"If it happens," he reminded her again. The mediation hearing was ten days away, and Mark wasn't optimistic that they would come to any agreement. The pressure would be on in the two weeks afterward before the trial date.

Mark ran into the hotel to get Francisco and Dahlia's bag so she didn't have to go upstairs, and they took off for Stinson as soon as they were in the car. Mark could see her relax visibly as they drove, and by the time they were on the winding road, she was herself again. He was pleased to see that she had come through it impressively and was the perfect witness he had believed she would be. He was proud to be defending her.

They stopped in the village to buy groceries. He had promised to cook steaks on the barbecue, and she was going to cook the rest. And as soon as they walked into the house, he took her in his arms and kissed her. "You were terrific and I'm proud of you," he said, and she smiled.

"I wish it would all just go away," she said.

"Then we wouldn't be here together," he reminded her, and she sighed. They went to change their clothes. She had bought black baggy sweatpants she could wear over her cast, and put on a pink sweater with them. The air was cool at night at the beach.

He made the steaks while she made a salad to go with them, and they ate dinner on the deck. They could see stars peeking through the thin veil of smoke overhead, and they didn't bother to watch the news. They were tired of all the bad news and tragic stories they'd been seeing for three weeks. The reports never changed, only the direction of the wind to fan the flames in new directions. It was a vicious trick of nature.

They put their dishes in the dishwasher and went to bed and made love, and in the morning, Mark took a run on the beach with the dog, and she made him an omelet when he got back. They went to buy the newspaper after breakfast and saw that the fire had added another county to devour, and another thousand people had been evacuated.

"That's North Marin," Mark commented to Dahlia when he read the paper, "just north of here."

"Is it close?"

"Close enough, but the wind is pushing it away from here." The flames had demolished an entire development of houses and a hotel during the night, like an insatiable beast.

They sat on the deck and read all afternoon, and Mark looked over at her and smiled, and they wound up back in bed before dinner. They barbecued again, chicken this time, and they were just sitting down to eat when they both noticed the smell of smoke. Mark looked up and saw streaks of black smoke in the sky.

"I think the wind has shifted," he commented as they ate, and she was taking their plates into the kitchen, walking on her cast without the crutches, when Mark looked at the hills above them, and saw a rim of fire all along the ridge. They watched it race across the crest of the hill above them. "Shit, get your bag, Dahlia, we've got to leave. There are only two ways out of here, past those hills or the way we came. I'm not going to wait till the fire comes down the hill." There was enough dry grass to feed it, and they could sit in the ocean if they had to, and watch the beach houses burn, but he wasn't waiting for that. He turned off the barbecue and told her to hurry. They piled into the car with her bag and his briefcase and Francisco, and a few bottles of water and a bowl she grabbed for the dog, and headed out of the gated community toward the winding road. Mark kept glancing up at the hills, at the flames that were getting brighter and coming closer as he stepped on the gas, and they reached the hairpin turns in the road within minutes. At any time, the flames could race down the hill and surround them, or cut them off and jump the road, and they'd be trapped.

"Do you think we should go back?" Dahlia asked him, as they raced around the turns, and she prayed that no one was coming in the opposite direction and would hit them. She was silent as she watched him handle the road at full speed. The hills above them were fully in flames now, and there were embers flying, and rocks that hit the car and bounced off. Mark didn't take his eyes off the road for a second. He was trying to outrun the fire before it blocked them in the forest around them. They could hear sirens in the distance.

"Are you okay?" he asked tersely as he sped through each hairpin turn.

"Yes," she said, and didn't want to distract him. "Are you?" He nodded and kept driving, going faster, and skidded around the last bend, as they reached the straight stretch of road past Muir Woods, and he went faster. The next ten minutes were the scariest she'd ever experienced, but she didn't say a word. There was a bright glow of fire behind them in the distance, and darkness ahead, which Mark suspected was smoke. He kept going, and five minutes later they were at the entrance to the freeway, and two firefighters and a police officer flagged them down.

"How bad is it back there?" one of the firefighters asked him.

"It's bad and it's coming this way fast. I don't know how but we outran it."

"Is there anyone behind you?"

"Not that I saw. I don't know how many people are there tonight. And it took us by surprise. We saw the flames and ran."

"Smart, or you could have spent the night on the beach in the water. The others won't be able to get out soon. We're going to airlift anyone there off the beach by helicopter." Dahlia hoped Mark wouldn't lose his lovely house, but all he had wanted was to get them both out and to safety. As he got on the freeway, there was heavy smoke overhead but they could still see the road. The wind had fully shifted in an hour, and the fires were in Marin County.

Mark didn't speak until he had gotten them across the bridge safely and back into the city.

"Well, so much for a peaceful weekend at the beach." He smiled wryly at her. "Sorry for the scary ride."

"You were amazing."

"I just wanted to get you out of there as fast as I could."

"Do you think the house will be okay?" she asked him.

"I hope so. But you mean more to me than the house. Everything's insured. So, what'll it be? My place or yours?" he asked her with a grin. "We certainly don't lead a dull life. Life in an inferno." They decided that they might be safer at the hotel and could always go to his place in the morning, which they did. There was a cloud of black smoke hanging over Marin County, and the air quality had gone up to red again. Another hundred thousand acres had burned during the night.

They stayed at his place the next day and watched old movies and ordered in Thai food. "This is like living through a war," he said. But they forgot about it for a while, as they nestled in his big bed, with Francisco lying at the foot, snoring, and Mark set him down gently on the floor so they could make love. They spent most of Sunday in bed in his apartment, to avoid the toxic air. They couldn't even open the door to the terrace, it was so bad by Sunday morning.

On Monday morning the mediation hearing was a week away. Time was running away from them, like the fires all around them. Mark wanted to stop time. They had three and a half weeks left in the time capsule fate had given them.

He looked at Dahlia across the breakfast table before he got dressed, and he looked serious. "I love you, Dahlia. I was so afraid on Friday night that something terrible would happen. Thank God it didn't."

"I love you too," she said softly, and she had no idea what to do about it. There was nothing they could do. Their lives were firmly carved out, six thousand miles apart. She had been thinking about it more and more with each passing day. Each day that brought them closer to when she'd have to leave. Having to leave in a few weeks was starting to be real. "Can you handle that?" she asked him, since he had avoided loving and being loved for most of his life, especially the last twenty years.

"Probably not," he said with a wry grin, and leaned over to kiss her across the table. "But I'm willing to try."

"Me too," Dahlia said with a smile. And then he looked serious again.

"What are you going to do about your married boyfriend

when you go back to Paris?" It had been worrying him and he needed to ask her, since she never mentioned it. This was their time, she didn't want to think about Philippe.

"I don't know yet how it will play out, or what I'll do, but I'm not going back to him. I want to tell him in person. I think after six years, he deserves that. It won't break his heart—it'll be an inconvenience. He'll have to find a new one. I'm replaceable," she said matter-of-factly. Mark looked relieved when she said it. It had been gnawing at him.

"Will it break your heart?" he asked her.

"No, it won't. Nor his. Leaving you will break mine," she said, and they looked across the table at each other.

"To be continued," he said, and got up to dress for work. He had a meeting, and her comment required a bigger answer than he could give her at the moment.

He kissed her when he left for work, looking very distinguished, and happy about their exchange over breakfast. He had been worried about Philippe, and he liked her answer.

As Dahlia cleared away the breakfast dishes in Mark's apartment in San Francisco, her son Charles walked into Delphine's office at Lambert in Paris. It was six o'clock, and he'd been waiting all day for her to be free. She was finally alone in her office. He walked in and slid into a chair across from her desk, looking like disaster had struck.

"What's wrong? Are you going to complain about my department's bills again?"

"Catherine is pregnant," he said in one breath. "Mom is going to have a fit."

"What do you want? Never mind Mom. You're thirty years old. Do you love Catherine enough to have a child with her? Do you want to marry her?" He looked pale and didn't answer.

"It's a lot to take on."

"You need to figure it out for yourself. Don't tell Mom right now, she's got enough going on to worry her."

"Catherine has wanted another child for a long time. She's turning forty in two months. She feels like it's her last chance. And I wasn't planning to marry her."

"It's not her last chance. I have a friend who just had a baby at forty-nine." Delphine was practical and more mature than her brother. He looked confused and worried. At thirty, he was still naïve about women.

"I don't know what I want," he admitted to her.

"You need to figure it out, for you. Not for Mom or Catherine." Charles and Catherine had been living together for three years. He had never considered the future with her.

"I love her, but a child is a big commitment." Delphine grinned at him in response.

"That's for sure." They talked about it. They both knew

that their mother disapproved of his girlfriend. She wasn't from their milieu, but he lived with her and said he loved her. But enough to marry her? He wasn't sure. He gave Delphine a hug and went back to his office, no closer to a decision than before. But it was a relief to share his worry with his sister.

Delphine thought about him on the way home. He was two years older than she was, but he was still a baby. He had no real responsibilities except his job. He was serious about it, but he had walked into it. Their mother made everything so easy for all of them, and she forgave them everything and let them grow up at their own speed. Delphine had been married for five years, had a husband and two children, and a big job of her own. Having children made such a big difference. You couldn't play at growing up then, you had to be there for them.

Her husband Francois expected her to be an adult. She listened to his business problems, told him what she thought. They made decisions together, fought over the children sometimes. His parents had never helped him with his start-ups. He had to figure it out for himself. He was thirty-five, and he sometimes resented how easy Delphine's mother had made life for all of them. It had given them a great start, but they had no experience at problem-solving and had to fly on their own now. And she didn't think

Charles was ready for that, with a woman nine years older, and she babied him too. If he decided to have the child with her, he would have to stand up and be a man—and she couldn't see Catherine being willing to give up the baby for him because he wasn't ready. He'd either have to take a giant leap into adulthood now, or admit he wasn't up to it and just support her. If he stayed and faced it with her, maybe he would grow up. If he married Catherine, their mother wasn't going to be happy about it, and he'd have to face that too.

He had created a man-sized mess, and now he had to deal with it. She didn't envy him, as she drove home to her husband and two little girls, Annabelle and Penny. They were two and four years old, and a full-time job and commitment—and Francois was great with them. They both had big jobs. They loved and respected each other, which made it all work. She had no idea what her brother was going to do, and neither did he. A child was forever, which was one hell of a long time. And he wasn't at all sure he wanted to give up his freedom for Catherine.

Chapter 15

The mediation hearing went exactly as Mark expected it to. It was all about showmanship, threats, and flexing muscles to show strength and not compromise. Mark had warned Dahlia before that Nicasio's lawyer would be tough, nasty, threatening, trying to convince them that they had everything to win at trial. It was basically a legally sanctioned shakedown to make Dahlia give them the five million they wanted from her personally, and to get the car rental company to give her an equal amount. Marilyn Nicasio wanted to walk away with ten million dollars, minus a third to her sleazy lawyer. That was her dream. Mark guessed that the reality was that she wanted a million from each and would be thrilled. She would quit her job, live high on the hog as long as the money lasted, and if she got lucky she would find a guy who was willing to marry her and support her before the money from the accident ran out.

The reality was that her injuries didn't warrant that kind of damages. A broken ankle and broken arm just didn't bring that kind of sympathy or price, particularly since she was in great part at fault by not wearing her seatbelt. Her whiplash was the oldest story in personal injury and hard to prove, and no one cared about her nightmares or her daughter's, and Dahlia had them too. And all of her daughter's injuries could have been avoided if her mother had made her wear a seatbelt. Their injuries were more Marilyn's fault than Dahlia's. Marilyn Nicasio wasn't an appealing witness and didn't elicit sympathy. Dahlia's dignity, lack of complaints, and restraint from trying to sue the car rental company because of the airbags that didn't open, or the trucking company, were far more impressive. She had integrity and it showed. Marilyn Nicasio was greedy, and that showed too.

She remained aggressive, nasty, and demanding during the entire mediation. She was rude to the mediator, told her own lawyer to shut up when he disagreed with her, and called Dahlia a rich bitch, which didn't endear her to anyone. From her side's standpoint, the mediation was a bust, and she was going to be an unsympathetic witness who'd be hard to control. From Mark's viewpoint, he hadn't expected anything different—in fact, he was pleased by how badly she'd behaved. Dahlia had been a lady and a star, which surprised no one. The mediator thanked them all for their time, with a look of extreme aggravation, dismissed them, and wrote a full report to the judge of the proceedings.

Mark was amused. Marilyn Nicasio was going to be a nightmare witness on the stand in front of a jury.

From that day on, they were on real time until the trial. Having been denied the settlement they hoped for, Marilyn's side would be heatedly trying to negotiate for the next two weeks. They didn't want to go to trial and take a risk. They wanted to settle and no one was willing to settle with them. They had a lot riding on one horse, and officially Dahlia wasn't afraid of a trial. Mark knew that, by then, Nicasio's lawyer would be beginning to sweat. His silk suit would be soaking wet. A third of nothing was nothing, which was his risk as a contingency lawyer. If Marilyn got nothing, so did he. Attorneys of Mark's stature were paid for their time and skill, win or lose, and contingency lawyers didn't have big wins every time. Lawyers like Mark were much more likely to convince a jury and go home winners.

On Dahlia's side, their investigator was working overtime to find out whatever he could about Marilyn to put the squeeze on her and her lawyer before the trial to drop the suit. Mark had faith in him that he would drop a plum in their lap in time, and he tried to convince Dahlia of that. She was worried as she waited, and just to get her out of the hotel and distract her, he suggested another weekend in Stinson, while he prepared a rough version of his opening statement for the trial, which he firmly believed he'd never use.

They hadn't been to the beach since the fire on the hills. It never reached his gated community, and the firefighters managed to stop it on the hills and beat it back. The tides had begun to turn in Napa, Sonoma, and Marin Counties. The winds had been favorable, and the fires were now ten percent contained. It wasn't enough, and they were far from over, but the air quality had improved slightly, and they were trying to beat back the fires every day. In the past month, three million acres had burned. The same had happened two years before, and it could happen again.

As Mark and Dahlia drove along the familiar hairpin turns, the hillside was charred from the road to the crest of the hills above it, and it reminded them both of their wild ride back two weeks before. The house looked pristine inside when they entered it, but needed a good power wash outside from the smoke. They unloaded the groceries, and Francisco rolled in the sand and barked at the birds, delighted to be back.

Mark bent to kiss Dahlia as she finished putting the groceries away. "Hamilton Special tonight," he announced. "Burgers." It made her wonder as she did constantly now what she would do when she was back in Paris, when there was no Stinson Beach and no Mark. In the past four weeks, being with him had become her life. She no longer went to her office, working remotely with her staff, and he was always on her mind. From the moment he came home from the office, her time was his. She was leading the life of a couple with a man she loved and would never see again, or maybe one day when he came to Paris for a holiday. More than that, she was leading the life of a woman with no children. Or children who were adults she hadn't seen in two months and could fend for themselves. They were doing a very decent job of it, and she hardly spoke to them now. Her whole life didn't revolve around them the way it had for thirty years. They didn't need her in the same way anymore and it was healthy for them, and for her.

It all made sense with Mark, and without him, none of it would. She had a worldwide company to run six thousand miles away. She and Mark had taken a risk, but what would they do with it now? San Francisco was too far to commute. They might have pulled it off from New York, commuting to each other on alternate weekends. But California and Paris were worlds apart, twelve hours by plane with a nine-hour time difference. There was no way it could work, and they both knew it. They were staying off the subject, because there was no solution, only heartbreak ahead. They hadn't thought of that when they threw their hearts over the wall. They had proven to themselves and each other that they were capable of being close. But there would be no way to be close geographically after the trial. The reality was cruel. They had won the lottery with a bogus ticket and there was no prize, except the love they had for each other.

Dahlia had a big date on Monday to take off the cast. Her leg felt strong now, although she had been warned it would look a mess when the cast came off, shriveled and dry, and she'd have to do physical therapy to get back its strength and muscle tone, but the bone would be fine.

She walked on the beach with Mark for a short distance and didn't care if she got sand in the cast since it was coming off in two days. She put a garbage bag around it anyway, and walked along the water's edge with Mark. She kept taking photos of him with her phone when he wasn't looking or asleep, to take with her. She still couldn't believe the day was coming when she'd have to leave.

Alex's wedding was in two weeks. Everything was set, and they'd had more acceptances than they'd had for

August first. Everyone would be back from vacation by September first. Alex hadn't said thank you to her mother yet for the smooth transition and probably never would. It wasn't in her DNA to be grateful or pleasant. She thought everything she had was her due. She was the only one of Dahlia's children to feel that way, and all of them recognized their sister as the narcissist she was. She had talent and beauty and redeeming features, but gratitude wasn't one of them, particularly to her mother, on whom she blamed all the ills of the world, and her life. Dahlia didn't expect anything from her anymore. She just wanted to give her the best wedding she could. She was her child, for better or worse, and she loved them all. Some were easier to love, like Delphine. Emma was an enigma all of her own. And Charles wasn't fully cooked yet. He had a lot of growing up to do. Alex had a cruel side, which she unleashed on her mother at the slightest provocation, or with none at all.

Mark and Dahlia stopped at the edge of the water and sat down on the dry sand.

"I'll be happy to get rid of this." She pointed to her cast. "I won't miss it."

"I'm thinking of having it bronzed, in honor of the day I met you." He knew the fires would always remind him of her, and the dog. He had no idea what to do with the rest of his life without her, but he accepted that that was how it was going to be. And going back to the way he had been no longer worked. He loved the closeness they shared. It didn't scare him anymore, with her. And with anyone else, the closeness would be pointless. He was in love with her.

"It's hard, isn't it? Harder than we thought," she said, looking out to sea. "I thought it would be easy for six weeks, and then we'd go back to who we were before. It would be fun."

"It is fun, with you," he said to her, and she leaned against him.

"You made me different," she said softly.

"We made each other different. It's the combination," he said, "of all the different elements. I'm better because of you, and more. And I'm going to be less without you."

"Me too. Maybe this is all you get sometimes. A moment. A day. A year. Six weeks." She and Jean-Luc had had five years. Others had fifty. This time she and Mark only got six weeks. They had to make it enough and take it with them, and feel blessed instead of cheated when it ended. She was working on it and so was he.

"I'll race you," he said, as they headed back to the house. "Winner take all," he teased her, as she stumped along with her cast and the garbage bag over it.

"Very funny. Maybe I will go to jail, and then you can visit me."

"No, you'll go back to your kids and your job and your perfume. Just don't let Alex torture you, or go back to that married jerk. He doesn't deserve you. Maybe I don't either," he said. She hardly ever thought of Philippe now. He felt like part of another lifetime, ancient history. It made no sense anymore. It never did.

"It's weird. You made me feel American again. I haven't felt that way since I was a kid, in college, before we moved back." But she couldn't imagine a life in California with him, full-time. She had responsibilities in France, and a family business to run. She took their business seriously, and Delphine and Charles weren't ready to run it yet on their own. One day, but not yet. And by the time they were, she and Mark would be too old to chase a dream. They had taken a risk, and she wasn't sure if they had won or lost. If they had won, winning hurt.

The weekend at the beach was peaceful and just what they needed before the impending storm of the next week. They closed the door regretfully on Sunday afternoon. They would be in trial, or waiting for the verdict, the following week, and they wouldn't come to the beach house. Or if the trial was canceled, she'd be on a plane, back to Paris. She looked around for a last time, and had tears in her eyes when they left, and she was quiet on the drive home. They stayed at his apartment that night. They couldn't bear to be apart now. Either way, it was their last week. The trial was starting on Wednesday.

Mark had a busy day on Monday, dealing with other matters, and wrapping up the final details before the trial. Dahlia went to the hospital for her appointment. They took off the cast and X-rayed her leg. It had healed perfectly, and she walked out on two feet. It felt weird not to have it on, and when Mark came home from work, she pointed.

"Look, two legs. And the broken one doesn't look as weird as they said it would."

"It looks good to me," he said, and kissed her. They had dinner at the apartment, and he worked on his opening statement, just in case. His cellphone rang at ten o'clock that night. He was in his study, working. It was Harry, their private detective.

"You're all set. We hit gold." Harry sounded pleased with himself and had a right to be.

"Whatcha got? Dahlia never hit her. Nicasio backed up?" Mark joked with him.

Harry laughed. "Better than that. Full house. The sad news first. Johnny Block, the truck driver, had a nasty heroin habit. I've got the autopsy. It took forever to get it. He was high as a kite. That's probably why he hit her, as much as the smoke. He plowed right into her, maybe nodded out at the wheel, we'll never know, but the likelihood is that he hit her first. They'd never get 'beyond a reasonable doubt' with that going on, and the charming Ms. Nicasio has been back at work wearing a jet-black wig for the last three weeks. She's collecting a paycheck, which was dumb of her, so she lied. And her daughter has been out for summer vacation, not trauma, and her casts came off a week ago. She's going back to school, right on schedule, her school is expecting her. Ms. Nicasio is no longer wearing the boot, to work or anywhere else. The ankle was declared healed two weeks ago, and I'm not sure about the arm, but I have a feeling the sling is purely decorative. And we have a great photo of her at her aerobics class. She's been going to a spinning class, and she goes to yoga at the Y, so I think the whiplash is bullshit too. There goes your trial and her ten million dollars right out the window, on wings. And I've got photos for most of it." Mark was grinning from ear to ear as he listened.

"You are, once again, a genius," he complimented the detective.

"No, I just know the right people who like to talk and follow other people around. I'll shoot you an email with the written report and all the documentation. You'll have it by the morning. Sleep tight. Sweet dreams."

“Thank you,” Mark said, and went to find Dahlia. She was half asleep in front of the TV, and he touched her gently to wake her.

“Oh, sorry. I was just resting.”

“I’ve got some good news,” he said gently. “Harry, the investigator, just came through.” He read her the list—he had written it all down so he didn’t forget anything—and she stared at him in amazement.

“Is it over?”

“It’s going to be. They can’t walk into a courtroom with that pile of shit. They’re going to be scrambling like crazy. I’ll call her lawyer tomorrow. They’ll be begging us to settle. They can’t go to trial,” he said, and she was wide-awake. They talked about it, and Dahlia felt sorry for the young truck driver. He was twenty-four years old.

They talked about all of it for an hour and then went to bed. Mark got up early and went to the office. He called Herb Mayer, the head counsel for the insurance company, at nine A.M. sharp and shared the information with him. Herb was delighted. It was better than they could have hoped. He was going to contact Marilyn’s attorney and suggest a meeting in his office. Mark said he’d be there. The negotiation was beginning in earnest.

Herb confirmed the meeting to him twenty minutes later,

and Mark was there five minutes early. Herb congratulated him on the good work.

The shyster lawyer was the last to arrive, and looked nervous, confronted by the big guns. He was outclassed the moment he sat down and they told him the lay of the land and how it was going to work. The car rental's insurance company was offering ten thousand dollars in damages to Ms. Nicasio, and ten thousand to her daughter, and Mark said that Ms. de Beaumont was willing not to press charges of fraud against Ms. Nicasio and was offering her nothing.

Her lawyer squealed like a little pig and was begging for mercy within an hour. He stood to make ten thousand on the case, which no one cared about. He begged for a hundred thousand for each of his clients and Herb Mayer laughed at him. The car rental company offered a hundred thousand to Dahlia for her injuries since the airbags malfunctioned, and Mark said two hundred thousand or they would sue, and he threatened Nicasio's lawyer with a defamation of character suit, and extortion. Herb agreed immediately to the two hundred thousand for Dahlia, because he knew she could ruin them if she chose to. They raised their offer to twenty-five thousand each for Marilyn and Tiffany Nicasio. And they notified the court that the matter had been settled amicably, and the contingency lawyer withdrew the civil suit.

It was a productive morning, and everybody went away happy. Mark called Dahlia and she was at the hotel, organizing what she needed to pack. Francisco had half a suitcase just for his things.

"I'll be there in ten minutes," Mark told her, and rang the doorbell of the suite ten minutes later. He was beaming when she opened it. He couldn't wait to tell her. It was a spectacular victory. "The trial is canceled and the civil suit is withdrawn. Marilyn and Tiffany get twenty-five thousand each, which is more than they deserve, minus half to their lawyer, and you get two hundred thousand for your broken leg, and I magnanimously agreed not to press charges of fraud, extortion, and defamation of character on Ms. Nicasio. It's a clean sweep."

"But I didn't want money." Dahlia looked upset and Mark laughed at her.

"You deserve it. Their fucking airbags were defective, and you've been stomping around in a cast for a month and a half. Enjoy it." She sat down on the couch and looked at him.

"I have a better idea. I want to give the two hundred thousand to the girl, in trust. She can use it for her education one day. And her mother can't touch it, and the lawyer doesn't get a penny of it. It's a gift."

"Are you serious?" He was shocked.

"Yes. One day she'll need it, to get away from that awful

woman. And she'll never see that kind of money again. I don't need it. She does."

"They're not going to believe this."

"And make some bank a trustee. No one touches that money until she's twenty-one or uses it for college before that."

"Are you sure?"

"Yes, I am."

"You are amazing." It was only one of the many reasons why he loved her. She was an incredibly decent person.

"Let's have lunch somewhere and celebrate," he said, and she looked suddenly sad.

"What are we celebrating? I have to go now." He looked like he'd been hit by a wrecking ball when she said it. "It's over. And I have to go back to Paris. The wedding is in two weeks, and I've been gone for two months. I have no excuse to stay now." She looked devastated.

"When are you leaving?" He looked panicked. She thought about it for a minute.

"They're still in the south of France till next week. This is their last weekend, and I said I'd join them. I'll stay with you. Let's go to Stinson this weekend, and I'll leave on Monday. That gives us six days, including today. And then I have to go. I need to be in Paris the week of the wedding. I already have my outfit. I'm all set."

"Six days," he said sadly, and then he pulled her into his arms and held her. "I love you, Dahlia."

"I love you too. Thank you for doing such a fantastic job. I really thought I'd go to jail at first, before the hearing."

"I knew that wouldn't happen, and that awful woman doesn't deserve a penny. And Tiffany is a very lucky little girl."

"Maybe it will make a difference for her one day."

Mark notified Marilyn's lawyer of Dahlia's gift to Tiffany, and he couldn't believe it either. "Guys like you always get the good clients," he said in a whining tone. And guys like him didn't deserve them.

They ended up having lunch in the suite so they could be alone, and after they ate, he went back to the office. He had a mountain of work on his desk and a rock on his heart. He couldn't bear the thought of her leaving, but he knew she had to.

She moved into his apartment that afternoon, and left all her suitcases at the hotel, most of them packed with things she didn't need. Mark wanted her with him for every moment they could share, and he was grateful for the extra week without a trial.

"You don't mind missing out on the south of France with your kids?" he asked her that night.

"I'd rather be with you. They've been doing fine without

me, and I want to be with you." And she had years to be in the south with them, and none with him.

Every day and night that they spent together was precious. They walked along the waterfront, and took long walks at night when he got home. And on Friday at noon, they left for the beach for their last weekend together. The weather was glorious and the sky was finally clear. The fires were twenty percent contained now. The air quality was green. They walked the length of the beach at Stinson. Her leg got tired, but it didn't hurt.

Every moment with him was bittersweet, knowing what she would be missing for the rest of time. He wanted to visit her in Paris, but their deal had been that they would say goodbye after six weeks and move on with their lives where they belonged.

"We were just supposed to have a good time, and not fall in love," he reminded her.

"We screwed it up," she said mournfully. "Both of us."

"We certainly did." He was madly in love, and so was she.

"We have to live up to our deal," she said sadly. "There's no way to make it work at this distance, and we're both too young to retire. You can't give up your career, and I can't give up mine. Maybe my kids could take over in five years, but they're not ready now."

"So we make a date to meet in five years?" He looked at her and she shook her head.

"No. I'll love you forever, and be grateful that we had these six weeks. That was the deal."

"That's pathetic," but he didn't have a solution either.

There were tears in her eyes when they left the house on Sunday and drove back to the city. They spent the last night at the hotel. She had to leave at two P.M. to check in at three for a five o'clock flight. Mark drove her to the airport. They checked her luggage in at the curb, and Francisco was in his travel bag. Mark stayed with her until she had to go through security. There were no words left to say, and she couldn't speak when she left him. He kissed her, and she wanted to die in his arms, and never live another day without him. But she had to follow her duty, and not her heart, and she loved her children too, and the business her mother had left her and her grandfather had built. She had to take care of it for the next generation. It was a sacred obligation to her.

"I love you," was all she could say. "Thank you. I really will love you forever."

"Oh, Dahlia," he said, with tears in his eyes. "This is crazy. I can't let you go."

"We have to," she said, as tears slid down her cheeks.

"I know. I'll come to Paris sometime soon," he promised,

and she clung to him, and then she stood back and looked at him with a brave smile. "I love you," he said, and she nodded and walked away. She turned as she went into security, and he was still standing there. They were both smiling and crying, and then she walked through and disappeared.

Chapter 16

The plane landed at Charles de Gaulle airport at five in the morning local time, on Tuesday. Dahlia went through customs and immigration with her French passport. She was home, even if it didn't feel that way, and she couldn't let any of them know how she felt. If she'd been older or younger she would have stayed in San Francisco with Mark, but she couldn't. She had changed in two months. Everything felt different now, and it wouldn't be the same without him. Her car and driver were waiting at the airport. She walked Francisco for a few minutes, and then got in the car with him. She sent Mark a text. It was seven-thirty P.M. for him. He was lying in bed, and heard it come in. "Safely arrived. Nothing is the same. I will always love you." And he answered her immediately. "I am always with you. I love you too." They were like two kids madly in love. In a way it was silly, but it was wonderful too. She had never thought it could happen at her age, but it had. It was just miserable luck that they lived so far apart, and had obligations they couldn't leave: her children and her work, and his. And now they had to be grown-up about it. But she was sure she would never know the same joy again.

The house on the rue de Grenelle was quiet when she got home at six-thirty in the morning. Emma was asleep. Henri the butler gave her a hug when he came to work at seven, and the bags disappeared to her room. She took a bath and changed, and Francisco stayed close to her, not knowing where he was. She wore a chic gray suit to the office and was there at nine. She walked into Delphine's office, and Delphine let out a scream and rushed to hug her mother, and for a minute Dahlia was glad to be home. This was why she had come home. Delphine looked tanned and well after a month in the south of France. Charles heard Delphine scream and came to see his mother a little later and hugged her too. He was more restrained, but he was happy to see her.

"You look great, Mom. And the mess is all over?"

"It is, and I didn't pay a penny in settlement."

"How did you manage that?" Charles asked her.

"I had a great lawyer," she said quietly.

"That'll probably cost you more than the settlement," he said cynically, and she didn't tell him that Mark had insisted on doing it for free. They had argued about it for days, but he was adamant and said he wasn't going to charge the woman he loved legal fees. In the end, she gave in and thanked him profusely.

Agnes cried when she saw Dahlia, and everything for the wedding was on track. It was in four days, and there was nothing left for her to do.

Dahlia sat at her desk and felt like an imposter. It didn't feel like her desk or her office anymore after two months away, and so much had happened.

"How's your leg?" Delphine asked her.

"A little skinnier than the other one, but I have exercises to do, and it doesn't hurt. I'm fine." Fine, but now she had a broken heart, which was worse.

There were little stacks of messages on her desk. Everyone had been informed that she was returning, and she had done enough by email while she was away to keep abreast of what was going on, and nothing happened in France in August. Most people had come home the Sunday before, and some people wouldn't be back for another week. No one had missed her.

She had brought Francisco to the office with her, and he sniffed around, and wagged his tail when he met people.

And at seven o'clock she went home, as she did every night. Emma was back, and came bounding into her room to say hello. Her hair was still pink and she was bubbling over with excitement about her show. It was going to be in October, and she had a lot of work to get ready. In a way, it was like nothing had changed, and Dahlia hadn't been gone at all. It was a strange feeling. She had texted Alex too, to say she was coming home, but there was no word of welcome. She would see her at the wedding if not before. Alex would have to prove a point and punish her for not coming home earlier as planned, so she could get married in August. In the end, it had worked out much better for September, and there were more guests coming than originally.

She had seen three of her children by that night, and she had an omelet and a cup of soup for dinner, alone in the dining room. She had forgotten how lonely and solitary her life was, with grown children who were busy, a job that filled her days but not her nights, and a man she only saw two days a week. She spent weekends alone most of the time, except if she visited Delphine if she and her family weren't in the country, or Emma had nothing else to do and agreed to go to a gallery with her. For years it had been enough, but it no longer was. There was no one to walk with, to sleep with, to talk to, to cook with and eat with, and make love and laugh with. She had come home to the solitary sentence that had been her life for so long that she no longer noticed it, and now she noticed it acutely. It was deprivation of everything she and Mark had shared and she'd come to love. It was everything she had given up to come home, and her family would never know.

She'd had Agnes invite them all to dinner on Thursday night, for an informal dinner at home. They would all have plans on Friday night with their friends before the wedding. And she might have to have dinner with Paul's parents, Alex's in-laws, so she had kept the night free. The full social season would begin in a few weeks, as Paris came alive again after the summer.

She texted Philippe that night. "Just got home today. Would love to see you. Does tomorrow work for you?" He responded very quickly with, "Perfect. Love to, welcome home!" Their usual nights were Monday and Thursday, and he didn't like to deviate from the schedule, but they hadn't seen each other in two months.

She couldn't sleep that night and kept wondering what Mark was doing, and calculating the time difference, but it seemed cruel to keep contacting him, and she was trying not to. It was hard to believe she had come home that morning. It already felt as though she had never left. She was right back in the same routine. And by the end of the week, California and everything that had happened there would seem like a dream.

Francisco was lying on her bed, waiting for her, and looked as though he felt lost too. He didn't know where he was. All his familiar places and people were gone again.

"We'll both get used to it soon," she whispered to him, and he snuggled close to her when she got into bed. It was only three in the afternoon in San Francisco, and Mark would be in the office, but she didn't call him, and after she lay awake for a long time, she fell asleep.

Dahlia's alarm clock woke her as it always did at seven o'clock. She showered and dressed and had breakfast on a tray in her home office, and checked her emails. There was nothing she particularly wanted to read, and went through them quickly. Mark hadn't written to her, as they'd agreed. Only in emergencies or dire need were they going to contact each other.

She left for the office promptly at nine o'clock and was at her desk twenty minutes later when Charles strode into her office with a purposeful look.

"Can I speak to you?" he asked, looking increasingly nervous, and she went to kiss him, and then sat down at her desk again. She was sure he was going to tell her about some enormous expense that had to stop, some part of business that was out of control or someone who had done something that had to be addressed. She hoped it was nothing worse. He looked extremely serious. "I have something to tell you," he said in a very adult tone. He seemed older and less carefree than when she left. "Catherine and I are getting married. She's having a baby, and she wants to keep it. I don't think that's right, to have the baby out of wedlock. We want to get married. I know you don't approve of her, and that she's nine years older, but I've given it a lot of thought, and it's what I want to do." It was a heavy hit for her second day back, but she tried to be equal to it and not overreact. She hesitated for a minute and looked at him squarely.

"Is it really what you want, or do you feel obligated, as though it's what you 'should' do? There's a big difference, Charles. What do *you* want to do?" It was the same question Delphine had asked him, which surprised him, coming from his mother. He had been sure she'd have a fit, but she wasn't. He had been braced for it. She was astonishingly calm, not happy, but sensible and down-to-earth.

"It's what I want," he said more gently. "I love her. I don't care that she's nearly ten years older. And I want to be married to have our baby. I think I might adopt her daughter too. She doesn't see her father and he seems to have disappeared. We don't want a big wedding like Alex, just a small civil ceremony with the family and a few friends. We could do it at the house, if that's all right with you."

"Of course it is. It's your home too. And if it's what you really want, you have my blessing. And I'm sure Catherine and I will get used to each other, when she's part of the family." She had made no effort so far in three years, so Dahlia hadn't either. She had assumed that Catherine was temporary, even after three years. And she might have been, without the baby, but not now. Charles stared at his mother as she said it. Something had changed. She seemed more open to letting them do what they wanted. He couldn't have imagined her doing that before. She fully accepted his decision and respected his choice. He was at heart a traditional and moral man, aware of his responsibilities and willing to fulfill them. And he loved Catherine more than he had realized before.

"Thank you, Mom." He came around and kissed her and she stood up and hugged him with tears in her eyes.

"Sometimes you have to take a risk, Charlie. And you have to be with the person you love. I had that with your father, and I want that for you." They chatted for a few more minutes and he left and went straight to Delphine.

"Oh my God, I just told Mom about the baby and marrying Catherine and she was fine with it, she gave me her blessing. I thought she was going to kill me. She was really sweet about it."

"She's a sweet person, and I think she's willing to let us grow up now," Delphine said quietly. "I think she's grown up too. I think it was hard to be away this summer. She went through a lot. That changes you. She just wants us to be happy, all of us. That's all she ever wanted." Alex had never understood it, and Charles never thought about it.

"I know it sounds crazy because she's so much older, but I love Catherine. And I didn't think I was ready for a baby but maybe I am."

"You can't send it back once it's here," she reminded him, and he laughed.

"If it cries too much and drives me crazy, I'll drop it off at your house. You're good with kids."

"No, you don't! Catherine knows what she's doing, she's already had a child. Anyway, I'm glad you told Mom, and she was nice about it." Delphine had been nervous about it too. She had never been a fan of Catherine's.

"Well, that's one worry taken care of." He headed for his office then, with a lighter step and a big smile. And he called Catherine and told her the news.

In her office, Dahlia was hoping that he was doing the right thing. He seemed like such an innocent to her, and a child, but he was a grown man, and she had to respect what he wanted, and let him fly on his own. She couldn't have done that before, but she was ready to now.

Agnes came in with a cup of coffee for her, and Dahlia told her the news. "We have another wedding to plan. Charles is getting married. He just wants a small civil ceremony and lunch at the house."

"With Catherine?" Agnes knew how Dahlia felt about her.

"Yes. I'm trying to respect his choice and his right to make his own decisions. They all seem to have managed pretty well without me this summer."

"Maybe it was good for you too. They're growing up. And Delphine did such a good job."

"I know she did." Dahlia smiled at her. There was a certain sense of freedom about letting them try their own wings.

The day flew by with everything she had to do, and she left at seven and just had time to wash her face, brush her hair, and put on lipstick when Philippe arrived. Henri showed him into the library as always, and brought him a glass of red wine, the Château Haut-Brion he loved. They kept cases of it in the wine cellar for him. Philippe kissed her on both cheeks as soon as she walked into the room and he looked genuinely happy to see her.

"My God, I thought you were never coming back, you were gone forever."

"You were away for most of it, so you can't complain," she reminded him. "When did you get back?"

"Two days ago," he said with a laugh. "How did all the legal mess work out? I didn't hear from you after a while, but I assumed you were taking care of it and were in good hands." But he had hardly called to check on her. He was having fun in the south of France.

"It all got resolved. I didn't get sued. I didn't have to pay a settlement. In fact, they gave me one."

"You must have had a good lawyer," he said. He looked very jovial, and he thought she looked beautiful. He was looking forward to having sex with her after dinner. It had been too long.

"I did have a good lawyer. And it was stressful, but it all worked out."

He told her about the people she knew that he'd seen in Cap-Ferrat. He'd had a pleasant, relaxing summer, and he didn't mention his wife. He was happy to be back now, and ready to resume his routine with Dahlia. Monday and Thursday nights and occasional special events.

They had a very good dinner of duck, one of his favorites, which she'd ordered for him. She wanted to end it on a nice note. He put his hand on hers after dinner, always his signal to her that he was ready to go upstairs. "We can skip dessert," he said slyly. He was hungry for her—it had been two months. But she realized more than ever now how limited and shallow their relationship had been. It was mostly about sex twice a week and he'd go home to his wife, and having someone fun and intelligent to go to parties with. But he was always on loan, and never hers. And he didn't love her, and she didn't love him. She liked him a lot, and had a deep affection for him, but it wasn't enough, and never had been.

"We're not going upstairs tonight," she said to him gently, and he looked surprised.

"Are you tired, darling? Of course, you just got back yesterday, and you probably went straight to the office."

"I did, you know me." She smiled at him.

"Yes, I do." He was too much of a gentleman to make a fuss about being put off.

She looked him in the eye and spoke to him honestly. "I can't do this anymore, Philippe. It doesn't feel right. It's dishonest to Jacqueline, and for us too. I make it easy for you to stay married to her. I provide what she doesn't. I want to be more than that in someone's life, more than just a filler, or a stand-in, or an add-on. You're not in love with me, and you never will be. I don't want to be someone's girl on the side hiding in a closet, while you stay married."

"I do love you, darling. I just don't want to get married."

"You *are* married. You forget that you are every Monday

and Thursday night, and you remember as soon as you go home, or to Cap-Ferrat with her all summer. I deserve better than that."

"I can't get divorced," he said, still looking surprised by what she was saying. "Our families and Julien would be shocked. No one in our family has ever gotten divorced. I've always told you that."

"Yes, you did, and I thought it wouldn't bother me, but it does."

"Is there someone else?" he asked her, and he didn't like that idea.

"Yes," she said. "Me. I don't want to live your lie with you anymore. I wanted to be honest with you and see you to tell you."

"No more Mondays and Thursdays?" He looked crestfallen.

"No, no more."

"I'll miss you," he said. But she had been reminded now of what real love was. She didn't want to settle for less. It made her feel cheap, but she didn't say that to him. He had done his best and lived up to what he'd said in the beginning. He hadn't changed. She had. "Well, let me know if you change your mind. You might get bored with all those dull bachelors we know."

"You'd be the first one I'd call," she said, and he smiled

and got up regretfully. If she wasn't going to sleep with him, he had no interest in being there. It was very clear how little she had meant to him. She was just a convenience, and a woman he wanted to show off with. She realized even more now how demeaning it had been. Her relationship with Mark had been clean and respectful. With Philippe, it never was. He made his way to the front door, and she went with him. She kissed his cheek and smiled. She had no bad feelings toward him. He wasn't a bad man, she just didn't want to play anymore, or be his toy.

"Thank you for dinner," he said, and lowered his voice discreetly, "and for six very amusing years." She didn't want "amusing" now. She wanted real. He opened the door and left, and she went upstairs to Francisco waiting for her, and she felt independent and strong. She'd rather be alone now than the plaything of a married man. It was done. She felt better immediately. She almost texted Mark to tell him, but decided not to. It made no difference now for them. It was just the right thing to do. Mark was gone. And so was Philippe. She was alone.

Chapter 17

The dinner on Thursday night at Dahlia's house was relaxed and fun and boisterous. All four of her children were there, and Delphine's husband Francois, the groom-to-be Paul, and Catherine, the mother of Charles's baby, that Dahlia had just learned about. The table looked beautiful with silver and crystal gleaming. The food was delicious, prepared by a party chef she used at times to entertain to make it seem special. She wanted them all to remember how good it felt to be together. It was a happy time after being away from them for two months, which seemed like an eternity to her now. They all showed up nicely dressed, out of respect for their mother. Emma wore a black skirt and top and her Doc Martens and pink hair. They were individuals with talents and lives of their own now, and partners Dahlia didn't always love, but that suited them. She had no right to pick or choose or condemn or criticize. They had a right to their own choices in life and she wanted to respect them. She couldn't protect them all the time, no matter how much she loved them. They had to have their own victories and make their mistakes. She had never wanted to control them, but she didn't want to let them go. She knew she had to now. The summer in California had taught her that. They had done fine without her, some better than others. Even Emma was trying her wings with her art, and having her first gallery show, a major accomplishment for her.

She toasted them all at the end of dinner and told them how proud she was of all of them, and they could tell she meant it.

And Alex finally spoke to her before dinner.

"It looks like you and Agnes pulled it off, Mom," she said quietly, more subdued than usual.

"It sounds like everything is in place. It's the first thing I checked when I got back. I want you to have a beautiful wedding, and I hope you know that. I'm sorry I couldn't come back sooner. I came home as soon as I could."

"I'm sorry I got so upset about it. I thought you were going to cancel my wedding." It still didn't justify the hurtful things she had said. But that was Alex. She'd do it again.

"No, just postpone it," Dahlia said gently. "I want you to have the best life can give you."

"Thank you, Maman," Alex said, and hugged her. And for now, the war was over, until the next time when she didn't get her way and took out nuclear weapons because things weren't going as she wanted. Dahlia was still smarting from her words, and Alex looked happy as the focus of everyone's attention. Dahlia hoped everything would go smoothly for her on Saturday. Their family dinner was a nice prelude and what she had missed most while she was in California. In a way, she had given up a man she loved for them, to be with them, and they would never even know it. It was a sacrifice Dahlia had made in silence, her gift to them.

The wedding was as beautiful as Alex had hoped and Dahlia had planned, with a great deal of help from Agnes to pull it off successfully. It was flawless. The church of Sainte-Clothilde was filled with flowers, with balls of lily of the valley at the end of each pew. And Alex carried a huge bouquet of them, to go with the dress that fit perfectly. Even her shoes were exquisite with lily of the valley on them. Dior had gone all out and made all the adjustments Alex wanted.

The guests were excited and happy for them, and people came impeccably dressed. The food and wines were wonderful, and the florist had done a masterful job at the château where they held the reception. People danced until four in the morning. The paparazzi were kept away, and Dahlia looked distinguished and elegant in a navy-blue lace haute couture gown, with sapphires that had been her mother's on her neck and ears. Not a single detail was overlooked. Nothing went wrong. The weather was balmy and warm, and Alex came to find her mother and tell her that it was even better than she'd dreamed it would be. No one would have guessed the agony it had been planning it, or how unkind Alex had been to her in the process. It was a magical night, just as every bride's wedding should be. Dahlia wished that Mark could have seen it and been there with her. Charles walked his sister down the aisle, and Delphine and Emma were her witnesses. Delphine was the maid of honor, and her two little girls were the flower girls, with Delphine guiding them down the aisle holding satin baskets of rose petals. They were what they always had been and Dahlia had worked so hard for, a family, with all its flaws and mistakes, and strengths which prevailed in the end. And Dahlia was grateful she had made it home in time for the wedding. She would have been heartbroken to miss it, and Alex would never have forgiven her.

There was nothing to forgive at her wedding. It was as close to perfect as anyone could get.

Dahlia had walked into the church alone, and she left the reception at the château quietly at two in the morning, having greeted all of the two hundred and fifty guests. Charles had danced with her once, and thanked her again for being so reasonable about Catherine and the baby. Catherine looked very respectable in a simple black dress. The baby didn't show yet.

Dahlia's driver took her home and it was a good feeling knowing that the evening had been a success. Nothing could have been added or subtracted. Francisco was waiting for her, asleep on her bed, and he wagged his tail when he saw her, and cuddled up next to her when she got into bed.

The flowers at the wedding had been exceptionally beautiful, white orchids and lily of the valley and hydrangeas in elegant arrangements on every table. As she closed her eyes, she could see all of it, and knew that it would be an unforgettable memory for Alex too. It was exactly what Dahlia had wanted for her, and now it was Alex's turn to make a good life for herself. Dahlia hoped they all would. And Alex and Paul were leaving on their honeymoon in Greece the next day, on the yacht they were borrowing.

Dahlia drifted off to sleep with the dog she had brought

back from California. The wedding was a suitable conclusion to a happy time. It really had been perfect.

She dreamed of Mark that night and walking down the beach at Stinson with him. She wished that she were still there with him. She knew that there would never be another man like him in her life, or another love.

Chapter 18

On Monday after the wedding, Delphine and Agnes were still talking about how beautiful it had been. Delphine had had a spectacular wedding herself five years before, with four hundred guests. Francois' parents were very social, and people from all over Europe had been there, aristocrats and royals, the cream of Paris society. And Alex's wedding was exactly as she wanted it, with good friends, people she and Paul both knew from work, and a number of celebrities.

"You did a beautiful job," Delphine told Agnes, and then they all got to work. They had a busy week ahead. Dahlia had meetings lined up all afternoon. She was putting away her wedding file when Agnes buzzed her and told her that the video screens for her two P.M. meeting had just been delivered to the conference room and they wanted her to check them and direct their placement.

"Can't you do it?" Dahlia asked her.

"If you don't like the way they're set up, you'll be frantic to have me get the delivery people back to correct it. You'd better take a look now while they're here." Dahlia had so much to do, and Delphine wanted to meet with her during lunch to talk about the youth line she was creating, which was important too. There weren't enough hours in the day to do it all. She hurried out of her office, and down the hall to the conference room. The screens weren't set up when she got there, there was no one around, and she was about to leave when she saw him standing at the far end of the room, looking at her and smiling. It was Mark. Her breath caught as he walked toward her with a purposeful expression and when he reached her, he kissed her and she didn't stop him. She was too stunned seeing him to know what to think. All she knew was how much she loved him.

"What are you doing here?" she asked him, breathless from the shock of his being there, and from the kiss.

"You told me to take a risk and I did. It was worth it. You were right. We won the lottery, Dahlia. We did it. It was scary as hell, and it still is. But life isn't worth a damn if you don't take a risk, so here I am. And you can have me thrown out in five minutes if you want to. I can work remotely from here and fly to San Francisco when I need to. I've done it before with clients all over the world, and it worked fine. You need to be here with your business and your kids. I can do a lot from here if you're willing to give it a try. I'm tired of playing it safe and the dead ends. I was wasting my life before I met you. You showed me that. I don't want to play that game anymore. I want a real life with you. What do you say? Will you risk it with me? If you hate it or it doesn't work for you, I'll leave. I love you. I don't want to lose you or give you up. It took me two minutes to figure that out when you left. I've been working out how to do this ever since. What do you think?" He was terrified of her answer, as she gazed at him in disbelief. She was smiling and couldn't stop.

"I think you're crazy and I love you, and I don't want to lose you either. Can you really do this? I can give you office space, and you could work here. I don't want to be without you. And I don't have to be here all the time. My kids did fine without me this summer for two months. They're grown up. I didn't see that before. I want to be here to run the business and guide them and teach them how. But I want more than that in my life. I need you, Mark," she said softly. She had never said that to anyone before.

"I need you too." He was willing to admit it without shame. "Shall we roll the dice and take a chance?" Asking her that was the bravest thing he'd ever done. She nodded and he kissed her and stood holding her for a long time. He knew that wherever they were together was home. He had found her amid the fires and the smoke in an army surplus tent, and he didn't want to let her go. She was the woman he'd been waiting for, and a little curly black dog had come through the fires to find them and had brought them luck. And he was never going to let that go now that he had found her.

She pulled away for a minute then and looked at him. "How did you get past Agnes, to trick me to coming to the conference room?" She was usually a very efficient guard at the palace gates. "What did you tell her?" He smiled when she asked.

"I told her that I was your lawyer in San Francisco and I'm in love with you, and I needed five minutes with you, as a surprise, and if you wanted me thrown out, I'd go willingly. I think she was so shocked that she agreed to do it. She must be a romantic at heart because when she left me in the conference room, she wished me luck. I think she knew that I was telling the truth when I said I love you." His honesty and courage were impossible to resist, and Dahlia didn't want to. They weren't betting on six weeks this time. This time all the chips were on the table, they were betting on a lifetime. Winner take all.

Danielle Steel

Have you liked Danielle Steel on Facebook?

Be the first to know about Danielle's latest books, access exclusive competitions and stay in touch with news about Danielle.

www.facebook.com/DanielleSteelOfficial

NEVER SAY NEVER

When life can change in an instant . . .

When Oona Kelly Webster's husband drops a bombshell that shatters their twenty-five-year marriage, she travels to the charming village of Milly-la-Forêt in France, where they had planned to celebrate their silver wedding anniversary together, alone. When the world comes to a standstill due to a terrifying pandemic, her only comfort is that she can remain in France, where the beautiful surroundings slowly begin to heal her. And when a chance encounter with her new neighbour, a well-known Hollywood actor, blossoms into something deeper than friendship, Oona wrestles with the risks of opening her heart again . . .

Coming soon

PURE STEEL. PURE HEART.

ABOUT THE AUTHOR

DANIELLE STEEL has been hailed as one of the world's most popular authors, with a billion copies of her novels sold. Her many international bestsellers include *Triangle, Joy* and *Resurrection*. She is also the author of *His Bright Light*, the story of her son Nick Traina's life and death; *A Gift of Hope*, a memoir of her work with the homeless; and the children's books *Pretty Minnie in Paris* and *Pretty Minnie in Hollywood*. Danielle divides her time between Paris and her home in northern California.

daniellesteel.com

Facebook.com/DanielleSteelOfficial

X: @daniellesteel

Instagram: @officialdaniellesteel